THE
CORPORATE
KID

NEIL
SHULMAN
SUSAN
WRATHALL

The Corporate Kid

www.whitman.com

© 2012 Whitman Publishing, LLC
3101 Clairmont Road, Suite G
Atlanta GA 30329

ISBN: 0794836194
Printed in the United States of America

WHITMAN®

For a complete catalog of Whitman Publishing books, visit us online at www.whitman.com, or scan the QR code at left.

To my wife, Anna Zoe Haugo, and my son, Myles Verdandi Shulman, who are pillars of ethics and empathy.

—Neil Shulman

I dedicate this book to my daughters, Sophia and Simone, who bring joy and meaning to my life.

—Susan Wrathall

1

Bill Bradford sped up the six-lane highway in his silver Jaguar XK8 coupe. A casual click of a button sent the windows sliding down, and he breathed in the hot summer air. He was feeling good about himself. This morning, for the first time in months, he'd been back on top of his game—an energetic round of golf was one of his favorite ways to negotiate a business deal. "I actually felt relaxed out there," Bill thought. Heck, relaxation itself was a change of pace these days; his nerves had been jangled by angry protestors marching outside his company's headquarters. This morning, out on the green, he had managed to forget about them for a while. Now, speeding along the highway, Bill made a conscious decision: he was going to mentally check out for the rest of the afternoon. "No more business today," he said out loud. "Let the good times roll!" He switched his Alpine Sound System over to Sirius, found a classic-rock station, and cranked the radio up, pressing his foot down on the accelerator and zipping happily around the Sunday drivers in their slower-moving cars.

On the south side of town, the warmth inside Holy Trinity Church was getting to Ramona Sullivan. The air felt thick with humidity, and the architecture of the hundred-year-old church—which was drafty in the winter and stuffy in the summer—bottled up the heat. It was early summer now and the temperatures were already high and overwhelming. Big, old-fashioned electric fans set up around the outside aisles did little more than stir the hot soup of air.

Sweat trickled down Ramona's neck. She tried to concentrate on the sermon, but there was a wiggling next to her. She glanced over at her two children.

Charles, her son and the oldest, was fanning his face with a song leaflet. Ramona smiled to herself, proud of her handsome child. Then the smile faded a bit. They were growing up fast. Too fast for her. It felt like just yesterday Charles had been running around in diapers, and overnight he'd grown into a teenager. At fifteen he still had a slender boyish frame, but his facial expressions and manner often had a grownup air. She looked down and realized his good Sunday pants were too short on him. He must have grown an inch—maybe two—in the last month. "Charles is a good boy," she thought. He didn't complain about his old clothes. "He knows we can't afford new ones." It was remarkable how much he looked like his father. Ramona closed her eyes, remembering her husband.

She'd see if she could pick up another shift or two and buy that boy some new pants.

A heavy sigh interrupted Ramona's thoughts—it was her Gracie. At twelve, her daughter was already too smart for her own good, and not as easygoing as Charles. From the looks of her, Gracie had given up on today's sermon, in favor of a more intriguing subject: Ramona saw her smile shyly at a boy a few rows back. She gently swatted her, and Gracie quickly looked back up front. "I need to keep an eye on that one," Ramona thought. Her daughter was pretty, smart, and wily—not a good combination. And that boy Gracie was eyeing: Kayden. He was a nice boy but he was already good-looking and too confident for his age. Ramona could tell Gracie had a crush. She remembered when she was that age; she shuddered and then looked back, narrowing her eyes at the boy.

Charles looked up. "Who you giving the stink-eye, Mama?" he whispered.

"Don't you fuss about me."

"I thought we were supposed to be paying attention?" Charles replied.

"Oh, I am, believe me."

Down the row, Ramona's mother—Charles's grand-mother, Lorraine—leaned forward, gave the two of them a stern look, and faced forward again. Ramona winked at Charles. He rolled his eyes at his mother, trying to make her laugh, and reached over to hold her hand. They sat back in their seats, smiling.

———————————

A short time later, the congregation poured out of the old church's front doors. Ramona waited to shake the pastor's hand, with Charles and Gracie standing behind her; Charles a little more patiently than Gracie, who seemed keen to prance by Kayden. Ramona shot her a disapproving look. They said their good-days to the pastor and his wife and headed outside into the summer air.

Bill Bradford drove on, looking around. His golf game had been at the country club of a business friend, south of the city—a nice enough place, but a little outside his usual perimeter. On the way home, a long stretch of 85-North was closed for summer roadwork (an annual annoyance), forcing Bill off the highway and onto twisting side streets that never seemed to detour back to a main road. Now he was most definitely lost. He switched on his GPS, and its pleasant robot-woman voice started its commands.

"Turn left after one hundred feet," she said coolly, and Bill complied.

Shortly after that she calmly told him to "Turn right after ten feet"—which would have put him over a bridge railing and, a short free-fall later, into a side stream of the Chattahoochee River.

"Piece of junk!" Bill shut off the defective GPS in frustration.

Just then his cell phone, lying in the passenger seat, rang with "The Girl From Ipanema." He leaned over to grab it but it slipped from his fingers to the floor.

Down a bit further . . . reaching sideways to scoop it up . . . taking his eyes off the road. As Bill came back up to a sitting position, he opened the phone and barely said "Hello" before he saw—

—*a woman walking out in front of his car.*

"Whoa, there!" he yelled. He hit the brakes hard.

As he swerved the wheel, his Jaguar swung around, skidding sideways, and the passenger-side bumper smacked the woman with force as he screeched to a halt. She flew into the air and landed with a sickening *thump* on the asphalt, her purse tumbling after her, blown open from the impact, sending church notes and photos of her children—a handsome fifteen-year-old boy and a pretty twelve-year-old girl—floating like leaves to the ground.

Inside the car, an anxious voice buzzed from Bill Bradford's cell phone. "Bill? Bill? What's happening? Say something!" Bill was dazed. He heard the tiny voice but he had no idea where the phone was, which direction his car was facing, or whether he had just killed a woman.

Charles Sullivan stood on the sidewalk near the silver sports car. He was stunned. He had watched the whole scene unfold in slow motion, and now his mind tried to process the information: a car had hit his mother. For a moment the world fell silent. Time moved very slowly. Charles ran but he couldn't move fast enough. It was like he was treading through water toward his mother, who lay frighteningly crumpled in the middle of the road. His sister Gracie was crying out but he didn't have time to stop and try to comfort her. Their grandmother ran over in painful slow-motion to hold Gracie tight in her arms.

Charles had to help Mama. She wasn't moving; her hat had been blown off her head; there was blood all over her face. From the steps of the church a woman screamed, high-pitched and then low, like a wailing siren. Charles heard an old man yelling nearby; his cries were too loud, too panicked for a gentle Sunday morning. "Somebody call 911. *Somebody call an ambulance!*"

Inside the car, the tiny voice persisted until Bill silently picked up his phone and turned it off, dropping it in his lap. He didn't need his wife to add to the confusion at the moment. For an instant he had a powerful impulse to put the car in reverse and peel off in the opposite direction. Instead, he made himself turn the engine off. He tore his eyes away from the motionless figure in the road and tried to focus his thoughts. With a growing sense of panic he noticed the street filling with people, surrounding his car, converging on the woman, looking toward him. He instinctively locked his doors, with a loud "click."

Bill was not in his safe, neatly manicured neighborhood, and in fact he had no idea what neighborhood this was, exactly. He gripped his phone tightly and opened it, starting to call 911—but then thought better of it and punched in another number. The phone rang and rang. "Pick up," Bill commanded quietly. "Please pick up!"

The ringing stopped and rolled over to voicemail. He left a hurried message, his voice cracking: "Morrie, it's Bill. I've hit someone with my car. What should I do? This is a time when I really need my lawyer. Please, please call me." Hanging up, he cursed to himself. "This is not what I need," he thought, "another scandal." He hoped the woman wasn't dead. He couldn't tell. There were too many people around her. He opened his phone again and punched 911.

"Nine one one," a woman's voice answered efficiently. "Please state your emergency."

"Yes, there's been an accident."

Bill looked around at the people now surrounding the woman and his car. He double-checked that he'd locked the doors. "I think I may be in danger," he said nervously.

"Sir, where are you located?"

Bill peered around, seeking street signs, then said, "Washington and Cleveland, maybe fifteen or twenty miles south of downtown Atlanta?"

"What is the nature of the accident?" the dispatcher continued.

"A woman got hit by a car. I accidentally hit her and now there are people all around. Something's going to happen. Hurry!" Bill pleaded. "Please hurry!"

"Sir, what is your name? Are you in danger? Describe what's happening."

"William Bradford. There are so many people . . . so many *black* people, surrounding my car. Tell them to hurry!" He looked out his window with a growing sense of panic, hoping this new car was everything it was cracked up to be. *Impossible to break into*, the suave salesman had assured him.

"Sir, are they threatening you?" the dispatcher asked with an edge of alarm to her voice.

"They're banging on my car! They're—"

"With weapons? Bats? Clubs? Do they have *guns? Sir?*" The dispatcher quickly called in a patrol car along with the ambulance. This could get really ugly.

"Uh, well," Bill said, less sure of himself now. "Looks like a cane . . . and . . . and an umbrella."

"Say what?"

Bill gulped as he stared at the worried, creased faces outside of his window. A toothless old man dressed in a grey suit and red bowtie stood holding his cane up in the air and waving it around as his wife rapped on the window with her sun-shielding parasol. She wobbled unsteadily and held on to her husband for balance. She was eighty if she was a day.

"Sir? Are you still there?" The dispatcher hoped the silence didn't mean bad news.

Bill continued to look around and noticed that off to the right of his car was an old church. With its doors open. Putting two and two together, he realized his mistake.

"Oh, actually, I think church just let out," he said sheepishly. "These people are all dressed up and . . . and mostly old," he admitted.

Sudden laughter burst from the phone as the dispatcher tried to collect herself. "Sir, have you been knocked on the head?" she managed to sputter out.

"No," he said stiffly.

"Well, you best get out of your car and check on that woman you hit," she said, remembering the seriousness of the call. "You'll be all right. The paramedics are on their way. And those folks just spent all morning with the Lord . . . they ain't gonna hurt you."

Charles knelt down to get a closer look at his mother. "She's breathing!" he whispered. That was good. Gracie had stopped screaming and was sobbing quietly in the arms of Lorraine. Charles made eye contact with his grandmother and nodded, telling her silently that his mother was alive. Lorraine's shoulders sagged with momentary relief. Charles could hear the sirens. Help was coming. Then he looked up at the silver car that hit his mother. The driver was still sitting inside. He hadn't even come out to check on her, to see if she was okay. "He looks like he's scared to death we'll eat him." Anger burned inside Charles. He was going to talk to that man. He got up off his knees and marched over to the car.

Bill sat, shaking, in his Jaguar. He'd hung up on the emergency dispatcher and now was clutching the cell phone uselessly in his hands. Suddenly someone was knocking on the driver's side window—*clack, clack, clack.* It was a boy dressed in a dark blue suit, his white shirt unbuttoned at the neck and his maroon tie wildly loosened. The boy was no more than fifteen, but his expression made him look older and threateningly bigger. He stared into Bill's eyes and banged against the window. *Clack, clack, clack.*

"What?" Bill asked stupidly, shrugging his shoulders helplessly. "I called 911. They should be here any second."

The boy replied in a muffled voice through the window, "I can't hear you."

Bill rolled his window down an inch and repeated himself. "I called 911."

"You better get out of your car and see about my mama," the boy said loudly, so as to be heard. He forced his hands into the crack. *"Get out of the car!"* His face was set with anger. If Bill had looked more closely at him he would have seen tears forming in the corners of his almond-shaped eyes.

As the businessman recoiled in fear he was relieved to see an ambulance pulling onto the street in front of him. He unlocked the car and cautiously stepped out, holding the door open in case he had to jump back in;

but no one came forward. Several people, including the angry boy, simply stood looking at him.

"You hit my mama." The boy was trembling, but he made no move.

"She ran out," Bill protested. "I tried to stop. It wasn't my fault." Then he wondered why he was defending himself to a child. He saw a police car pulling up and breathed a sigh of relief. He was safe. No one would dare attack him now.

———————————

Charles stood and watched as the EMTs quickly and skillfully loaded his mother onto a stretcher and pushed her into the back of the ambulance. He wiped away his tears and tightened his mouth to stop it from trembling. One minute they'd been talking about what to eat for Sunday dinner, and the next minute all he could hear was the squeal of brakes, and all he could see was a flash of silver. Why did nobody see the car approaching? It seemed to have come around the corner out of nowhere.

His grandmother gripped his shoulder and interrupted his thoughts.

"Charles. Charles, listen to me. I'm going with your mama in the ambulance. You take Gracie back home and stay there. You hear me?" She was trying not to cry in front of the children. Lorraine Jackson looked sternly at her grandson, forcing him to acknowledge what she'd said.

Charles nodded numbly. "Yes, Grandma." He was too frightened to argue.

Gracie clung onto their grandmother, almost afraid to let go. The worried woman pried the child off her arm and placed her hand into her brother's. "Gracie. *Gracie!* You go home with Charles, you hear? Your mama is going to be okay, but I need to be with her. You mind your brother now. I'll come 'round later and check in on you. Matter of fact, when you get home, go down the hall and let Juanita know what happened. Stay with her, if you want, 'til I get there."

With that she left the children and got into the passenger seat of the ambulance. The vehicle took off with its sirens piercing the Sunday afternoon quiet. Charles tugged his still-sobbing sister along with him and walked over to where the sleek Jaguar was parked sideways in the middle of the street. Several young men, not from the church, had appeared out of nowhere, admiring the expensive sports car and discussing its features. "That's about seventy grand right there," a muscular boy of about sixteen said admiringly, walking around the entire car. They eyed the Jag hungrily.

Charles watched the tall white man, the driver of the Jaguar, in his khaki slacks and navy golf shirt, standing next to the patrol car. "I hope they arrest him," Charles muttered angrily under his breath. The policeman took his statement and then—wait, did the officer laugh? "Typical," thought Charles. Glancing at his sister, seeing her tired, tear-stained face, he gripped her hand tighter. He didn't know why he hadn't gone home yet, but he wanted to see what—if anything—would happen to the man who had hurt their mama.

Finally, the man shook the officer's hand and walked back toward his car. He glanced briefly at the crowd of people who had gathered, but avoided any eye contact as he attempted to stuff his wallet in his back pocket with a shaky hand. Lowering himself into the plush leather seat, he slammed his door shut and locked it again. He started the car, carefully turned it to face the proper way, and slowly made his way down Cleveland Avenue until the silver sports car could no longer be seen. The policeman followed him in his cruiser.

Charles and Gracie walked over to the spot where the car had been and it was then that Charles noticed the brown leather wallet lying on the street. Impulsively he picked it up and stuffed it into his back pocket. Gracie looked at him curiously. "What's that?"

Charles shook his head impatiently. "Nothing. It's nothing. Let's go."

He didn't notice that the young men who had scattered to the sidewalk had seen him pick something up.

A number of older ladies offered to walk them to their apartment but Charles politely declined. With that, he and Gracie turned and headed home.

A short walk and a few flights of stairs later, Charles and Gracie arrived outside their modest apartment. They heard the cries of a baby down the hall and a couple yelling at each other a floor down. Charles sighed and wriggled his keys inside the locks. When they got inside, Gracie flopped onto the couch and turned on the TV. Charles closed the door and looked around. Right now his mama should have been starting their Sunday dinner. The kitchen was quiet and their small apartment felt more cramped than usual. He went to the fridge to get a drink, opened it, and found not much there. A glass of tap water would do the trick—his throat was really dry. He looked at the phone with an idea to call the hospital and check in, and then remembered their phone service had been disconnected again.

Charles wished there was something he could do to help his mama. How much work would she have to miss because of the accident? Would she even be able to work again at all? He'd put in for a worker's permit to help bring in money, but nobody seemed to want to hire a fifteen-year-old kid. And now, with the hospital, there would be extra bills. Mama worked so hard. Some nights she'd come home and have to turn around a few hours later to go to her other job. She'd look so tired, but she always managed to straighten up her back and give them a good dinner. They were never without lots of love. He sighed, wishing there was something, anything, he could do.

And then he remembered the wallet in his pocket.

"I'll be right back, Gracie," Charles called as he walked into the bathroom. He locked the door to the tiny room and removed the wallet from his shirt. He stared at it without opening it. Turning it over, he wondered why he had taken it. Finally, curiosity got the better of him and he opened it up. Inside he saw an array of cards and some banknotes. Charles pulled out the currency and counted it: $352. The cash included two hundred-dollar bills. That was the most money he'd ever seen and he'd certainly never seen a hundred-dollar bill before. He counted it again just to make sure. The things he could do with that money! He imagined a full refrigerator. He could buy Mama something nice. Maybe take her to a good dinner and help her pay some of those bills.

Suddenly Gracie was pounding on the door. "Charles, what are you doing in there? I need to pee."

"Just a minute!"

"No, I need to pee real bad. Let me in!" She was jumping up and down outside the door.

Stuffing the money back in the wallet, Charles made up his mind. He put the wallet back in his pocket, and unlocked the door to let his sister in. "Go pee, Gracie! And stop your hollering."

She slammed the door behind her. As Charles walked down the hallway he felt heavy and he wondered how his family was going to survive.

2

As soon as Lorraine stepped into the ambulance and sat in the passenger seat she found herself nose to nose with a fat bulldog, strapped in with a homemade seatbelt. She gasped when he leaned over and licked her enthusiastically across her face with his warm, wet tongue. She was *not*—had never been, and wasn't planning to be—a dog lover. If the vehicle hadn't immediately lurched into motion she would have jumped out then and there.

"Can I ride in the back with my daughter?" she asked the driver, a burly man with muttonchops and a scraggly ponytail left over from the 1960s.

He threw her a look with one bushy eyebrow raised. "You ain't goin' nowhere, little lady," he barked. "This bird's flown the coop. Now hang on and pray for an easy landing!"

Lorraine spent the next two minutes holding up her left arm as a shield against the licking canine, and moving as far to the edge of her seat as possible. The driver weaved in and out of traffic with the sirens wailing and his slobbery dog inching closer to Lorraine, waiting for a chance to lick again. Finally she couldn't take it any more.

"Why is this nasty animal in here?" she gasped.

The driver put his arm protectively around his furry companion. "Babysitter called in sick this morning," he bellowed over the siren. "This is Winston, and he's not nasty—are you, boy? Give Daddy smooches!"

Lorraine looked on incredulously as the big man lowered his face, barely keeping one eye on the road, and let the dog lick all over him. With their heads close to each other, she saw the driver and his dog resembled each other. She thought of all the germs in the dog's mouth and shivered in disgust.

"Watch where you're going!" she cried.

"Don't worry, sister," he yelled back, straightening up but keeping one hand on the bulldog's wrinkled head. "This ain't Cowboy Bob's first day at the rodeo." He released his dog and blew the ambulance's horn to clear the road.

"Whoops, hold on, ladies and gentlemen!" Bob wrestled the steering wheel with both hands. "Hot coffee, comin' through!"

As they veered around a corner Lorraine gripped the side of her seat, but couldn't stop from leaning against Winston anyway. The bulldog quickly licked her face again until she managed to push him away. They couldn't get to the hospital fast enough.

As they sped along, Bob reached over to turn up the radio, and suddenly "Start Me Up" by the Rolling Stones was competing with the wailing siren. Lorraine felt a pounding headache coming on. She had never been a

Stones fan. She didn't understand what everyone saw in that skinny white man with the big mouth prancing around on stage. Now here he was, on a Sunday, no less, screaming into her ear. If having her daughter hit by a car wasn't bad enough, the ride up front was qualifying as a first-rate nightmare.

"It's—it's Sunday! Do we really have to listen to this mess?"

No comment from Bob because he suddenly hit the brakes and extended his left arm out the window with his middle finger saluting a driver in an old, battered station wagon. "Shake a leg, Grandpa!" he shouted. "*Get out of the road!*"

An elderly man with huge hearing aids stared in confusion at the ambulance driver. Adjusting his glasses, he squinted, then smiled and waved back.

"Sweet Mother Sheboygan," Bob grumbled. "Some days I don't know why I get out of bed!"

Lorraine looked up in the direction of the sky and muttered, "Lord, just get us to the hospital safe."

Bill Bradford breathed a sigh of relief as he approached his home. As he went to pull into the driveway of the two-story colonial red-brick house he stopped abruptly—cars were blocking the entrance to his garage. In fact, now that he looked around, they were parked all along the street. He was forced to park several houses down. Shaking his head disgustedly, he walked up to his home. Something was going on, but what? Why was Paige always playing hostess to her league meetings and social events? Didn't anyone else have a house?

He flung the door open impatiently, but when he stepped into the entrance hall no one was there. He heard the low noise of a crowd in the backyard, with the telltale sound of splashing from the pool. "Paige?" He yelled into the empty house. Where was his wife? What a hellacious morning this had been. This was when a wife needed to be there. And he still hadn't heard from Morrie. Here he was in the middle of a real crisis and no one seemed to care. He strode angrily through the living room, and the kitchen, until finally he reached the sliding door that led to the outside.

He could hear shrieks and laughter coming from out by the pool. On the patio and spilling onto the lawn were neighbors and their kids, and other people he didn't even recognize. Why would Paige invite these strangers here and not even tell him? Really fuming now, Bill walked briskly outside, looking for his wife. There she was, in a pink sundress and sandals, talking to a slight middle-aged man he had never seen before.

"Paige," he called out to his wife.

The pretty blond woman, with her hair up in a girl-ish ponytail, turned around and her smile froze as she looked at the expression on her husband's face. "Honey, there you are. I tried calling you back," she said through a thin smile. She asked in a bit more of a whisper, "Are you all right? What happened?" Then, realizing she was ignoring her guest, she put her hand apologetically on the arm of the man next to her. "Michael, this is my husband, Mr. Bradford. I mean . . . Bill," she finished nervously.

She turned to her husband, "Bill, this is Michael. He's Scott's father. You remember Scott, from Andrew's class?"

Bill gave the man the most basic of greetings. "Nice to meet you. Will you excuse us?" he said with barely veiled tension in his voice. Then he turned to his wife. "Paige?"

"Good to see you again," she said apologetically, and she scurried after her husband.

Once inside, Bill turned on his wife. "What's going on, Paige? Do you have any idea what kind of day I've had? How could you invite all these . . . these strangers . . . here without even asking me?"

Paige looked confused. "But Bill, you've known about this party for weeks. Today is. . . ." She trailed off. Surely he realized what day it was?

Suddenly they were interrupted by their son Andrew. He burst noisily through the back door wearing only his red swim trunks. He was soaking wet, fresh out of the pool. "Dad! You made it! You're home!" The wiry boy with a big smile flung himself onto his father, but let go when he realized his hug wasn't being returned.

Bill shook him off. "Andrew. You're dripping wet and ruining the floor."

Andrew recoiled from the sharpness. "Sorry, Dad, I just. . . ."

Bill lashed out, "Can't you see I'm trying to talk to your mother? Now go back outside and leave us alone." Bill looked at his son with a stony expression.

The boy opened his mouth in surprise. "But, Dad."

"I *said* go outside," Bill hissed, pointing his finger to the door.

Andrew gave his father a disappointed and hurt look and stormed back outside.

Paige turned to face Bill. She knew her husband worked hard, and she always tried to give him the benefit of the doubt when he was in one of his tense moods. He put in so many hours running his company, Hospitals of America. He provided for them, gave her a roof over her head, and gave their son everything he needed and more. Paige could take the occasional outbreak of frustration aimed at her—but not at Andrew.

"I'm sorry you're having a bad day," she said reproachfully, "but since you've apparently forgotten, it's your son's birthday! Those people outside are his friends and their parents. So if you'll excuse me, I must go see to our visitors."

Bill's face fell as the realization dawned on him. He'd totally forgotten about the party with the way the day had gone. Now he'd really screwed up. He barely whispered, "I'm sorry." But Paige didn't hear him as she slid the patio door shut.

As she stepped outside she took a beat to compose herself, and put on her best Junior Leaguer smile. She had guests to attend to.

Bob pulled the ambulance up to the ramp at Regional Hospital and braked with a screech of his tires. Lorraine found herself holding onto Winston—she wasn't clear if she was keeping him from flying through the windshield or if she was hanging on for her own safety. With her heart pounding, she released her hold on the animal, unfastened her seatbelt, and grabbed her blue purse before stepping out of the vehicle.

On the sidewalk, she tried to regain some sense of her composure. She straightened her blue straw wide-brimmed hat with the sunflower, and smoothed her bright, form-fitting blue-and-yellow patterned dress over her curvaceous figure.

Out of nowhere came a whistle, followed by, "Pretty mama, you're looking *good!*"

Lorraine whirled around and saw a tired-looking group of men slouching by the side of the building. Two of them were sitting slumped over. The other two, who appeared to be in their twenties or thirties, leered at her. Frowning, Lorraine looked them up and down and said, "Y'all are pitiful. Haven't you got something better to do? It's Sunday, why aren't you in church?"

One of them began walking toward her unsteadily. She could smell a combination of alcohol and body odor even from several feet away. Suddenly Winston, who had been waiting patiently in the ambulance, jumped out and rushed up to the man, snarling, baring his teeth. The man stopped and raised his arms above his head as if Winston were a police officer.

"That's right, move on back," Lorraine threatened. "This dog is a vicious attack animal and there's no telling what's on his mind. I think he's hungry."

The man stumbled over his own feet as he hurried around the corner, out of sight. Winston barked loudly to emphasize his point. Lorraine had a glimmer of why a person might want a dog. The animal walked over to her and looked up. "Yeah, you're all right, Winston," she said, patting him briefly on his head. "You're a big boy. You happy? Now, where's my baby?"

Bob and the attendants emerged from the back of the ambulance, wheeling Ramona's stretcher up the ramp into the emergency room. As the doors to the back of the vehicle slammed shut, Lorraine scurried behind, straining to see her daughter. When she finally caught up, she grasped Ramona's hand. "Mama," came her whisper. "Don't worry, I'll be all right." Ramona tried to smile but then winced in pain as the front of the stretcher hit a bump.

"Can't you be careful!" Lorraine snapped. "My poor little girl." As if the ride to the hospital hadn't been enough, now they had to add more pain.

As they rushed in, a petite Asian nurse conferred with the EMT. Other nurses were taking Ramona's blood pressure and examining her body. They asked her questions and she gave weak answers. They threw around some phrases she didn't quite know. She just heard, "broken leg, ribs, spleen."

"What is going on?" Lorraine demanded, but a nurse gently held her back.

"Please, ma'am, let us do our job," she said, continuing to tend to Ramona.

She passed off some paperwork and the petite nurse turned to Lorraine. "Your daughter has an internal rupture and needs surgery right away." The nurse put her arm behind Lorraine to guide her away from the stretcher. Lorraine turned to follow Ramona, who was being wheeled away. The nurse took her arm and said assertively, "I'm sorry, ma'am, you can't follow her in there."

Wrenching her arm free, she scowled at the woman. "Let me go. That's my daughter. I need to be with my daughter!"

"Ma'am, I know you're concerned," she replied, and, showing that she wasn't going to be easily moved, she continued calmly. "But I just can't let you follow her into the operating room. I'm sorry. Now, if you'll please come with me to the front desk, we'll need you to fill out some forms. Your daughter is in good hands. We'll let you know when you can see her." The nurse was used to dealing with emotional and sometimes unruly family members. With a backward glance over her shoulder, Lorraine reluctantly followed.

After the Bradfords' birthday-party guests had gone, Bill found his son lying down in his bedroom.

"Andrew?" he said as he entered. But Andrew just turned over to look at the wall and away from his father.

"*Son.*"

There was no movement from the boy. Bill sat down on the edge of the bed.

"Sit up when I'm talking to you," Bill said, trying to keep his irritation from showing. Couldn't the boy see he was sorry? Kids could be so selfish. Andrew didn't know what kind of day he'd had.

Finally Andrew sat up and glared at him but refused to speak. He looked both angry and hurt—just like he did sometimes when he was a baby, Bill thought. He remembered how Andrew, as a fat little toddler, used to make that same face.

"Andrew, look. I came up to say . . . well, what I want to say is . . . happy birthday. Okay? I'm sorry I missed your birthday party, son." Bill held out his hand in reconciliation.

Andrew began to say it was okay when suddenly Bill's cell phone rang. He looked at the caller ID. It was Morrie. He put his hand up to his son in a gesture of "Hold that thought."

"I have to take this," he said as he walked briskly out of the room.

"Whatever, Dad." Andrew rolled back over onto his stomach and pulled the pillow over his head.

Bill closed the door to his home office. He explained to Morrie what had happened with the car accident. Morrie listened carefully and then said reassuringly, "Look, Bill. I'll get in touch with the insurance company. You said she walked in front of your car."

"Um, yes," said Bill, remembering with some hesitation how he had been reaching down on the floor to find his phone just before he'd hit her.

"So she was in the middle of the street. That's jaywalking. It's not your fault. This should be pretty easy. Seems open and shut. I'll make sure it gets taken care of quickly."

"Okay. Do it fast and do it quietly. I just don't want it to get to the press or anything. They love this stuff."

"Yes, I understand completely," said Morrie.

"Especially with everything going on. I'm already under enough fire for outsourcing jobs. Something like this, well, it's the last thing I need." Bill sighed.

"Stop worrying. That's why you pay me the big bucks. I'll take care of it."

"Thanks, Morrie." Bill hung up the phone. Morrie had been performing miracles for him, legally speaking, for years, and he seemed confident he could take care of this. Bill leaned back in his chair, relieved.

Charles lay down on his bed. He needed to think. He took out the wallet and examined it. A driver's license was tucked inside; Charles saw the thin, serious smile of the man who had hit his mother. A confident, rich-looking man. He read the name next to the photo: William Thomas Bradford II. He stared at it for a moment. Then he found a business card: Bill Bradford, CEO . . . Peachtree Avenue . . . "Probably a big office in the city," Charles thought. He took the cash out again and counted it. "It would serve that guy right if I kept his money." He remembered the way the man had stared at him, at everyone from the church. "Locking himself inside his fancy car like we were going to mob him. He just thinks we're a bunch of poor thugs."

Then he had another thought: stealing his wallet was just what Mr. Bigshot Bradford would expect him to do.

As he mused, he failed to notice that Gracie had quietly stepped into the doorway. He looked up and realized she was standing there staring at him. He tried to hide the wallet. She looked down at him suspiciously and folded her arms.

"Don't you knock?" Charles snapped.

Gracie smirked. She stood her ground, narrowing her eyes. "What is that you're hiding?"

"None of your business," snarled Charles. "Now get out." But Gracie was too quick—she reached behind him and before he could stop her she was snatching the wallet from his hands.

She held it in front of her and gasped, "I knew it! You stole that man's wallet!"

"I did not steal it," said Charles defensively. "Give it here." He tried to grab it back but Gracie fled down the hallway to the kitchen.

Suddenly there was a knock at the front door. "Charles, Gracie! Open up. It's Juanita."

The two exchanged glances. It was their neighbor. Gracie judged the situation. She wasn't going to get to the bottom of this if Juanita saw the wallet. Charles could tell she wanted information. He looked her in the eye. "You going to keep your mouth shut, little girl?"

Gracie's mouth curled. She'd won. She nodded at him and slyly slid the wallet into her pocket. As soon as the wallet was out of sight, Charles opened the door.

A short, plump Hispanic woman rushed in and embraced the two children, enveloping them in her arms. "Shhhh . . . that's okay, babies," she said soothingly, "you can cry. Cry it out." Charles and Gracie squirmed awkwardly. She was suffocating them in her ample bosom.

After a moment Charles managed to wriggle away, but Juanita continued hugging Gracie. "One of your church ladies called, told me to come check on you," she explained. "How are you doing?" Gracie tried to respond but the noise was muffled. Juanita looked down and released her.

"We're okay," Gracie said again, more clearly.

Charles looked away, realizing that he had forgotten all about his mother for a moment. He felt guilty. Some quiet tears fell from Gracie's eyes. She must be feeling guilty too, he thought. "But we haven't heard anything about our mama. Do you think you can call the hospital, Miss Juanita?"

"Phone got cut off again, huh?" she said, feeling sorry for the two children. They must be so worried about their mother.

Charles nodded, embarrassed. "Yeah. Last week. Mama had a paycheck coming. . . ."

Juanita held up her hand. "No need, honey, I understand," she said. The woman looked at the tired children and sighed. It wasn't that she minded that they used her phone; it just happened so often. She knew it couldn't be easy for their mother to raise two children by herself.

"They take her to Regional?"

"I think so," Charles said.

"I'll be right back," Juanita said. "Now, don't you two be ashamed to cry. Let it all out, don't keep it bottled up. Own it, and let it out, that's what that doctor on TV says." Her slippers padded softly on the wooden floor as she started into the hallway. Then she quickly stuck her head back in: "Own it and let it out."

They watched her go. In their dilapidated apartment building there were only a few neighbors they were even allowed to talk to. Mostly, the Sullivans just kept to themselves. It was safer that way, Mama advised them. Nobody would be getting into anybody's business, so there'd be less drama all around. And, judging from the terrible fights they heard going on, Mama was right.

As soon as Juanita left their apartment, Gracie whirled around, wiped her tears, and said, "Now talk."

Charles motioned for her to come into the bathroom with him, just in case their neighbor came back too quickly. Once she was inside, he shut the door almost all the way. "You promise you won't talk to anyone about this. I mean *nobody*."

Gracie frowned and nodded. "I promise, I promise."

Charles put out his hand. "Give it back to me first."

Gracie shook her head. She was enjoying the power she had over her brother. Charles reached for the wallet and tried to grab it out of her hands. She was too quick. He grabbed the ribbon on the back of her lavender dress and hung on tightly. "Give it back, Gracie!"

She resisted, but wasn't willing to have her best dress torn up. As soon as she quit struggling he snatched the open wallet out of her hands. He fumbled with it and it fell to the ground, spilling its contents. Cash was scattered all over their bathroom floor. Gracie gasped, "Look at all that money. We're rich! Charles, we're rich!"

Just at that moment they could hear voices. Another woman's high-pitched voice mingled with Juanita's.

"Oh, where are those poor babies? Lord have mercy! I feel terrible! Are you sure there's nothing I can do? I can do something! You've got to let me help. Where are they? *Charles? Gracie?* It's me—Mrs. Carter."

They could hear the talkative woman walk through their apartment with her high heels. *Clickety-click, clickety-click.* Quickly, without even thinking, Charles started scooping up the cash and dropping it into the tub. Gracie, following his lead, did the same. In five seconds all the money was picked up. They heard the woman approaching. "Juanita, I apologize, but if you'll excuse me I need to use the lady's room. I've just come from church and I haven't had a chance all day. . . ." Without waiting for an answer she headed their way. *Clickety-click, clickety-click.*

Charles grabbed Gracie, hopped into the tub, and pulled the shower curtain closed. Giving her his meanest look, he held his index finger across his lips and shook his head at her. And in case she didn't understand that, he took the same finger and made a slicing motion across his throat and pointed at her. Gracie wanted to say something to him so bad, but the look in his eyes stopped her cold. Biting the insides of her cheek to keep from reacting she held his gaze. She'd never let him scare her. Or, at least, never let him know if he did.

Mrs. Carter seemed in no hurry; in fact, she opened up a few drawers in the bathroom searching for something, coming dangerously close to the shower curtain. If she'd angled her head just a little bit she would have seen the two children crouched down in the tub in their Sunday best, surrounded by money. Finally, she looked under the sink and there it was—the toilet paper. She took her time putting on the roll. Both children were hoping this would be a fast trip. Otherwise . . . Gracie covered her nose, just in case.

Fortunately, once she got going she was quick. Gracie had to put her hand in her mouth to stifle her desire to laugh. Their neighbor washed her hands and out she went.

Mrs. Carter walked back down the hallway. They could hear parts of a quiet conversation. Juanita was puzzled about where they'd gone and said she'd leave them a note and come back later. She assured Mrs. Carter the kids were well taken care of. As soon as they heard the front door close again, both children breathed a sigh of relief.

Charles started gathering up the money. He was careful to place it back carefully into the wallet, the big bills first, so it all lay in order. He remembered that's how the man had it. It was important to keep it just the same.

Gracie whispered harshly at him, "What're you doing? Why are you putting that money back like that?"

Charles didn't even glance at her. He knew this would happen, but now there was no helping it. She shoved him roughly, but still he didn't respond.

"You better listen to me, Charles! I want some of that money! Give me some of it. You better not keep it all to yourself. That's not fair. Then I really will tell."

Once it was all back in order Charles folded the wallet and held it firmly in his hand. "I'm not keeping any of it," he said finally.

Gracie stopped in the middle of what she had been saying and stared at him with her mouth hanging open. Charles repeated, "I said, I'm not keeping any of it. What part of that don't you understand, Little Miss Greedy?"

"But, but . . . that must be five hundred dollars in there," she said in a high-pitched voice.

"Three hundred and fifty two," Charles corrected.

"Whatever, that's still a lot of money, Charles! What about our phone? We need stuff. I need some clothes. And Mama could use it." She could see she was losing the battle. "It isn't for me. *She* needs it," she finished lamely, seeing that Charles stared at her skeptically.

"You don't know anything, do you?" Charles asked with disgust. "You ought to be ashamed of yourself."

Gracie didn't know how to respond. How could he not want to keep it? It almost made her dizzy thinking about everything that money could buy. But she knew that Charles saw right through her. She had visions of clothes and a new radio and a bicycle . . . and . . . it had nothing to do with Mama and everything to do with her.

She made another attempt at reason. "Charles. He hit our mama! He doesn't deserve to have his money back. Think about that fancy car he drives . . . he doesn't need this money. It's chicken feed to him. He spends that on lunch, I bet. He spends that in one hour."

Charles said nothing, so she continued, feeling like maybe he was seeing it her way now. "Look, can we at least keep a little? He won't even know. That'd be fair. We get some, he gets some. We can use it to buy Mama something. You know, something real nice. She needs something nice. . . ."

"Gracie, I *said* I am not keeping it. It isn't mine. It isn't yours. It's that man's. Period." Before she could start whining again he continued, "The best gift we can ever give Mama is to show her that she's a good mama. The *best* mama."

"But. . . ."

"How did she raise us? She sure didn't teach us to steal. Do you ever listen to her? Or in church? Would she be proud of us for taking that wallet? Yes, the guy's a jerk, but that doesn't mean we should steal from him. Where have you been, huh?" Charles glared at his little sister.

"I—"

"Did Mama teach us to steal?"

"No, but—"

"Not buts, Gracie. It's not right and Mama would be so ashamed of us."

Gulping, Gracie thought of her mama and how she'd looked the couple of times she'd let her down. She knew Charles was right, even if she did want that money more than anything. Her face burning with shame, Gracie stared at her lap and shook her head.

Charles continued, "And I'm not going to let that man be right. You saw how he looked at us. I bet you he's reporting his wallet stolen right now instead of wondering if he might have dropped it running back to his car to escape the big, bad ghetto. I won't be just another black kid who stole his wallet. I don't know if you can understand that." Charles paused. "We're better than that, Gracie. You understand?"

Gracie continued to look down. Charles ventured, "You got anything else to say?"

Tears rolled down her cheeks and dripped onto her good dress. Again, she shook her head wordlessly. Life was so unfair sometimes. Was it wrong to want some new things and for the phone to work? She knew it wasn't right to steal, but why did everyone else get everything? She couldn't help feeling selfish. She liked to look pretty instead of wearing clothes that sometimes had holes despite Mama's ability to mend almost anything. And now with Mama hurt, what would they do? Gracie let out a sob.

Charles wouldn't allow himself to feel sorry for her. He pulled her into a hug.

"Give it back to the man," Gracie whispered almost inaudibly.

Charles left his sister to pout in the bathroom and walked into the kitchen. On the counter he saw a piece of paper—the handwritten note from Juanita. It read, "Spoke to the hospital. Your mom is in surgery. I'm going to get you some dinner. Be back soon."

Surgery, that was serious. Charles closed his eyes and prayed silently for his mother.

Lorraine felt like she'd been sitting for hours on one of the waiting room's stiff, ugly, orange plastic chairs. Why was it that hospital chairs were always so uncomfortable? "Makes no sense," she thought. "All you ever do in a hospital is sit and wait. They should invest in some rich Corinthian leather." Her dress was rumpled and her back ached. Her hand was cramped from doing paperwork on enough forms to wallpaper an emergency room. She'd called to check in on the kids but realized the phone was dead. She felt frustrated and ineffective. She looked around at all the other faces in the waiting room. Each one seemed to share her frustration and anxiety. A couple was seated across the way, facing her. The mother was crying quietly onto her husband's shoulder. They'd come in with a sick boy earlier and Lorraine could see on the woman's face that she was worried about her child. They made eye contact and Lorraine gave her a weak, sympathetic smile. She knew just what she felt like. At least that woman had a shoulder to cry on. She looked up at the clock again. "Why don't they come out and tell me what's going on?" she grumbled.

Finally she tossed down the three-months-old copy of *Reader's Digest* she'd been reading and marched up to the desk of the new receptionist who'd just come on shift.

"Excuse me."

The woman smiled back at her politely, with professional courtesy, but without emotion. Lorraine regarded the plain young woman: pale skin, light-blue eyes, glasses, and mousy hair framing an unsmiling face devoid of makeup. Lorraine scoffed, thinking, "This woman needs a makeover." Under different circumstances she might have offered a subtle hint or two, but today she couldn't be bothered.

"I'm waiting to hear news about my daughter, Ramona Sullivan," she said abruptly.

The lady moved slowly. "She needs some energy pills, too," thought Lorraine. She looked at Lorraine a few seconds before slowly reaching onto her desk and pulling out several forms. As she glanced through them at the slowest of speeds she said, "Can you repeat the patient's name?"

"Ra. Mona. Sulli. Van. With an S." Then, just to be safe: "And an R."

The woman put down the stack of forms. She hadn't found Ramona's name there. She typed the name into her computer and searched her screen. "And you are?"

"Her mother," said Lorraine, trying to be patient. It was proving difficult.

"Ah, here we go: Sullivan. I believe she's still in surgery." The woman didn't look up from her computer screen.

"But can you tell me exactly where she is? How the surgery is going? And if maybe all the doctors in this hospital have gone on their lunch breaks?"

The receptionist ignored the sarcasm. "I'm afraid I don't have that information. I just show her status here as still in surgery. The doctor will be out afterwards to inform you." She gestured back to the waiting area. "If you'll just have a seat over there."

"I have been waiting so long I actually started counting the number of cracks in your comfortable plastic chairs."

"Ma'am, surgery can take several hours. I'm sure the doctors are doing everything they can and will be out as soon as possible to update you on your daughter's status."

Reluctantly, Lorraine turned to go back to the waiting area. How could this woman say it all so matter-of-factly?

"Oh, ma'am, one moment. I see here we still need some additional information about your daughter."

Lorraine turned back to the woman. "I filled out all the forms you gave me."

"But you didn't fill in the insurance information," said the receptionist, with pursed lips. Lorraine was finding this woman more exasperating than ever.

The receptionist continued to look at her expectantly. Lorraine paused as the woman waited for an answer. "Well, she doesn't have any insurance."

"Medicaid card?"

"No."

The woman frowned, the most expressive facial gesture she'd made since Lorraine saw her. "Has she been here before?"

Lorraine nodded. "Yes, about a year ago."

"I'll need to pull up her record. Do you mind waiting for a moment."

Lorraine looked back at the woman as if to say, where else would I go? Her nerves were shot. Trying to curb her impatience, she closed her eyes. Instinctively, she pulled her Bible out of her purse and said a silent prayer both for her daughter's well being and for whatever was going to pop out of this woman's mouth next. She waited with closed eyes. She was interrupted by the monotone voice, but she finished up and said a quiet "Amen" before opening her eyes.

"Our records show that Miss Sullivan owes—"

"It's *Mrs*. Sullivan. Missus, as in she was married, but her husband passed." Lorraine needed to clarify that and keep her baby's dignity intact.

Without breaking stride, the woman continued, "*Mrs*. Sullivan owes the hospital eight thousand dollars." She stared at Lorraine and arched her left eyebrow. She lowered her voice. "It says here that numerous attempts have been made to contact *Mrs*. Sullivan, but apparently her phone has been disconnected. Bills have been sent out every month, but none have been returned. In fact, there have been no recent payments whatsoever on this bill, and it's over a year old."

Lorraine slumped. She should have realized this was coming. Accusations were all over the woman's face.

"Ma'am," the receptionist said. "What does she intend to do about it? We can't have this." She folded her arms and squeezed her lips as if she'd tasted something sour.

Something about her voice made Lorraine stand up straight and narrow her dark eyes. She knew what the woman was assuming about her daughter. Passing judgment when she didn't even know her.

"My baby works *two* jobs to keep her kids fed and clothed. She's not on welfare. Nobody gives her any help. Nobody gives her any insurance even though she's a good worker. She's doing the job of both mama and daddy. Every penny she has goes to her family. My daughter's a good person. Best woman you'd ever want to meet. She pays when she can but lately there's less work. I don't need to explain myself to you. Don't you sit there and ask me *what does she intend to do about it!*"

Lorraine was in a fury now. She was yelling and she realized that people were starting to look at them. All of the anxiety and frustration of the past several hours bubbled over. She placed the palms of her hands flat on the woman's desk as she leaned over and stared her down. "Yes, she had surgery over a year ago. She had breast cancer. They went in and had a tumor removed. Thank God," here she raised her eyes upward and her right palm in salute, "it wasn't full-blown cancer all over. Just a lot of pain. But she was out long enough so she lost her job. She's strong, though. She got well and found not one but two jobs. And when she could, she paid what she could. And now there's no telling what's wrong with her. I just pray she lives. She's been in surgery for hours. And you're here talking some mess about some *bill?*"

The woman's pale cheeks began getting a pink tinge, and she rolled her chair slowly away from the edge of her desk. "Well. I understand how you're feeling, Mrs.—?"

"Jackson."

"Mrs. Jackson, but I also have a job. Mine is to take information so that we can get people to pay their bills. We can't run a hospital where people don't pay their bills. This isn't a free clinic. Medical care costs money. More money when we have to continue to offset the costs by—"

Lorraine fumed. "Oh, I see. You just wanted to rub my nose in it. I see how you are."

The woman ignored the jibe and continued. "I understand that your daughter is having hard times. I'm sure we can work out a payment plan or some sort of means to help your daughter pay. I'll see that someone comes to speak with you about that. Any questions you might have beyond that can be directed to our administrative office. They're closed for the rest of the day, unfortunately, but open tomorrow at eight a.m. In the meantime," she said, glancing down at Lorraine's Bible, held tightly in her fist, "perhaps you'd like to visit our chapel while you're waiting?"

Lorraine answered icily, "I just came from church. But thank you for your kind concern."

"Maybe the chaplain could come talk with you . . . in the . . . the waiting room?" the woman suggested hesitantly.

"The waiting room?" Lorraine returned. "I should air my concerns in the waiting room in front of God and everybody?" Her voice was becoming high pitched again.

The receptionist was trying to delicately extricate herself from the situation. The brightly clothed woman looked as if she were ready to explode. Didn't people understand she was only doing her job? First thing tomorrow she was going to see if she could be transferred to another department. She looked up at the woman, hoping she was ready to sit down.

Lorraine never let her eyes leave the receptionist's face. "That woman's veins are as cold as ice," she thought. "She just sees numbers and forms and dollars signs. But I shouldn't have blown up at her like that. Her cold heart probably makes her well suited for her job." She needed to calm down.

"Well, maybe some prayer would do me some good." She read the woman's nametag. "Send him over, Sandra. I'll be in the chapel." She turned on her heel and flounced down the hallway with her head held high. That's all she needed was some overweight, has-been, wannabe chaplain spouting off about patience being a virtue. *Puh-lease. . . .*

Oliver French heard himself being paged. He was in the Intensive Care Unit visiting with a dying man. The man had been a parishioner of his years ago. Instead of talking about the afterlife, the thin man in the bed had the chaplain in stitches as he regaled him with tales from his youth. "Yeah, boy, I sure was a wild one, I'm telling you," he said with a huge, toothless grin. "Ain't got any regrets, though. No sir. If I wanted to do something I did it. Simple as that."

Oliver took the man's bony hands in his and said, "Well, we can all learn from that. I don't know when I've laughed so hard." He wiped the tears from the corners of his eyes. "I have to go. They just paged me. I'll visit you later today, okay, Jack?"

Oliver was reluctant to leave his friend but the man was falling asleep quickly. Jack already had his eyes closed, worn out from his storytelling. He waved feebly in response.

Out in the hallway Oliver wondered what new reason there was for the page. He always anticipated the worst. Even though he had retired from full-time parish duties, he knew in his heart that "once you're a minister, you're always a minister," and for very personal reasons he considered hospital visits a ministerial duty. They were rarely easy. He guessed it was probably someone close to dying and the family wanted him there to pray with them. His mind wandered to a story Jack had been telling him. He chuckled to himself. A passing nurse looked at him with a judgmental stare. He stopped smiling and tried to look serious. That Jack!

Going to the front desk, he noticed the receptionist looked flustered. Hmmm. Must be pretty serious.

"Sandra. You paged me?"

She put her hands on her cheeks in an effort to cool them off. "Yes, a middle-aged woman. She's over in the chapel. Lots of yelling. It took all my prodding to get her to go in there and wait for you. She needed some . . . some quiet time."

"A little high strung?"

"Wound tighter than a spring," she said drily. "She screamed at me all when I told her about a bill her daughter owes. I'm just doing my job. Don't these people understand that? And her daughter is still in surgery. Only thing I could do to get her to calm down was to say you were coming."

"And how serious is her daughter?"

"Car accident, broken leg and ruptured spleen, but it looks like the ambulance got her quickly. Everything's under control. She's being worked on."

"Where do you need me to go, then?" Oliver asked. "Visit her daughter when she gets out, or . . . ?"

Wide-eyed now, Sandra said in a rush, "No! Please find that woman and calm her down so she doesn't come back here. She was carrying around a Bible so I thought you might help set her straight."

The chaplain nodded. "Who is she?"

"Bright blue hat. You can't miss her. Loud. Just loud."

———

Moments later Oliver walked into the chapel. There were only a few people praying quietly inside—but even in a crowded room he would have spotted her immediately. Bright blue hat, perky yellow flower, stylish dress. Dang. Sandra hadn't said the woman was beautiful. She looked to be in her late forties or early fifties, just a little younger than him. He tried to put such thoughts out of his head. He wasn't here to admire her; he had a job to do and that was to help soothe this woman's fears.

Lorraine sat miserably in a corner with her Bible in her hand. "Shouldn't have gone off on that woman like that. I'm surprised she didn't call the police," she thought. "That would take the cake if, on top of everything else, I got arrested." She just wished there was something she could do. *Oh Lord, please, please, help my baby. Don't let anything happen to my baby.* A tear streamed down her face. *Please help us.*

At that moment Oliver cleared his throat and interrupted her thoughts. Looking up, she gazed into the warmest pair of brown eyes she'd ever seen. Thick, dark lashes, strong nose, straight white teeth, full lips, and dark chocolate skin.

Oliver stood looking at the woman with the tear-stained face. "I'm Oliver French, the hospital's chaplain on call." He was waiting for her to get loud.

"Yes," she said softly. "Lorraine." And then, regaining her composure: "Lorraine Jackson." She held out her hand. He gripped it gently and then held on to help her up. For a moment, it seemed neither of them wanted to be the first to let go.

Oliver cleared his throat. "Sandra said you were worried about your daughter. How can I be of service to you?"

Lorraine looked around at the other people in the chapel. Oliver could tell she was reluctant to converse here.

"Would you like to talk with me? We can take a walk outside, if you'd like."

"But my daughter," said Lorraine with concern.

Oliver put her arm in his and gestured down the hall as they walked. "We'll just be outside." He nodded in Sandra's direction at the reception desk. "Sandra will know where to find us."

"Oh, well, then, that would be lovely," she said as she grabbed hold of his bicep through his black jacket. "Thank you."

An hour or so later, Lorraine and Oliver walked back into the crowded waiting room. Lorraine's demeanor had changed altogether. She was holding his arm and laughing. Sitting at the reception desk, Sandra allowed herself a smile of relief. She knew she could count on

Reverend French. He had a soothing way with people that calmed their nerves and brought them strength— the perfect hospital chaplain. Sandra turned back to her papers.

In the waiting area, Lorraine turned to Oliver and gave him one of her famous you're-the-only-one-in-this-room smiles and said, "I feel so much better. Thank you, Reverend."

The chaplain beamed happily. "Call me Oliver, please. And I'll see what I can find out about your daughter." As he turned to walk over to the front desk, Lorraine heard her daughter's name being called by a skinny nurse with a clipboard in her hand.

"Is there anyone here for Ramona Sullivan?"

Lorraine rushed over. Oliver followed but kept his distance to give her privacy.

"Yes?" said Lorraine to the nurse, hopefully. "I'm her mother."

"Your daughter is all right. She's out of surgery and in the recovery room. You can go in and see her now. She should be just waking up." The nurse turned to lead Lorraine away.

Lorraine glanced back at Oliver expectantly. She didn't want to leave him so soon. Oliver said, not moving, "Don't worry, I'll stop by her room later to see how you both are getting along."

Lorraine gave a meaningful smile and said, "I'd like that. Thank you," and then turned, following the nurse down the hallway.

Loraine was not prepared for the sight that met her eyes in the recovery room. Her baby's ginger-brown skin was black and blue. Her left cheek was scratched and bruised. Her eye was swollen and her lip was bruised. Her leg was in a cast held up in some contraption with what looked like a metal brace around it. She had tubes up her nose and an IV attached to her arm. She seemed to be breathing softly. Was she sleeping? Lorraine wasn't sure what to do. More than anything she wanted to hug her daughter, but she was afraid to even touch her. She choked back a sob.

Just then a doctor came over to her. "Are you Mrs. Sullivan's mother?" he asked.

"Yes," she whispered.

"I'm Doctor Hartford. I performed the surgery on your daughter's spleen."

"How is she?" Lorraine managed to get out.

The doctor gave her a quick run-down. "We were able to repair her spleen during surgery, which is good. Her leg is broken in two places and needed to have some pins put in it. We had to reset the leg, and the pins will help keep it in place while the bone heals. Her face is badly bruised, as you can see, but she shouldn't have any scarring. We'll need to keep her here for a day or two to make sure she recovers fully from the surgery and make sure no infection sets in. This cast will have to stay on about six weeks, and then we'll pull the pins.

You'll need to have her take it easy to let her body mend."

He looked at the woman standing before him. This information hadn't comforted her, as it should have. She looked a bit woozy. He gave her a reassuring smile.

"But she'll be okay."

Lorraine let out the breath she didn't know she'd been holding.

"Why are her eyes closed like that?" she whispered.

The doctor continued to smile kindly, putting his hand on the shoulder of the worried woman. "She's just coming out of the anesthetic. We need to monitor her until she wakes up, but you can sit beside her until she does. It will probably be another half hour or so."

"Thank you." Then she remembered her grandson and granddaughter. They must be worried sick. She chased after the doctor but he was gone. She found a nurse and asked, "Would it be possible to use your phone? I need to call my grandchildren and let them know their mama is okay."

The nurse pointed to a phone in the hallway. "As long as it's local, you can use that one right there." Lorraine smiled her thanks. She realized she couldn't call the apartment but remembered that Juanita had called the hospital earlier and she phoned her.

Charles and Gracie were trying their best to be upbeat. They sat on the couch watching the TV in Juanita's apartment. She had insisted they stay with her until they heard about Ramona. She worried about them being on their own and crazed about their mother. She'd made them *arroz con pollo*, rice and chicken, which they barely ate.

Suddenly Juanita shouted out, "Oh, Dios mio!" causing Charles to look up.

Charles realized Juanita was reacting to her Mexican soap opera. She was thoroughly engaged and seemed very shocked with whatever had just happened—some woman had slapped a mustachioed man across the face. Charles wondered how long they'd be watching this. Neither he nor Gracie knew more than the most basic Spanish and yet they both had been sitting there for a while, not understanding a thing. Their minds had both been elsewhere, thinking about the same thing. He hoped his mother was okay.

Then the phone rang.

Juanita got out of her chair and picked up her phone. "*Buenas*." Her face changed. "Hello, Lorraine." Juanita looked over at the kids, giving them a weak smile in an effort to look hopeful. Charles and Gracie sat up straight, eager to hear what was being said. Juanita put a hand to her heart. "Oh, that's good news. I'm so glad to hear that. Yes. They're here. I'll tell them. Okay. Thank you, Lorraine. Goodbye. *Bendiciónes*."

Juanita hung up the phone and turned to Charles and Gracie with a smile on her face. "Your mama's okay," she exclaimed, and then went on to tell them about the surgery.

Some time later, Juanita walked them down the hall to their own apartment. As Charles climbed into bed, he couldn't remember the last time he'd been so tired. They would go to the hospital to see Mama tomorrow. He was relieved to know she was okay. He realized he'd been so worried all day he'd barely eaten. His stomach rumbled but he decided he was too tired to get up. He looked over at his bedside table and saw a lump of folded brown leather. As he nodded off, Charles told himself the first thing he'd do tomorrow was return that wallet.

5

Charles woke up early Monday morning and quickly got dressed. He tried to move quietly so he wouldn't wake his sister. He grabbed the wallet by his bedside and put it in his pocket, then picked up his shoes. Tiptoeing with them in his hand he made his way toward the front door. As he walked by his mother's bedroom he looked in and saw his grandma lying on top of the made bed, still in her Sunday clothes. He barely remembered her coming in; she must have been too tired to even undress. He knew she'd want to go back to the hospital as soon as she woke up. But the wallet was burning a hole in his pocket. He just wanted to be rid of it already.

He turned away from the bedroom and headed toward the front door, but then he decided he should leave a note: "Had to run an errand. Will meet you at the hospital." Just as he was signing his name he felt a hand on his shoulder. He jumped, then turned and saw it was Gracie, looking sleepy, dressed in an oversized blue-and-white t-shirt that reached her knees.

"Where are you going?" She was whispering, so as not to wake their grandmother.

Charles whispered back, "Taking care of some business. Go to bed."

Gracie rubbed her eyes. Her brother never got up early unless he was forced to. He was up to something.

"You better tell me. You can't just leave." She was fully alert now.

He pulled the wallet out of his pocket and held it out in front of him. "I'm going to find that man and take him back his wallet. You need to cover for me," he said urgently, keeping an eye on the bedroom where their grandma was sleeping.

"Cover for you?" Gracie stepped back and stared at her brother.

"His office is downtown somewhere. I don't know how long it'll take me to find it and come home. When Grandma wakes up you need to tell her something."

"But," she protested, "what about Mama? We're supposed to go see her this morning."

"I don't like having this man's wallet. I need to get it back to him today. But you can't tell anybody. It's just between you and me." Charles was itching to go.

Gracie glared at him, refusing to budge. "If Grandma wakes up," Charles realized, "there's no way I'll be able to leave." Why did Gracie have to be so stubborn? She was going to ruin everything.

"I'll come to the hospital as soon as I'm done."

Gracie felt secretly flattered. Her brother never needed her for anything and now he did. She hid her happiness and gave him a bored look. "What do I get out of it? I'm not covering for you for nothing."

"I'll bring something back for you," Charles said, relieved now that he had won. "I'll surprise you. C'mon. I gotta get going before this whole street wakes up and knows my business."

This seemed to placate her. "It's cool. I can handle this, Charles," Gracie said, pushing him out the door. "I'm not a little kid." She smiled to herself. If there was one thing she was good at it was telling a story. The trick was to keep your eyes on the other person the *whole* time and not give too many details. It worked every time.

Several hours earlier, Bill Bradford had woken up feeling sore, and his neck and back were stiff. It took him a moment to recall the events of the previous day. He grimaced. He'd probably hurt himself when he hit that lady. He looked across the bed for his wife, but Paige was already up. He could smell the scent of freshly brewed coffee. After trying to get the kinks out of his neck, he put on his workout gear to go on his usual morning run. He had been an athlete in school and made a point to keep himself in good shape, but lately it had been more about having some time to himself. He used it to clear his head. Today he really needed it.

Bill walked by his son's room as he headed toward the stairs. The door was closed. He paused for a moment outside, debating whether or not to look in, but decided against it. He needed to make up for missing his son's birthday. He pondered what to do as he made his way down the stairs.

Paige was in the kitchen reading something on her iPad. She was dressed in her workout gear: tight, very flattering black pants and a tank top. She'd no doubt take Andrew to a friend's house or something and then head out to her Pilates class. Bill took a moment to reflect on how beautiful his wife was. She looked up from her iPad and poured him a cup of coffee. After the party had wrapped up yesterday he'd told her some about what had happened with the accident. She'd listened attentively as always, not judging, just listening. It had been just what he needed.

"Feeling any better today?" she asked.

"Nothing a good run won't fix, thanks," he said as he took the coffee. He had a few sips and then stretched. Paige smiled. She knew her husband would talk about things if he wanted to.

"Can I make you something for breakfast?" she asked.

"No, I'm good."

Paige looked back at her iPad. "She's probably reading some mom blog," Bill chuckled to himself. He couldn't fathom why anyone would want to read about what other moms were doing. They all seemed to be stories about, well, things that seemed trivial and boring to him.

Bill smiled at the ease of their relationship. It had always been easy to be with Paige. That's what he'd liked about her when he met her all those years ago.

She was comfortable in her own skin. Not like all the high-strung society girls he'd spent most of his childhood and teenage years with. She'd liked him for *him* and only later did she learn he was the son of the famous William Bradford of Hospitals of America. He remembered back to when they were first married. Before Andrew. They'd really had a lot of fun together. And then he realized it had been a while since they'd done anything together—alone or as a family. "That's it!" he thought. He smiled to himself. He knew just the thing to make it up to Andrew for yesterday. Take a little vacation; maybe let Andrew bring a few friends. Paige deserved a getaway, too.

Bill popped up from his stretching. "Honey?" he said. "What do you think about taking a vacation? I feel terrible about forgetting Andrew's birthday yesterday. Maybe it would be a good present. Besides, we haven't done anything as a family in a while."

Paige looked up with a smile. "I think that would be great. Andrew would really enjoy that." She'd been worried all night about Andrew. He'd been really hurt by his father's behavior yesterday.

"Then it's settled," said Bill. With that he gave his wife a kiss on the cheek and headed out the door.

South of town, Charles waited for the #3 bus. He looked up and down the block nervously, and felt the wallet, tucked securely in the back pocket of his faded jeans. He wore a big orange shirt to make sure that the wallet was concealed. All he needed was for someone to see it and assume he stole it. He looked at the bus schedule again. Stepping off the curb he peered anxiously down the street, but the bus was nowhere in sight.

"What are you doing, boy?" someone said behind him. "You out early this morning."

Charles froze, recognizing the voice immediately. *Okay, think, think!* Slowly he turned around and nodded briefly at Davon. Davon was seventeen and ran with a rough crowd. He was also one of the boys who had been so interested in the Jaguar yesterday. "What's up, Davon," Charles said in a bored tone, adding a yawn for emphasis. *Where was that bus?*

Davon sidled up next to Charles and gripped his shoulder. "Not much, Charles. Just wondering what're you up to, that's all."

Charles shrugged. "Just chilling."

Davon snickered, "Yeah, right. You're up to something, boy. Where you going, huh?"

His heart was pounding so hard he thought Davon would hear it. "What you want, Davon?" Charles asked finally.

"I ain't playing," Davon said, tightening his grip. "What did you pick up yesterday?"

Charles hadn't learned the art of lying as well as his sister had, so instead of remaining cool he said heatedly, "What? I don't know what you're talking about!"

"Don't play me for a fool, boy," Davon growled, punching him lightly in the chest, his eyes narrowed into slits. "Me and my boys saw you pick up that dude's wallet. You think you're slick, don't you, keeping all that money for yourself? Well, I got news for you, boy."

"Oh, *that*," Charles said, staring innocently into Davon's hardened face. "We turned that in to the police."

"You *what*? Are you *crazy*? What did you do that for? You telling me the truth?" Davon gripped Charles's shirt and twisted it, bringing the boy close to his face.

Charles forced himself to stay put as he looked at Davon's disgusted expression. "You know how my grandma is," he explained, eyes wide.

"Y'all are sorry," Davon said, letting go and pushing Charles away from him. "Ain't that some mess! That's just pitiful."

Charles could see the bus approaching, and allowed himself a small glimmer of hope that he would live until it arrived. He wanted to get away from Davon as soon as possible. He was a bully and had beat up people for looking at him cross-eyed. The sooner Charles got out of here, the better.

Finally the bus pulled up, belching a cloud of foul-smelling gas. Climbing aboard, Charles ignored Davon standing on the sidewalk glaring after him. He turned his back on him and asked the driver how to get to 7501 Peachtree Avenue. Charles knew the local lines like the back of his hand but he'd never had much reason to head that far north, into downtown.

"That's a long way, son. It's gonna take you two transfers."

Charles held up a dollar. "Can I get there on this?"

"Sure, I'll give you a day pass. Have a seat. I'll call you when you got to get off," the heavyset man said, pulling the door shut.

The bus only had a few passengers so Charles picked a seat all the way in the back. Looking out the window he saw Davon flip his finger at him and saunter off. *Whew* . . . he had gotten off easy today. Looking at the other people he was relieved that he didn't recognize anyone. He didn't need any nosy folks knowing his business. He hated not going to see Mama right away, but the longer he kept the wallet the more he felt like a thief. He could have just turned it in to the police . . . but they had a way of twisting things around. Next thing he knew he'd be sitting like a dummy in detention, and that was no joke. But it was more than that; for some reason, he wanted to give it to the man himself. Just to look him in the eye and say, "See, we aren't like how you think we are." But now that he was on his way he felt anxious. It was a funny feeling having so much money. He had to get to Bill Bradford without anyone knowing anything. Except Gracie. "Little girl better handle business at her end," he thought worriedly.

After a few more stops an unsmiling, tall, well-built young man got on. Shades covering his eyes, gold earrings in both ears, hair braided back in cornrows. Attitude filling up the whole bus. Charles sighed. He just couldn't catch a break. First Davon and now TJ. Why was that no-good up so early? Charles could hear the beat of his music through his earphones as TJ walked down the aisle rapping out loud. "Go DJ, that's my DJ, go DJ, yeah, that's my DJ." *Lil Wayne.*

He slouched in his seat and stared out the window, hoping TJ wouldn't notice him. But that did no good, because here he came. "There's a whole bus," Charles thought, "why does he need to sit right *next* to me? Okay, stay cool." He slid his hand to the back pocket as he moved over and felt for the wallet. Still there. Good. He pushed it down further and then in a fluid move he brought his hand palm up. "What's up, TJ?"

The young man slapped his hand. "What's up yourself? Where you going? You ain't supposed to leave this hood, little man," he said laughing, turning off his headset.

Charles shrugged, as if he did this all the time. "Just taking care of some business, that's all. Where *you* going? Thought you'd be kicking it at the crib all day."

"You don't know nothing, Charles. I ain't going to be one of those lazy brothers staying home all the time. I'm finding me a job. *Today.*"

Charles looked at TJ, truly surprised. Maybe he'd misjudged him. And here he was mad at some rich white guy for assuming he was a criminal.

"Really? Where at?" Charles asked skeptically. As long as he'd known TJ he'd never held a job. And as far as he knew, TJ'd barely made it out of high school, and that was a couple of years ago. Charles knew more than anything that he didn't want to end up like Davon and TJ. First step, he knew, was making it through high school. Charles's grades had always been pretty good. His mama always said if you worked hard you could make it. He looked at TJ and realized he too was trying to make his life a little better.

"I'm for real," TJ protested. "Job Services. I've been taking some classes. They're going to hook me up with an electrician apprenticeship."

"Apprenticeship? What's that?"

"It's like you follow a guy who already knows how to do a job and you learn how to do it. Then one day, I can become a full electrician," TJ said with pride.

"That's cool," said Charles, holding out a fist so TJ could thump it with his own. He was impressed. Then a thought occurred to him. "You going to hook *me* up?"

TJ laughed. "You a baby. How old are you?"

Charles sat up straight. "Fifteen. I've been trying to get a work permit but can't get anyone to hire me."

"I know the feeling. Look, if I get something going, I'll be sure to help you out. Okay?"

Charles was so tempted to share his secret with TJ. "A job would gain me some respect," he thought. He really wanted to get some sort of work to help Mama. Maybe even save some money for college. But, he'd known TJ too long. No way could he ever tell him about the wallet. Even if TJ was a good guy, his friends weren't.

"Thanks, man."

At that moment the bus driver called, "Hey, you in the back! Your stop is coming up. Come up here so I can tell you what bus to catch next."

Charles stood up. "Catch you later, TJ."

He walked to the front and listened carefully to the bus driver, then hopped off the bus without a backward glance. He shook his head thinking about TJ. "You learn something new every day," he thought.

⸻

Charles followed the bus driver's instructions, and after two more bus rides found himself in the downtown business district, in the middle of some very tall buildings. He had no idea where he was because he'd never been to this part of the city before. He looked at the people rushing around him and saw that they were dressed in business suits and skirts. He felt very out of place. Nobody looked like this in his neighborhood, except on Sunday. Matter of fact, nobody *rushed* where he lived. Here everybody was running like a bee had stung them. Suddenly a woman ran into him, splashing some coffee on his shirt. "Great, now I look even more out of place," he thought. She looked up from her phone. "Oh, sorry. Shouldn't text and walk." She stepped around and kept going, looking back at her phone. Charles frowned. "That lady didn't even notice she spilled her coffee on me. People here sure are rude." He stood for a few more moments staring up at the buildings. He wasn't sure which way to go. As he stood there, a woman stopped and shoved a couple dollars into his hand.

"Here, honey, go buy yourself some breakfast," she said sweetly, then disappeared into the crowd before he could hand it back.

"Great, I must look homeless or something," Charles thought, looking at his baggy shirt, with its new coffee stain, and his faded jeans. "Now Mr. Bradford is really going to think I stole his wallet." He looked at the dollar bills. Well, at least now he could make good on his promise to bring something back for Gracie. He could pick up a candy bar or something on the way to the hospital.

He pulled the business card from his pants pocket and read it for the umpteenth time.

> Bill Bradford, CEO
> Hospitals of America, Inc.
> 7501 Peachtree Avenue, Suite 2600

While the driver's license had given Charles the man's home address, he'd decided to come to his office instead. "Bus probably doesn't even go to the part of town Bradford lives in," he thought. "And a black kid walking the streets there is sure to get picked up." More than anything else, he wanted to return the wallet as soon as possible. It was Monday, which meant the man was probably at work. Charles looked around at the street signs and saw Peachtree Avenue a block up. He started walking in that direction.

Inside his office, Bill prepped for his usual Monday morning staff meeting. His morning jog had helped him clear his head, but he still felt a little worn down and tired. Another spot of caffeine might help. He'd have his assistant run and grab him a coffee from the shop down the street. A good strong Americano, not the horrible stuff they brewed in the office. He reached into his pocket to look for his wallet so he could give her some money. He patted the pockets of his pants and then his coat. No wallet. He couldn't remember if he'd had it with him that morning. He looked in his desk drawer and tried to recall the last time he'd seen it. Suddenly he realized—the accident. He hit the intercom for his assistant. "Gladys. Gladys!" He slammed his fist on his desk. Now he'd lost his wallet. This was *not* what he needed.

As he walked, Charles noticed the street numbers getting bigger. He looked up a twenty-six-story building and saw a huge HOSPITALS OF AMERICA logo at the top. There it was. *7501.* Charles stopped and double-checked the card. He gulped. What if they wouldn't let him in? He hadn't even considered this until he gawked at the tall building with his neck craned back. As he walked toward the front he noticed a line of picketers outside. He looked at their signs and saw words like UNFAIR and GREED. Other signs had phrases like "I need my health care," "Workers' Rights," and "Shame on you, HOA." Charles wondered what this was about, but he knew he had a mission and couldn't pause to investigate. He hoped the crowd would let him through and he started to walk by.

One of the protestors stopped him as he tried to walk to the front door. He looked up, confused.

"Charles? Is that you?"

An older black woman carrying a sign was standing in front of him, holding his arm. They both smiled in recognition—it was his grandma's eldest sister.

"Aunt Etta! What are you doing here? Why are you carrying that sign?"

"Charles, what are *you* doing here? Aren't you supposed to be at home with your sister and your grandma? And what about your mama?" Then she put her hand on his shoulder. "I heard she got out of surgery okay."

Charles bowed his head and stared uncomfortably at the ground.

"I'm sorry about what happened to her," his great-aunt said gently. "So, what are you doing up here?"

He didn't want to lie, especially not to his mother's aunt, but he didn't want to tell her the truth, either.

"I . . . uh. . . ."

She tilted his head back so she could see his eyes. "You what?"

"Aunt Etta, I'm here to, um, meet with someone. I'm going to see Mama later this morning."

Etta gave him a stare that demanded answers, but Charles stood his ground. "That's all I can tell you." He pleaded with his eyes for her not to ask any more questions.

She released him. She was worried, but it wasn't her place to question his conviction. Whatever it was looked like it mattered to him a great deal. "You're a good boy, Charles. I got no reason to doubt you. Who are you trying to see?"

"Bill Bradford."

Her mouth fell open and she let go of her sign. It crashed to the ground. "*Naw*. Are you sure? Do you know who he is?"

"Not really."

"He's one of *the* Bradfords. His father, old Mr. William, is the man who founded this company."

Charles shrugged. "I just know he works here." Why was she looking at him like that?

Aunt Etta laughed as she picked up her sign and propped it on her shoulder. "Oh, Charles. You can't just walk up in there and go see Bill Bradford. He's the CEO!"

Charles frowned. He'd noticed that on the card, but just thought that was part of his name, one of those fancy rich-people names like King George III. "What's CEO mean?"

"Top dude. The *man*, Charles, you hear me? The *maaannn*."

"I don't get it, Aunt Etta," Charles said, looking puzzled.

"Chief Executive Officer, honey. He's the big dog here. Hospitals of America is his company. There's nobody above Mr. Bradford. He's the one we're mad at. He's why we're out here getting sore feet, carrying these signs. You know I'm not standing here working on my tan."

Charles chuckled, but he got serious when he read her hand-lettered sign: "I WANT TO KEEP MY JOB!"

He looked around at the other people slowly walking in a circle, some with children also carrying signs.

"Why are those kids here?"

"No one to watch them. It's summer. School is out. I guess their mamas felt strong enough about keeping their jobs that they brought the family."

"Are you getting fired?" Charles asked, concerned.

"Yes. Everyone here is. Mr. Bradford decided that he's going to outsource all his housekeeping staff."

"Do what?" Charles asked.

"Right now we work for Hospitals of America. We have a union. We've got benefits. Things like healthcare. In a few weeks Mr. Bradford is releasing all his house-keeping staff and contracting with another company to provide that same service for less money. It will cost less, so he can earn more. Never mind that we already do a good job and provide a quality service. His father never would have let this happen," she added, shaking her head. "Seems to me like Bill Bradford has forgotten where he came from."

"Can't you just work for that other company?" Charles asked, trying to make sense of it.

"It's not that easy, child. First off, who wants to hire a woman in her 60s with health issues? My boss knows I do a good job, but I'd have to prove myself to someone new. Most people just won't take that chance when there are younger, cheaper people they can hire. Second, even if they *do* hire me they won't give me benefits because there won't be any union. Third, I don't qualify for Medicaid. I won't be able to see the doctor or the dentist. Can't get my medicine. . . ."

"And you got bad high blood pressure," Charles added.

"You know I need my pills. All that'll go away. That's why I need my job," she said, waving her sign for emphasis.

Charles didn't know what to say. Between his mother and now Aunt Etta, it seemed like Mr. Bradford had caused a lot of trouble for his family, that was for sure.

"How do you know Bill Bradford, Charles?"

"He's the one who hit my mama yesterday," Charles answered softly.

"He *what?* He's the one hit your mama? You sure?" she asked skeptically. Suddenly she looked at him with real concern. Was this boy going to do something dangerous, out of anger? Teenage boys could be so reckless. "Oh, Charles. Are you here to cause trouble? You don't know who you're dealing with. I wouldn't go in there. Whatever's worrying you, just let it alone. Go on home, child."

Charles shook his head. He realized she was thinking he was out to enact some sort of revenge. He had to calm her down or she'd run and call his grandmother. He put his hand on her arm and looked her calmly in the eye. "I can't do that, Aunt Etta. I can only promise you I'm not going to do anything wrong."

She nodded a reluctant okay and watched the boy walk away. She said a prayer for Charles as he went to the building and disappeared through the revolving door.

Charles paused as he entered the foyer. The immensity of it was overwhelming. He stood in awe of the high ceilings. The walls rose taller than any he'd ever seen. And the marble, and the rich furniture, and the fixtures. He'd never seen anything this impressive. He tried to keep his mouth closed. He was supposed to be blending in but couldn't help but stare. As he walked toward the elevators he saw a hefty guard in uniform monitoring the entranceway. That man would question him for sure. Charles stopped in his tracks as he considered what to do next. How was he going to find out what floor to go to without drawing attention to himself? He watched as people walked in and out of the building, some stopping at the desk and asking for directions. His ears perked up when a businesswoman checked in for a meeting with Bill Bradford. The man at the reception desk signed her in and pointed to the elevators, saying, "All the way to the top. Press number 26."

As the woman waited for the elevator, Charles stood unnoticed in the background until the guard was distracted by another person asking for help. He quickly scooted around the desk and dashed into the elevator just as the door was ready to close. The woman looked startled, so he gave her his best smile. She nodded at him curtly and gave him a cool half-smile, stretching her thin lips into an even thinner line.

Finally they reached the top without any other passengers and exited the elevator. Charles lingered as she walked away, and wondered where to go next. The businesswoman walked up to a receptionist and told the woman her name. The receptionist picked up her phone. "Gladys? Mr. Bradford's nine a.m. meeting is here to see him."

So whoever worked for Mr. Bradford was named Gladys. He needed to find her, he guessed. But how would he get by the receptionist? She hung up the phone, and then looked up at the waiting businesswoman. She gestured toward the chairs in the waiting area. "If you'll just have a seat, Mr. Bradford will be with you momentarily. Can I get you something to drink?"

The woman looked up from her BlackBerry and said shortly, "Coffee, please. Black." Then she looked back down.

The receptionist got up to fetch the coffee and Charles took the opportunity to rush by her desk toward the offices inside. The businesswoman was staring intently at her phone screen, and barely noticed him.

Charles walked by a series of offices. He marveled at the view outside the windows. He could see all of downtown from here. No one working in the offices seemed to even notice the scenery. No one glanced at him. They were all staring at their computers or talking on the phone. Continuing down the long hallway, he checked the signs outside each door but none of them was the one he wanted. At the end of the hall was a glass door marked BILL BRADFORD, CEO, that appeared to lead into a waiting area with yet another office inside that. No one was on guard here. He opened the door hesitantly, only to be met by a stern-looking woman dressed in a drab, black dress, her grey hair pulled back severely into a bun, sitting at a desk.

If Gladys was surprised to see a young man standing before her, she didn't show it. She looked at Charles without expression, like the consummate professional she was. She was well trained in her job and greeted everyone equally, with the same respect. "May I help you, sir?"

Charles wiped his sweaty palms on his shirt and tried to appear confident even though he didn't feel that way. "Yes, ma'am. I need to see Bill Bradford."

This time the woman raised an eyebrow in surprise, but kept her voice neutral. "I see. Do you have an appointment?"

"No, ma'am."

"Is he expecting you?"

"No, ma'am."

"What do you need to see him about?"

Charles shifted on his feet uncomfortably. "It's personal. It'll just take a minute."

The woman stared at him, waiting for more. Her job was to protect Mr. Bradford and run interference on anyone coming to see him. Whether it was this kid or Fred the annoying vice president down the hall, it didn't matter. She would not let this boy pass without Mr. Bradford's say so. Charles could see she wasn't to be gotten around. "Please," he said. "I promise I'm a good kid. I have something of his and I want to return it, is all." He held out the wallet for her to see. She reached to take it from him but he pulled back. "If it's okay, ma'am, I'd like to return it myself."

Gladys's expression barely changed. She frowned just a little and picked up her phone. "Uh-oh," thought, Charles, "here she goes, calling Security." He had to force himself to stand still and not fidget.

"Mr. Bradford? There's a young man here to see you," she said. Then, covering the mouthpiece, she asked Charles, "What's your name?"

"Charles Sullivan."

"Mr. Charles Sullivan. No, he doesn't have an appointment, I'm afraid. He said it would only take a minute. Yes, yes. I see. All right then."

She shook her head and said regretfully, "He's very busy. Why don't you leave the wallet with me, and I'll make sure he gets it."

"Gladys!" said a woman's voice. It was then that Charles noticed another desk off in the corner. There sat a much younger woman. "I'm sure we can fit the poor boy in for a minute," she said, tossing her long blond hair over her shoulder, and chewing vigorously on a mouthful of gum. Gladys stiffened her back and gave the young woman, Sheila, a cold look. "Remember the chain of command," she had often told Sheila. "I am Mr. Bradford's personal assistant, and you are his secretary." And how many times did she need to talk to her about chewing gum? This was an office, not a high-school football game.

Just then Bill Bradford himself came bursting out of his office and barked at Sheila, "Did either of you talk to my wife? Has she found my wallet? We need to start calling to cancel my credit cards and report them stolen."

Bill looked over and saw Charles. "Who are you?"

"Charles Sullivan," he managed to squeak out. Mr. Bradford had that effect on people.

"This is the young man who wanted to see you," said Gladys, again without expression.

Bill rubbed his eyes, trying not to become more exasperated than he already was. The kid was obviously lost. Did it really take both Gladys and Sheila to help one lost kid? Hadn't he been clear to make him go away?

"Ah, yes," he said, waving his hand dismissively. "I'm afraid you'll have to come back another time."

"No, sir. Aren't you Bill Bradford?" Charles asked, finding his voice.

"Yes, but—" Suddenly Bill realized that this was the same boy who had stood outside his car yesterday, yelling at him to come out. How in the world . . . ?

Charles reached underneath his shirt, remembering suddenly what he had come for. Bill jumped and scrambled underneath his assistant's desk with a thud as his knees hit the ground.

"Don't shoot! It was an accident! *Don't shoot!*" His muffled voice sounded terrified. The women shrieked in reaction to Bill and looked at him, frightened.

Charles jumped back himself and then, catching his breath, started laughing. "Nobody's here to shoot you. I just came to give you back your wallet."

Bill glanced around the edge of the desk to confirm that the boy was indeed holding a wallet. He got up off the floor, trying to look composed. Sheila coughed and spit out her chewing gum. She'd almost choked on it in her shock.

Bill brushed the dust off his pants and smoothed his appearance. He then reached out and took the wallet from Charles. "I see."

Everyone, including Gladys, looked at Bill expectantly. Did the boy have more to communicate? Bill saw no one seemed to be moving and, with nothing else to say at the moment, he gestured for Charles to follow him into his office. Charles nodded thanks to Gladys and followed.

The door closed behind them. And for the first time in a long time, Gladys cracked a smile.

Charles followed Bill and stood inside the doorway. He had never seen anything like this. The room seemed as big as the Sullivans' entire apartment. Bill took great pride in his office. It had been furnished sparing no expense, with thick, colorful oriental rugs decorating the highly polished wooden floor. The light-green walls held original oil paintings, displayed alongside numerous awards, and bookshelves lined the perimeter of the room. One of the desks held an extensive computer system, while a larger desk, made from mahogany, had framed photographs, stacks of papers, and two telephones. The view of the city from the huge floor-length window was spectacular.

Charles surveyed the scene in awe, forgetting for a moment why he was there. So *this* is where a CEO worked.

Bill sat behind his desk and motioned for Charles to sit down on the other side at one of two chairs. They stared at each other. "What does this boy want?" thought Bill. "He's only a teenager." Did the boy steal the wallet so he could come and confront him? He wondered if Charles would attack him now that there were no witnesses. "I can take him if it comes to that," he thought.

"How did you get my wallet?"

"It fell out when you got in your car yesterday," Charles said.

Bill opened the wallet and looked through his cash and cards. Then he checked it all again.

"You didn't take anything?" he asked suspiciously.

Without hesitation Charles answered, "I took a dollar out so I could ride the bus up here to bring it back to you. Other than that, it's all there."

Bill narrowed his eyes at the youngster in the baggy clothes. What was the catch? He saw the coffee stain on the kid's shirt. Didn't he have any clean clothes? He looked like a vagrant. Maybe he wanted money.

"I guess you expect some kind of reward. You didn't come all this way just to give me back my wallet."

Charles looked puzzled. "No, sir, I just wanted to return it to you."

Bill stared at him quizzically. Surely that couldn't be it. "Is that all?"

Charles shrugged. "It's your wallet."

"What are you—some kind of a saint?" Bill said a bit mockingly.

Charles knew he was being insulted, but he couldn't figure out why.

"You didn't come here and expect nothing," Bill insisted. "Now tell me the truth."

"It was just the right thing to do." Charles got up. "So I'll be on my way," he said quietly, turning toward the door. He didn't know what he'd expected but he felt frustrated for some reason.

He stopped and looked back at the man behind the large desk, and spoke again. "I guess I also came here because of the way you looked at me, at all of us, yesterday." He hesitated. "I just didn't want you to think that we stole your wallet, is all. Just because someone is poor doesn't mean we think stealing is the right thing to do."

Now Bill felt a little uncomfortable. "At least let me give you some money for the bus?"

"No thank you, sir, I have a day pass."

"Are you sure I can't give you a reward?"

"Hard work, that's how I'll get my money. As soon as I can get a worker's permit, I'll get a job. Not just by having some rich man give me a handout. You have your wallet back, so I'll be on my way." Charles headed toward the door.

"That's it?" Bill said. On one hand he was anxious for the boy to leave—but on the other, he also wanted to understand.

Charles looked back, frustrated. He shook his head. "You know, here you are a *CEO* and you don't have any manners," he said. Bill frowned as Charles continued. "You haven't thanked me. And, you haven't even asked me one thing about my mama. I returned your wallet and you still can't believe I did it for no other reason than what I already told you."

Bill opened his mouth to protest, but Charles had already shut the door behind him.

As Bill stared at the closed door he felt guilt weigh down on him. The boy was right. Even if the woman had walked in front of his car, he'd hit the boy's mother and he didn't ask how she was doing. What was wrong with him? He'd been so worried Charles was going to knife him or something, but in the end he seemed like a good kid. Why wouldn't he take the money? It would have made it all so much easier. Bill knew the insurance company wouldn't give her a dime if things went his way and the accident was defined as her fault. Morrie was a good lawyer. He wondered if there was anything to do. Impulsively he picked up his phone. "Sheila! Call the security guard down on the main level. Tell him to stop that boy from leaving the building."

"But, what—" Sheila began to ask.

"Now! Call him now and get that kid back up here!" Bill slammed down the phone.

In the next office Sheila blew a bubble and punched in a call to Security. "Howard, watch for a black boy about fifteen years old coming off the elevators. Mr. Bradford said not to let him out of the building. Sounds serious. He needs him back in his office. The kid's name is Charles, by the way. Thanks, hon." Pop! went a bubble.

Charles had barely stepped off the elevator when the burly security guard grabbed him roughly by the arm. "Hey, let go of me!" he protested.

"Your name Charles?" he asked.

"Yes, why?" Charles said, trying to shake off the man's grip.

"You're not going anywhere. You need to come with me," the guard said, not releasing his grip.

Charles's heart was pounding and his stomach tightened into a knot. He had a terrible urge to pee. He should've known they were going to pin something on him.

"I didn't do anything! *Let me go!*" He tried squirming out of the man's grasp, but gave up.

A crowd of people stood and watched, many of them looking at Charles accusingly and shaking their heads. Charles avoided their hostile glances and focused on the floor. Even though he knew he was innocent he felt really embarrassed in front of all these people. He knew their expressions; he'd seen them aimed at him before. Half of them just assumed he must have stolen something. He and the guard waited in front of the elevator for what seemed like eternity until finally the doors opened. The guard pushed Charles in, pressing number 26. Even when the doors closed Howard kept his grip tight on Charles's arm. When they reached the twenty-sixth floor he marched him passed a shocked Gladys and over to Sheila's desk.

"Here he is," Howard announced, shoving Charles in front of him.

Sheila lifted up her phone. "Mr. Bradford, Howard's here with that boy."

Not even glancing at Charles, she gave Howard a big smile and said, "He'll be right out."

***

Bill strode out of his office and when he saw the look of terror on the boy's face—and the satisfied smirk on the guard's—he shouted, "Let go of him! Why are you holding him like that? What's wrong with you?"

Howard looked stunned as he released his hold on Charles. "I thought—"

"All I said was I needed Charles back up here. I didn't say he'd done anything wrong."

He looked accusingly from Sheila to Howard and shook his head in disgust.

"Come with me, Charles," he said in a more subdued tone. "I want to talk to you."

Charles looked at Sheila and Howard, who both hadn't said one word. He was trying to read the expressions on their faces. Fear, he decided. They were definitely afraid of Mr. Bradford.

"I'm not in trouble?" Charles asked, without making a move. He rubbed his arm where he could still feel Howard's painful grip.

"No. You're not. This will only take a minute."

Letting out a long, pent-up sigh of relief, Charles followed Bill into his office, but not before he leveled a meaningful gaze at Howard, causing the man to turn away in discomfort.

They entered the office and Bill closed the door. This time he gestured for Charles to sit on a couch in the sitting area of the office. Bill settled down next to him in a chair. Looking Charles in the eye, he said, "You were right. I forgot my manners. Let me start over. First of all, thank you for returning my wallet. It was a very big thing of you to do." Bill waited for Charles to respond, but the boy only stared at him without expression. Clearing his throat, he continued, "Second of all, how is your mother?"

"She's doing okay," Charles said simply. "Her leg's broken and her spleen was damaged, but they fixed it. She should be in the hospital another day or two and then she can come home. I was on my way to see her today but came here first."

"Well, I'm glad to hear that she's recovering." Bill paused as if he was unsure of what he was going to say next. "Uh, Charles."

Charles waited uncomfortably, wondering if he was going to be in trouble after all. Could this be some kind of a setup? Why was Mr. Bradford looking and acting so strange?

"Charles, I understand you won't let me give you money. I respect that. You're proud and have a good head on your shoulders. My father was that way. He started this company from nothing, and look at it now. Everyone starts somewhere. They say, *give* a man a fish and you feed him for a day. *Teach* a man to fish and you feed him for a lifetime. So if I can't give you money, maybe I can teach you to fish."

Charles was more confused than before. He'd dragged him back here to talk. What was all this about fish? Bill saw the confused look on Charles's face.

"Meaning maybe I can give you experience. I'd like to give you that start, so I've decided to give you *one share* in this company. It will come to you in the mail in the next few days."

Charles furrowed his brow. Share? Fish? What on earth was this man talking about? At least it no longer seemed like he was in trouble.

When Charles made no response, Bill asked, trying to not sound condescending, "Do you know what I'm giving you?"

Charles shook his head. "No, sir."

"I'm giving you a piece of my company," Bill said proudly, smiling now. "Everyone who owns a share owns a piece of Hospitals of America. Each share is worth money."

"Why are you giving *me* a share?" Charles asked mistrustfully.

"Hospitals of America is a very important corporation, Charles, and has been for years. Owning a share is a good thing. You returned something important to me. Not many people would have done that," Bill conceded. "So, as a reward I'm giving you a share. If you want to learn about business and hard work, it's a good place to start. See how a company is run. How business decisions are made."

Charles took this all in and nodded. It was fair, he decided. "How much is my share worth?"

Bill took a newspaper from his desk and pulled out the financial section and pointed to HOA. "See? That's us. Now look here. This number says that today it's worth $45.85."

Charles looked at the numbers carefully. Next to that number it said -4.15. Pointing to it, he asked, "Why does it say minus 4.15?"

Bill scowled and set the paper back down on his desk. "Our stock was doing great. In fact it was up past $50.00 a share only a week ago. Since May we've been going downhill. And those protestors outside aren't helping."

"What do you mean?"

"Bad publicity. They're making us look bad. Makes people worried about the stability of the company. I'll be glad to finally get rid of them," Bill said bitterly.

Charles listened carefully, but made no comment. He didn't want to start trouble. At the same time, his aunt was one of the people being gotten rid of.

"So," Bill continued, handing him an envelope, "this is a letter stating that I've given you one share of HOA. Give Sheila your address and watch the mail carefully for your certificate. Our next shareholders meeting is next week. You should attend."

Bill stood up. Clearly that was the indication to leave.

"Thank you, Mr. Bradford," Charles said solemnly, taking the proffered paper. He still wasn't sure what to make of it, but the man seemed to think it was really important and so he shook his hand.

Bill was surprised at the youngster's firm grip. "You won't have any trouble finding your way out?"

"No, sir," Charles said, and closed the door behind him.

Sheila was sitting at her desk filing her nails. When she saw Charles, her face reddened and she said, "Hey, Charles . . . I'm really sorry about the mix-up." She shrugged her shoulders apologetically.

"It's all good," Charles said lightly, relieved to be out of Mr. Bradford's office. He wrote down his mailing address and then turned to leave.

"Wait!" Sheila said, before the boy walked out. Reaching in her drawer, she held out a peace offering. "Gum?"

She seemed to need his forgiveness. He took a piece and said, "Thank you," then he walked quickly back down the hallway.

A short time later, Charles got off the bus across the street from the hospital. He was still confused by the events of the last couple of hours, but he put them out of his mind. The wallet was back where it belonged and he was glad to be rid of it. Now he needed to see his mama. He strode across the street toward the entrance. As he walked inside he saw a gift shop. Remembering the dollars in his pocket, he went inside and bought two candy bars: one for his sister as thanks for helping him out, and the other for his mama.

Charles paused for a moment outside his mother's room. He heard Gracie and his grandmother talking inside. Then he heard a small giggle from Gracie. So at least they weren't going to be crying or something. He took a deep breath and went inside.

The first thing he noticed was his mother's leg in a huge cast. For a moment he felt scared. He remembered the year before, when he'd felt so sure she was going to die from cancer.

Ramona looked up and saw him first. "Hey, baby," she said weakly.

Lorraine and Gracie turned around.

"There you are!" said Lorraine. She stood and looked at Charles reproachfully. "What on earth did you have to do that was more important than seeing the woman who brought you into this world?"

Charles tried to think quickly for an excuse. Of course they were going to ask where he'd been. Why hadn't he thought something up? And what had Gracie said he was doing? He didn't want to conflict with her story. Why hadn't they coordinated? He looked at Gracie for help but his mother stepped in.

"Don't scold him, Mom," she said. "He's here now and that's all that matters." She reached out her arms with some effort. Charles carefully went in to hug her.

Ramona studied her son; she wondered where he'd been but decided to let it go. He had never given her any reason to doubt him before. Whatever it was, he must have had a good reason.

"How are you feeling?" Charles asked.

"Like I got run over," said Ramona, trying to smile.

"I don't think that's very funny," said Lorraine, but she smiled, too, in spite of herself. Charles and Gracie laughed. Their mother must be feeling better if she was able to joke around.

Charles heard another voice and noticed that a curtain separated the room. He saw another bed on the other side of the partition. There was a woman talking to a man.

"My roommate," said Ramona.

A nurse came and checked Ramona's chart and gave her some medication. She questioned her about her pain and then left as abruptly as she'd arrived.

Charles looked hopefully at his mother. "When are you coming home?"

"In a day or two."

"But I thought you had surgery to fix everything?"

"Well, they have to watch me a day or two more, just to be safe. They reset my leg and fixed up my spleen but they have to make sure nothing got into them and that I don't get an infection. Then I can go home."

He looked at the cast and the pins in his mother's leg. "Can you walk?"

"I'm going to be sitting in a wheelchair with a cast on for a few weeks."

Charles nodded, too upset to say anything. All sorts of questions were running through his mind, but he didn't want to add to the sad look on his mama's face. She had enough to worry about.

"How are you going to go back to work?" Gracie blurted out. It sure didn't look like Mama could wait tables or clean hotel rooms.

A cloud passed over Ramona's face and she stared out the window, looking away from her daughter's anxious face. Even working two jobs it had been hard enough keeping her little family clothed, housed, and fed. When the doctor told her she'd have to be in a wheelchair for at least six weeks she felt like she'd been hit all over again. She couldn't work, or even leave her apartment building. The elevator had been broken as long as she could remember, and living on the third floor meant she was going to be stuck up there once she got home. She tried to hide her panic from her kids but her mother met her eyes and understood.

"Hush, Gracie!" Lorraine admonished, giving her the eye, causing the young girl to stare at her feet. "Don't be worrying your mama with all those questions. We're going to figure something out. Now, I brought you here to cheer your mama up. Can you do that?"

Gracie nodded.

Charles was hoping his grandma would come up with some answers. Working at J.C. Penney full time, Lorraine could get them clothes at a discount. But how were they going to pay for their rent and their food? Ever since his dad had been killed as an innocent bystander in a bank robbery five years ago, life for the three of them hadn't been easy. His mama relied on him to help her out—especially with Gracie—but he didn't see how he could help her now.

Gracie sat there fuming. If Charles had just *kept* that money then they all wouldn't have to be stressing so much. Charles caught his sister shaking her head at him. He narrowed his eyes and stared her down, until she turned away. Lorraine studied her two grandchildren and sighed. "Listen!" she said in a tone that caused the children to look at her quickly. She reached into her purse. "Why don't you two go down to the cafeteria and buy yourselves some lunch and give me some time to visit with your mama." She looked at Gracie and Charles meaningfully. They understood it wasn't really a suggestion.

"Thanks, Grandma," Charles said, reaching for the money. He gestured for his sister to follow him out the door.

———

As soon as she was sure they were gone, Lorraine turned to her daughter. She saw the worry in Ramona's face.

Ramona caved. "Oh, Mama, what am I going to do?" She started to cry but then held her still-tender side and wept more carefully. "Some lady came by this morning talking about payment plans and bills. We don't even know what this is going to cost yet."

"I know, sugar, I know. We're going to figure it out." Lorraine gripped the Bible in her hand as she held her daughter in her arms.

———

Charles and Gracie waited for the elevator to come. Finally it dinged and the doors opened. They paused as a man stepped out. For reasons he couldn't totally explain, Charles immediately thought of a weasel—then, noticing the man's gut, he thought of a *fat* weasel. He and Gracie got into the elevator.

As the elevator closed behind him, Mason Smith walked purposefully down the hallway, his worn leather shoes clicking dramatically. The nurse at the front desk had said Mrs. Sullivan was on the fourth floor. He checked the room numbers and headed in the right direction. "She should be just down here. . . ." Mason took out his handkerchief and wiped the sweat from his forehead. He smoothed his hair and tried to surreptitiously check his breath and armpits. He sure wouldn't seem professional if he smelled. Didn't want to perpetuate the lawyer jokes. All clear. He smiled to himself smugly and continued down the hall.

Mason couldn't believe his good luck and, if all went well, he'd have to remember to thank Officer McKeon for the tip. A big-time CEO hits a poor, innocent black woman on her way out of church? A jury would eat this up. He smelled a payday coming his way. It had taken all his self-control not to show up yesterday—but he didn't want to seem too eager. He had to make the family think he truly cared about them. He hoped he wasn't too late. He'd bribed the officer not to tell anyone else about the potential case, but his competition had their ways.

Lorraine said a silent prayer asking for help. What was she going to do to help her baby? She closed her eyes. Behind her, someone coughed. She opened her eyes and Ramona looked up.

A stout man stood in the entrance to the room, dressed in a brown suit that seemed a little too tight around the middle. Lorraine wondered what this man was doing here.

"May I help you?" she asked with just a hint of annoyance.

The man walked inside and held out his hand in greeting. "Actually, ma'am, perhaps I can help *you*," he said. After shaking her hand a little too firmly, he reached into his coat pocket and produced a business card. "Mason Smith, counselor at law."

He turned to address Ramona. "And you must be Mrs. Sullivan."

"Um, yes."

"I hope you don't mind me coming to see you, Mrs. Sullivan. You see, I'm an attorney. I represent people such as yourself. People who've been in an accident."

"We didn't call for an attorney," said Lorraine, moving to defend her daughter.

Ramona put up her hand to soften her mother's outburst. "What she's trying to say is, while we appreciate your coming to see us, we don't have money for an attorney."

"Yes, ma'am, I'm only too familiar with the unfortunate circumstances of innocent victims thrown into perilous situations through no fault of their own. But my services are free."

"Free!?" thought Lorraine. Was this man for real?

The lawyer continued: "Mrs. Sullivan, I believe you are entitled to compensation for your pain and suffering. From what I understand, because of one man's negligence, you had to have surgery and will be off your feet for weeks. I think we all know, if I may speak boldly, that you could also lose your job. With bills piling up, that's no easy life for a single mother."

Lorraine wanted to speak up. How on earth did this man know all that? Sneaky lawyers. She didn't trust a single one of them—most especially this guy. At the same time, he was making a point. He was speaking to their fears about their future. Maybe she should hear him out. She looked at Ramona, who seemed to be thinking the same thing, and let the lawyer continue.

"Now, you might be wondering how I know all this," said Mason. "Let's just say that a good attorney has his sources. Sources which also tell me that the person who hit you—" He leaned in for dramatic effect. "—is none other than the chief executive officer of Hospitals of America." He paused and raised his eyebrows in a way that said, "What do you think of *that?*"

Ramona and Lorraine looked at one another with shared expressions of surprise.

"Oh, I know his type," Mason continued. "I've been in this business for a while, and I've seen it all. If I had to guess, he was texting while driving and didn't even bother to keep his eyes on the road. Men like that, Mrs. Sullivan, they think they're above justice. Now, why should a rich man be allowed to run over some poor single mother in the street, without making recompense? His powerful, expensive lawyers will make sure nothing happens to him. Probably not the first time, either."

Lorraine looked at him. "If that's so, Mr. Smith, then why are you here?"

Mason gave her an easy smile. "This is what I do. I represent the little man—or the little woman, as the case may be. The woman who works two jobs, who struggles to get by. I represent justice, ma'am, which is why I want to represent the Sullivan family. I want to help you show rich men like Bill Bradford that there's punishment for bad actions. If he makes a mistake, he needs to fix it." He gently placed his fingers on the railing of Ramona's bed. "Now, I won't be asking for more than you deserve. I just want to make sure you can walk out of here knowing that someone is watching out for you."

Mason looked at the two women. He'd been worried about the victim's mother, but now she seemed to be really engaged. The mistrust had left her face and she appeared to be thinking hard about what he'd said. "Dang, I'm good," he thought. He knew he had them.

Ramona looked at the bedside table, which held the payment-plan paperwork from the hospital. Hesitantly, she asked, "And your services are free?"

"I take my legal fees only after I win your case."

Ramona looked at her mother. Lorraine seemed to be thinking the same thing: maybe this was just the help they needed.

Mason Smith smiled and thought of the new car he would buy when he won the case.

A short time later, Lorraine stepped gratefully out into the hallway. Ramona was sleeping and Charles and Gracie were watching the TV in her hospital room. She was still unsure about this Mason Smith, and hoped they'd made the right decision. She decided to take a walk and clear her head a little.

Without realizing she had been headed there, Lorraine found herself standing at the entrance to the hospital chapel, where she'd been just the day before. After gazing into the quiet interior she hesitantly walked in and sat down in one of the pews. She bowed her head onto her folded hands, and began praying fervently for Ramona. All her pent-up worries and fears overcame her as she sat there alone and asked God for help and guidance on how to assist her daughter. While they'd agreed to let Mason Smith represent them, something about the man made her uneasy. Even so, if he could do what he claimed, it would be worth it. She wished she knew the right answer. She didn't even notice the tears rolling down her cheek.

A few minutes later, Lorraine felt a soft touch on her shoulder. She looked up into the warm eyes of Oliver French. Suddenly she felt embarrassed. Here that good-looking chaplain again and she had tears all over her face. She fumbled in her purse for a tissue or anything to quickly tidy up her tears, and found a handkerchief being dabbed gently on her cheeks. "I do hate to see a beautiful woman cry," he said, smiling.

"*Beautiful* is not a word I would use right now," thought Lorraine. She took a quick assessment of her appearance. She never was one of those women who went out in public in sweatpants or jeans, and now she was ashamed to find she didn't look her best. She had been in such a rush to get back to the hospital that morning, and then so frustrated with Charles and his strange errand that afternoon, that she'd barely given her clothing a second thought. Granted, her outfit was still way above what most other women did, but she could do better. She was wearing a modest dress and barely any makeup. At least she'd had her hair done Saturday for church, so that was all right.

"I look a sight," she said with a half smile.

Oliver French thought she was the most lovely creature he'd ever seen. Even a bit more beautiful than yesterday. She seemed a bit softer, more vulnerable, somehow. "Well, I'm not one to argue with a lady, but I would be remiss if I didn't tell you that I think you look beautiful."

Lorraine blushed. Was he flirting with her? In a hospital? She tried to remember herself. It was hard when confronted with such a handsome man.

"Now," said the chaplain, "why don't you tell me why you're crying?"

Lorraine found herself unable to talk. It was not in her nature to speak about her problems or to ask people for help. She hadn't depended on anyone else in years.

Oliver gestured for her to sit back and relax. Then he walked over and sat down in the pew next to her. "You're going through some tough times, aren't you?" he observed.

"I sure am," Lorraine agreed, averting her eyes, fearing her mascara would be streaked all down her face. "We'll get through it, we'll be all right," she added, more to reassure herself than the chaplain.

"Would it help to talk?"

Lorraine hesitated. She barely knew this man, but this was his job—to talk to people in need—and she felt comfortable with him. Safe. "I'm . . . I'm just real worried about my daughter," she admitted finally.

"Are her injuries more serious than you thought?"

Shaking her head, Lorraine said, "No. She's okay. Her leg's going to heal up fine and the surgeon fixed her spleen. It's just everything else."

The chaplain waited, knowing that if he was patient she would tell him what was wrong. Haltingly she began. "My daughter, Ramona, well, she hasn't had an easy time of it. Her husband died a few years back. Ever since, she's been working two jobs, raising two kids all on her own. She got over cancer a year ago and now this accident." She stopped as tears welled up again.

"Sounds like she's a strong woman," the chaplain said, shifting in his pew.

"Oh, she is, she is," Lorraine agreed, "but there's no way she can work for the next couple of months. She's going to be stuck in that apartment and I just know she'll lose her jobs." Sitting straight up, she reached in front of her and gripped the back of the pew. "I have never felt this helpless. I'm her mother. I'm supposed to take care of her but I can't do anything. The few pennies I have aren't going to solve her problems, but I'd give her every single one if she'd take them. And now some lawyer comes along offering to help us. For free. We need his help but I'm not sure it's the right decision. But then again, what choice do we have? If he can get her some money. . . . And I wish I had the answers. I wish I didn't feel so, so . . . helpless." Lorraine slumped back down in the pew and twisted the handkerchief over and over in her hands.

Oliver waited a moment to see if Lorraine would say anything more, but she just stared off, looking upset. They sat in silence for a while. Finally the chaplain spoke. "I know a bit about what you're feeling," he said thoughtfully. "When my wife was dying, I could only sit by and watch her suffer. By the time they realized she was dying it was too late. There was nothing the doctors could do but ease her pain. A husband's supposed to take care of his wife. Protect her. And I could only hold her hand. I'd never felt like less of a man. I told her once, before she died. I cried over her bed; I told her I was sorry that I couldn't help her. And she turned to me and she said, 'Oliver, I couldn't have made it this long without you by my side.'" He looked off in the distance. "Sometimes just being there is all we can do."

Lorraine looked at Oliver. His eyes glistened. She squeezed his hand. Genuinely smiling now, she uttered a heartfelt and humble, *"Thank you."*

Bill Bradford stared for a moment out the window. He looked down the twenty-six floors below him toward the protestors at the bottom. They looked like colorful ants. A week ago he'd have said to squash the ants and be rid of the mess. But suddenly the whole thing made him feel uneasy. He'd had a terrible meeting with the company's board of directors. Ever since HOA had announced they were outsourcing their housekeeping staff, their stock had been declining due to bad press. Who would have predicted that the cleaning people and their supporters could make such an impact? Day after day they stood there with their signs. Nothing deterred them—not the heat, not the rain. It was infuriating. Well, in a few weeks it would all be over, he consoled himself. He could deal with the board; they were worried about the stock value, pressuring him to get this union protest dealt with. As soon as he let them all go, it would just be a matter of time before the press would forget all about it and move on. The unions were costing the company money and he could save the company money with non-union workers in the same jobs. Their bottom line going up meant he kept his position and his influence. They just needed to close the deal with the new contractor and they could officially lay the whole group off.

His thoughts were interrupted as Gladys's voice pierced the silence: "Mr. Bradford?"

Bill reached over and pressed the intercom. "Yes?"

"Mr. Morrison is on line one."

Without responding to Gladys, Bill hit the button and picked up his phone. "Hey, Morrie." He hoped his lawyer would have something good to say after the morning he had. No such luck.

"Bill, bad news. I thought this whole car accident thing was going to be open and shut, but it turns out the woman has gotten herself an attorney. He just called me this afternoon. He's an ambulance chaser, a low-life. But he has a reputation for making people's lives miserable."

"What do you mean, 'miserable'?"

"Well, he's not what I would call a professional. He's about paydays and high-profile cases. He threatened to go to the press. He wants a trial. He's thinking big money. He sees 'CEO' and dollar signs. Now, he's nothing I can't handle, but I mean this might not go as quickly as I thought."

"The press? Is there a way to keep him quiet? Can't you just settle the whole thing? Pay them a little money and get him to go away?"

"If that's what you want. Yes, I can. But I think we should push back a little first. The man doesn't have a leg to stand on. She was jaywalking. Regardless of who *you* are and how poor *she* is, the fact remains it's her fault. I know these guys, Bill. They think they see easy money. A little strong-arming to show you aren't afraid, and he'll back right off."

Bill sat silently. He just wanted the whole thing over with. Sunday morning, before the accident, he'd finally felt like he was back on his game again; since the accident, he wasn't so sure. What was going on? He needed a vacation. He had to remember to tell Gladys or Sheila to book that trip to make up for Andrew's birthday.

"Bill?" said Morrie, breaking him out of his reverie.

Bill shook his head in an attempt to clear his thoughts. "Do whatever you think is best, Morrie. But keep this out of the papers. That's all I need."

"Sure, Bill," said Morrie. "No problem."

Bill hung up the phone and looked out the window again. He rose and checked his pockets for his wallet. Satisfied he had it, he walked toward the door. He needed to get some fresh air. He needed a coffee. As he walked out, Gladys looked up. "Can I help you, sir?"

"I need a coffee."

Gladys rose and grabbed her purse as if she would go get it. "Your usual?"

Bill shook her off and bade her to sit down. "No, I think I'll take a walk and get it myself," he said as he marched out the door.

As he walked down the hall, Gladys and Sheila leaned out of their chairs in confusion, watching him go.

Two days later, Ramona Sullivan was ready to go home. She sat awkwardly in the shade of the hospital's driveway overhang in her wheelchair, right leg extended, waiting impatiently for her mother to take her home. Trying to propel herself in the wheelchair was cumbersome and she had already bumped against the wall trying to maneuver herself out of the room. Finally the orderly insisted that he push her out. It was his job, after all. Ramona guessed she was going to have to get used to people taking care of her. She didn't like it one bit. But she had to admit she was still feeling weak and tired.

When they got outside she told him to leave her. "My mother is coming to get me," she said. The orderly had other people to attend to, so he left her off to the side of the entrance. It was a hot day and after waiting a few minutes in the sun, Ramona tried to move herself again. Struggling to undo the wheel lock, she finally managed to roll herself forward a little. She barely got under the shade of the overhang and gave up and stopped where she was. She sank back into the chair. Where was her mother? she wondered. She was anxious to be back home in her own apartment with her children.

Yesterday Lorraine had brought her a new outfit to wear home from the hospital. At the time Ramona thought it was silly, but now she felt good in the pale-yellow dress that fell loosely over her legs. Mom was right—again. "You'll be more comfortable in a dress, wearing that heavy cast," she'd said, "and it just never hurts to look your best." The color emphasized her warm, cinnamon-brown skin. Ramona smoothed her short afro and chuckled as she thought of her flamboyant mother. Lorraine was *never* caught not looking her best. *So where was she?*

Then she heard the *clickety-click-click* of high heels coming toward her along with the sound of heavier shoes walking at a relaxed pace. Ramona craned her neck to see down the breezeway and there she was, finally . . . with the hospital chaplain. Ramona reached up to hug her mother and smiled.

"Reverend French," she said, "it's a nice surprise for you to come and bid me *bon voyage*." The chaplain had been by to visit her a couple times in the hospital. He was a calming presence and she had enjoyed talking to him. He also hit it off with Charles and Gracie; he had taken them down to the cafeteria for lunch and the kids came back happy and obviously charmed. Now Ramona noticed how her mom was smiling at him.

Lorraine, who was decked out in pink from head to toe today, laughed merrily. "Baby, Oliver is taking us home. Isn't that sweet of him? We won't have to call a cab."

The chaplain unlatched the wheelchair lock and pushed Ramona in the direction of the parking lot.

'Oliver,' hmm? So it's like that. Ramona looked back at the two smiling people and said sweetly, "Well, that's real nice of you, uh, Oliver. Thank you." While she appreciated his giving them a ride, she was mostly just happy to be out of the hospital. *Please, just get me home.*

It was a hot, muggy summer day, but Bill Bradford sat comfortably in his plush leather chair in his air-conditioned office with the blinds turned to block out the sun. He frowned as he went over several financial statements. Things could definitely be better. The intercom buzzed and he picked up the phone quickly.

"Just reminding you that you need to leave soon for the benefit," his secretary announced.

"Thanks, Sheila. Let me know when the car gets here." Then he remembered he'd wanted her to look into cruises for that vacation with Andrew and Paige. "Oh, and I have some more things I need you or Gladys to take care of this afternoon," Bill said, looking at his notes.

"I'll be right there," Sheila said cheerfully, hiding her disappointment. *Now what?* She'd been looking forward to taking the rest of the afternoon off.

Bill grabbed a pile of papers, placed them in his briefcase, and snapped it shut. He was eager for this upcoming benefit. It would be good to get away for a couple of days, especially to Augusta for some golf.

Sheila knocked and entered, carrying his garment bag. "I can't believe you actually get to meet Rickie Fowler!" she gushed. "That's *so* exciting, Mr. Bradford. He's so cute."

Bill shook his head. The kids on the PGA tour got younger and younger. That boy seemed to spend more time on his hair. But he was a good golfer.

He stood up, taking one last look around his office, straightened his tie, and shut the door.

"Who else will be there?" Sheila asked eagerly, hungry for celebrity gossip. She was having dinner with some girlfriends tonight and it would be great to casually drop a few names. She didn't mind showing off what a powerful man she worked for.

"Oh, the usual crowd who shows up at these charity events," Bill said. "Mickelson and Stricker are big draws, of course, but they can't do it all themselves."

"No, of course not," she hastened to agree. Okay, no more names. "What's the cause?"

Bill paused. "Cancer, leukemia, something like that." He looked down at his list.

"Wow." She popped a bubble and then looked at her boss guiltily.

Bill wrinkled his nose.

"Sorry. Watermelon. It's really good. Want a piece?"

Bill didn't answer; just shook his head. If she wasn't trying so hard to quit smoking he'd make her quit this nasty gum habit. She tried really hard but sometimes she was so unprofessional. Gladys had reprimanded her about her phone manners more than once. She was too casual. But then at least she had personality, which was more than he could say for Gladys.

"What else do you need me to do?" Sheila asked, changing the subject, knowing she'd annoyed him.

Bill checked his day planner. "I want to take my wife and son on vacation. I need you to book a cruise for three—no, five—people, for the first week of August. Seven days, oh, wait, I need to be back that Monday. Make it five days. That's good enough."

"Where do you want to go, Mr. Bradford?"

"Somewhere in the Caribbean, I think. Get me some options. Does Disney have a cruise line?"

"I think so? I'll talk to the travel agent," Sheila said, trying to act efficient. She knew she should be asking more questions, but she hadn't been on that many trips herself other than once to the Grand Canyon as a teenager with her family.

"I'm thinking my family and two of my son's friends. Or maybe my in-laws."

"Should I call your wife to see if there's anywhere in particular she'd like?"

Bill brushed the question off. "She'll be happy with whatever I end up choosing."

Gladys interrupted. "Your car is here, sir."

Bill headed toward the elevators. Sheila hurried after him. "Just get me some potential itineraries and prices and I'll pick one."

Sheila nodded and jotted a few notes down and looked at him expectantly, wishing he would just *go*. The elevator came and he walked inside. He made no mention of goodbye and so Sheila followed him inside. He pressed "L" and continued.

"Now, this is very important," Bill said sternly. "Paige and I are donating money to the Arts Council because she wants our name on the new symphony hall. I guess all the other wives are getting them. Find out what they want to make that happen. This is our big one this year, but no need to go overboard. Do you understand?" Bill looked at her carefully, hoping she wouldn't screw this up. He wondered if he should have given the task to Gladys.

"Of course, Mr. Bradford," Sheila assured him. "I'll take care of that today as well." *Leave already!* She tilted her head, smiling at him pleasantly. Bill nodded a brusque farewell and left her standing in the lobby.

"Have a *great* time, Mr. Bradford," Sheila called out as she headed quickly back toward the elevators, relieved to finally have the weekend ahead of her. She pressed the button to go back upstairs. She glanced at her fingernails, wondering what color to paint them this afternoon at her manicure appointment, after she snuck out early. She'd had them pink for a while now and she was going out this weekend. She wondered if purple would be too much. She had a brand-new bright-purple dress she wanted to wear. She watched the elevator doors close, in deep debate with herself.

As Bill walked to the front doors, Howard, the security guard, intercepted him. "Mr. Bradford! Hold on a moment, sir."

Bill glared at the guard. "I'm in a bit of a hurry, Howard. My town car is waiting to take me to the airport."

"I know, sir. I just worried that you might have trouble getting through those picketers. There seems to be more than ever today. Just trying to warn you. Maybe I can have the car pull into the loading dock." Mr. Bradford could be so irritable. "If I hadn't told him," Howard thought resentfully, "then he'd be jumping down my throat for *not* telling him."

"That will take too long," Bill said, glancing impatiently at his watch. He looked out at the crowd. There were a lot of people out there. But he didn't want to lose any more time. He looked at Howard. While he was getting up in years, the security guard was still an imposing man. "Why don't you help me out through them? That should be enough. Don't you think?"

"Of course, sir," Howard answered. He wasn't so sure he would be enough to take on the mob if they went after Mr. Bradford. He already woke up with more aches and pains than he used to. Still, Mr. Bradford was the boss.

"Fine, then," Bill said curtly. "But hurry, let's hurry, I'm meeting Ira and Tom at the airport in 45 minutes." He started toward the door, but, seeing the swarm of people carrying signs, he stopped abruptly and turned toward the security guard.

"Don't worry, sir," Howard said reassuringly, "I'll make sure you don't miss your plane."

Bill sighed in frustration. He couldn't remember the last time he flew commercial. "We're taking our corporate jet. It's not going anywhere without me. But I want to be to our destination by four o'clock. Please—just get me through that crowd." Then he mumbled under his breath: "Won't they just go home?"

"You ever talk to those people out there, Mr. Bradford?" Howard asked as he nodded toward the group carrying signs.

Bill looked at the man incredulously. *"What?"*

"You know, have you sat down with them? Maybe work something out?"

"No." He sized up Howard. The man rarely spoke more than a few words and now he was asking presumptuous questions. "We have people who deal with their union leaders."

"I see," said Howard, as he looked down. He had just been trying to make conversation and it seemed he'd annoyed Mr. Bradford even more than he already was. "I'm sorry, sir. I just thought sometimes sitting down with two parties helps them work things out."

"Can we please just get through this crowd," Bill demanded through clenched teeth.

Howard shrugged, tugged on his hat, and opened the door. They were met by a burst of heat and angry voices. Bill looked straight ahead toward his goal. All he had to do was push through and he'd be on his way.

One of the protestors spotted him. He pointed and yelled above the crowd, "Hey! That's him!"

"That's *him!* It's Bill Bradford!"

The crowd thronged toward him like a strong wave in the ocean.

"Why won't you listen to us?" someone pleaded.

"*William* Bradford must be rolling in his grave," another shouted disgustedly.

"I need this job, Mr. Bradford! I need my health coverage."

All of a sudden signs were being stuck in his path, in front of his face. There were hands on him, tugging this way and that. Abruptly he realized that he was trapped in the middle, surrounded by so many desperate faces. There seemed to be every kind of person: women and men, young and old. Most of them looking at him like they hated him. Like they wanted to break every bone in his body, and held him responsible for all their troubles. "I'm going to die in here," Bill worried. "Smothered by this angry mob!" He waved them away, careful to keep his expression neutral in case the media was there. He tried not to look as scared as he was. People were actually tugging on his sleeves. *Where was Howard?*

"All right, all right. Outta the way . . . you heard me. Move it. Move outta the way," Howard yelled as he strong-armed his way toward Bill. "Let us pass or I'm calling the cops! Move out of the way!"

The crowd moved back to get out of the bull-like security guard's path. Bill followed him as closely as he could, ducked into the waiting town car, and slammed the door shut without another glance at the protestors or at Howard.

He sighed after the door was closed, trapping the noise outside. The driver locked the doors without being asked. The faces and signs were still up against his windows but all Bill heard was their dull thudding against the car. Inside at least he was safe. He could see Howard still pushing people back from the car. He stared at them, getting a closer look now that they couldn't see him. He was mostly disturbed by the anger he saw in their eyes. "It's not my personal fault they're being let go," he thought. "It's a business decision. It's what's best for the company. I can't let my father's company lose money." Why couldn't they understand that?

Bill was shaken. He looked at the driver and pulled himself back together. "Marcus, let's go. I'm even more late now than I was before."

Marcus turned around before putting the car in drive. He'd kept the car running while he waited, so they could leave immediately. "I'll get you there, Mr. Bradford, don't worry. Ain't no use in stressin'. You know me, I be dippin' and dappin' through all that traffic. We'll get there." Marcus's banter relaxed his passenger.

Bill chuckled. "Okay, let's dip and dap, then."

As they pulled into traffic, Bill relaxed more. He leaned back and felt the buzzing in his pocket as his cell phone rang. "Hello?"

"Bill, it's Morrie."

"News?"

"Ah, still reviewing the case. But as I said, Bill, Sullivan was jaywalking. Her attorney doesn't have a leg to stand on. Now, you said you weren't speeding?" Morrie queried.

Bill hesitated, trying to remember that fateful Sunday. "Uh . . . I can't remember. I don't think so."

"Well, they can tell from the skid marks how fast you were going."

Then Bill remembered how he'd been lost and playing with his GPS. He worried that the other attorney might discover something. "Morrie?"

"Yeah."

"I was, well, I mean I *was* kind of distracted. . . ."

"How so?"

Bill recalled those chaotic moments. "Paige had just called so I was on the cell."

"So? Who isn't?" Morrie laughed.

"Yeah, well. And I was trying to figure out my GPS," Bill continued.

"That Jag is a beaut, isn't she? I bet you love that sound system. I might just have to get one myself. Getting a little tired of the Benz. We'll see. Listen, Bill, I've got to go. Don't worry. There's no way anyone could know what you were doing in the car. I'll wrap this up. Just thought I'd check in with you one last time. I'll handle it. Ciao."

Bill clicked off the phone and stared out the window, his thoughts everywhere but on the scenery. He just wanted to get on that plane and get out of town.

An hour or so later, Bill Bradford was on the ground again. It had been a quick and painless flight once he'd gotten to the airport. He sat in the back of the car. He felt more relaxed. He'd had a cocktail on the plane, which had helped to numb his nerves after the encounter with the protestors. He checked his BlackBerry and saw an email come through from Sheila. It had a list of potential itineraries for the cruise. He picked the second of the three options and shot back a quick email telling her to book it. Then he called Paige.

"Hey, honey," his wife said. "How was your flight?"

"Fine," he answered abruptly.

"Andrew's *so* excited that you get to see some of the big stars. Do you think you could—"

"I'll see what I can do, Paige. Don't want to come across like some star-struck groupie," Bill said, rolling his eyes. "That reminds me. Schedule a dinner at that new Thai restaurant for next Friday. Reservations for four."

Paige scrambled for a pen and looked for a calendar. "Next Friday?"

"Yes. We need to meet with Robert Strom and his wife. Good PR, you know."

"Sure," Paige said evenly. It was a good thing he couldn't see her grimace. She did *not* enjoy dinners with the board chairman and his wife, as they were usually quite tedious.

"Oh, and I booked those tickets for our vacation," Bill boasted.

"Oh, Bill, that's—"

"We're going on a cruise! The first week in August. Grand Caymans, Aruba, the whole works," he told her enthusiastically.

Paige checked the calendar. Uh-oh . . . August was Andrew's soccer camp. "Uh, sweetie? That sounds wonderful, but could we do it the following week? You see—"

"Listen, Paige, whatever you have, move it. It's the only week I can get away. Tell Andrew to pick two friends. That is, unless you want to bring your mom and dad instead? I hope this will make up for screwing up his birthday." Bill chuckled.

Paige bit her lip. Andrew had been looking forward to that camp all year. All his friends were going to be there, his whole team. Then again, how often did Bill have time to get away and spend time with them? She saw Andrew come through the front door and decided to table the conversation for a later date. Paige pointed to the phone and mouthed, "It's your father." Andrew came over eagerly to say hi.

"All right. Oh, Bill, Andrew just walked in the door! He wants to—"

Bill saw another call coming in on his cell. It was the office. "I'm getting another call. Talk to you guys later." Bill switched over before she could respond.

Paige sat at the kitchen table with the receiver in her hand, listening to the dial tone. "Sorry, sweetie, Dad had to take another call."

"Typical," said Andrew as he opened up the fridge and grabbed a Coke.

Paige put the receiver back in the cradle and tried to put on a smile for her son. "But he said he hopes you have a great weekend. That's all," she said, digging her nails into the palm of her hand.

"Why do you have the calendar out?"

Paige looked at the month of August. "Your dad wants to take us all on a cruise," she answered brightly. "Down to the Caribbean islands. Won't that be fun?"

Andrew was intrigued. "Yeah, sure, that sounds fun."

"He even said you could invite two of your buddies; how's that?" Paige glanced expectantly at her son. This news seemed to further pique his interest.

"Cool. When are we going?"

Paige hesitated. "Well, it will be the first week in August."

Andrew stood behind her and looked at the calendar. "That's when my soccer camp is, Mom."

Paige looked at him hopefully. "It was the only time that works for your dad. You can always go back next year."

Andrew set his drink down on the counter and faced his mother. "No way, Mom. I've been looking forward to that all year. They're going to have the national team there and everything. And all my friends are going. Typical Dad: don't worry about what anyone else wants."

"I know, honey, but your father said—"

Andrew shook his head. "It's not fair, Mom. First he missed my birthday party and *now* he's trying to ruin my summer. It's not fair!"

Paige put her hand on her son's arm, but he shrugged it off. "Andrew—"

"Mom, why didn't you tell him no?" Andrew asked accusingly.

"I did try, but. . . ." Paige looked back down at the calendar.

"You never stand up to him!"

"Andrew!"

"You don't! And you don't stick up for me either! You just let him do whatever he wants."

"Don't talk to me like that," Paige said sharply. She was shocked at Andrew's harsh words. The two of them usually had such an easy rapport.

"*I'm not going*. You can't make me," he said, scowling at his mother, shaking.

Paige hung her head. "Just stop it, Andrew. What do you expect me to do? He's trying to make it up to you. He feels terrible about your birthday."

Andrew clenched his fists. "Then why doesn't he just ask me what *I* want? I don't want to go on a stupid cruise! And he'll just be on his dumb phone the whole time anyway."

"Andrew—"

But Andrew was already out of the room. Paige heard his bedroom door slam upstairs and she sighed. She just couldn't win.

Ramona sat glumly on her bed with her leg propped up on pillows. She had more pillows behind her back to help her sit up but she just couldn't get comfortable. Gracie had brought her magazines from the library and Charles was attentive to everything she needed, coming in every few minutes to see if she was hungry or thirsty. But still she felt down.

"This heat is unbearable," she thought to herself. "I feel like I'm trapped in a cage."

Ramona didn't want everyone to have to wait on her. She felt like a burden. She'd tried to keep herself busy with a bit of mending and reading, but couldn't stay focused; television got boring quickly; there was nothing left to do but sit and think. "When is Mason Smith going to call about the settlement?" That was the only thing keeping her from falling apart altogether—the hope that she might be able to pay their rent and not be put out on the street.

"Those hospital bills are coming, too," she knew. While she wanted them to stay away as long as possible, morbid curiosity demanded she at least know the amount.

"I wonder if the mail is here yet?" Ramona wished she could just walk down and get it herself. Instead she reluctantly called out to her son: "Charles?" She waited a moment and called out again, a bit louder. "Charles?"

"Yes, Mama," came the reply from the other room.

"Can you check to see if the mail's here? And what are you watching in there? It better not be 'South Park' or MTV," Ramona warned her son.

"I know, I know," Charles said as he came into her room and jumped gently onto her bed, being careful not to jostle her leg. "I would never break the rules while you're helpless and can't move to stop me!"

"Don't get smart with me, Prince Charles," Ramona joked.

"I can't help it, Mama. I was born smart!"

"You're getting big-headed, I know that."

"Okay, I'm getting the mail," he said, jumping down and trotting into the kitchen.

He grabbed the little mail key off its hook, and ran noisily down the flights of stairs. Unlocking the narrow door from a long row of boxes, he peered to see if there was anything inside, grabbed the handful of letters, slammed the metal door shut, and quickly ran back up to his apartment, taking the stairs two at a time.

Once inside, Charles locked the door and looked through the letters. All of a sudden he froze. The second piece of mail was addressed to MR. CHARLES SULLIVAN and it was from Hospitals of America.

"Why would they send me a letter?" he worried. "Am I in trouble? I bet they want their share back. Mr.

Bradford made a mistake. Or he was just playing a joke on me."

"Charles?" Ramona called. "Can I get my mail *today?*"

Impulsively he stuffed the envelope inside his back pocket, covering it with his shirt. Trying to look nonchalant, he walked into his mother's bedroom and handed her the rest of the mail. "Here you go, Mama."

Ramona shuffled through the envelopes, mumbling. "Bill, bill, bill . . . But nothing from the hospital." She wasn't sure if she was disappointed or relieved to push off the bad news one more day. Then she saw an envelope with a handwritten address. *A letter!* "Now ain't that nice. It's from my cousin Trish up in New York."

"Well, have fun catching up with Trish, Mama. You need anything?" Ramona shook her head no. Charles walked out, leaving his mother to her letter. He'd been watching a ballgame on TV, but now he couldn't concentrate on it. The other team had tied it up and they were going to extra innings, but Charles realized that he no longer cared who won. He needed to read that Hospitals of America letter, but he couldn't go into his room and close the door—he never did that. It would immediately make everyone suspicious. He needed to open the envelope in the bathroom. But his sister was taking a bath. If only Gracie would get out of there. . . .

He walked over to the bathroom door. "Girl! Hurry up," he shouted, banging on the door. "You've been in there too long."

Silence. Then finally he heard the sound of the tub being drained. He waited a few moments but the door still failed to open. He could hear Gracie singing to herself, ignoring him.

"Gracie, you *don't* sound good," Charles said irritably. "You ought to give your raggedy voice a rest." She was taking her time on purpose just to annoy him.

The sound stopped abruptly. Then she began singing at the top of her lungs: *"I've got sunshine on a cloudy day. . . ."*

Charles put his hands over his ears. That girl could get on his nerves something terrible! If Mama weren't nearby he'd let her know what's up. Why didn't Mama tell her to stop, anyhow? After a long musical set that included the whole of "My Girl" and part of a mocking "Don't Worry, Be Happy," he heard the door click. Finally, Gracie emerged from the steamy bathroom wearing blue shorts and a red t-shirt with a green towel wrapped around her head. She smirked at him, proud of herself.

"You're just jealous, Charles, because you sound like a rusty old toilet when you try to sing," she said, smiling smugly. Unfortunately for Charles, Gracie *did* have the voice in the family.

Charles glared at her. "Are you finished?"

Gracie just laughed as she walked into her bedroom and closed the door. Then she opened it a crack and said quickly, "A rusty old toilet that's *plugged up*," before slamming it shut and collapsing in giggles on her bed.

Charles sat on the edge of the tub and carefully opened the envelope. Folding out the letter, he read through it, frowned, and read it again. "Nothing about me being in trouble," he thought. "Nothing about having to give my share back." Inside the envelope was another piece a paper—an official-looking document with his name on it. Also in the envelope was a note about the "annual shareholders meeting." Hadn't Mr. Bradford said he should attend? What was the meeting for? He shook his head. What kind of mess was this?

Charles sat with his head in his hands. Who could he ask? Mama didn't need any more stress right now. Grandma . . . naw. All of a sudden he sat up. Reverend French! The two of them had hit it off at the hospital, and Charles could tell the chaplain was a smart man with experience in the world. He would know what to do.

Charles stuffed the letter inside the envelope, tucked it back in his pocket, and opened the door. Grandma would know where to find the chaplain. If he was lucky, he might even be visiting at her apartment, which was close enough to walk to.

"Mama?" Charles knocked softly on her bedroom door. "Can I run over to Grandma's?"

Ramona looked up from her letter. "What for? You getting tired of being cooped up here all day?"

"Yeah," he admitted, figuring that was a good excuse. It wasn't totally a lie, either; he *was* a little bored of sitting in the apartment and watching TV.

"You want to take Gracie?"

Charles looked at her with undisguised disappointment. If he took Gracie he wouldn't be able to talk to the reverend. "Mama. . . ."

Ramona looked at her son's crestfallen face. He'd been real good about helping her out with every little thing. And he had more patience than she would have had with a sister like Gracie. That little girl surely lived to provoke her big brother. She'd had a good laugh with her little song performance a moment ago. Ramona decided to let him free for a while.

"Never mind. Just go enjoy yourself, okay? See if Grandma needs help with anything." Ramona held her arms open for a hug. "You're a good boy. Now get out of here." If *she* couldn't leave the apartment, at least someone could.

Charles bent over awkwardly, trying not to bump his mother's cast. "Thanks, Mama. Love you."

"Love you too, baby. Be careful. Be *good!*"

Charles ran the two blocks to his grandmother's building. He arrived sweaty and out of breath. Inside the building he had just enough energy to walk up the two flights to her small apartment. He knocked loudly on the door.

A few moments later he heard the sound of footsteps coming near and a "Who is it?" from inside.

"It's me, Grandma," Charles panted.

Lorraine flung the door open. She was wearing a housecoat. "Is everything all right? Is your Mama all right? What's the matter with you?"

Charles just nodded and collapsed on her couch. "Yes, yes, everyone is fine. I . . . ran . . . all the way . . . over here."

"It's too hot to be running all around, Charles. What's your rush?"

"I just came to see how you're doing, Grandma," he explained innocently.

Lorraine stared like her eyes could see right through him. "Mmm hmm. Why'd you really come?" she asked, with her hands on her hips.

"What? A boy can't see his grandma?" he asked, sitting up straighter. "That's a shame, it really is."

"Charles."

"Mmm?"

"Okay, you've seen me."

"And?"

"Charles, what's going on? What do you *need*, child? Just spit it out."

He knew he could never lie to his grandma. She always found him out. It was like she was psychic or something. "I need to speak to Reverend French, Grandma," he said, getting right to the point.

"Oliver?" she said, surprised. "What for?"

"I just need to talk with him," the boy said evasively.

Lorraine eyed him carefully. What was this boy up to? "Well, he'll be over here in about 20 minutes because we're going on a picnic, so you better let me get ready. You know I got to sparkle a little bit, don't you?" She winked at him and disappeared into her bedroom.

"Sure, Grandma."

Lorraine hummed to herself as she picked out a bright purple-and-green sundress with matching sandals. She and Oliver saw each other nearly every day lately, and that suited her just fine. Putting on pink lipstick while she looked in the mirror, she smacked her lips together, pouted, smiled, and then smoothed her hair into place.

"Looking *good,* girlfriend," she said to her reflection.

"Who are you talking to in there, Grandma?"

"Myself! Who did you think?"

"You getting old, Grandma?" Charles teased.

Lorraine opened the door and stood in the doorway. "Not hardly. How do I look?"

Charles studied her a moment. "All right, I guess," he said indifferently.

"Humph. You know better than that. Now, *how do I look?*"

Charles laughed. "You're the prettiest grandma on the block. *Okay?*"

"Just remember, you can't compliment a woman too much, Charles. Don't be stingy."

"You're something else, Grandma, you know that? Now where's Reverend French? I don't have all day."

"He isn't coming to see *you*, so don't start. Make yourself useful if you're so antsy. Sink's full of dishes." Lorraine pointed to the kitchen.

Charles knew better than to argue. He turned on the water and squeezed some soap out of the bottle. Over the next few minutes he washed the dishes carefully and quickly and placed them on the drying rack—all the while glancing at the clock. He wiped his hands on a towel and looked up at the clock again with impatience. Where was Reverend French? Charles was getting tired of waiting. He realized he might have a better chance of a private conversation outside. "Hey, Grandma," he shouted, "I'm going outside to wait for him."

"Whatever you want, sugar," she called back.

＊＊＊

As it happened, Oliver had just pulled up onto Lorraine's street. As he parked his car outside the apartment he noticed Charles standing by himself underneath the big oak tree. He hesitated before walking over. He didn't want to intrude on the boy's privacy, but something about the way Charles stared at the ground made the reverend want to acknowledge him.

"How're you doing, son?"

Charles looked up, as if he were just noticing him. "Hey, Reverend French. I know you're going on a picnic with Grandma." He hesitated. "But actually I really wanted to talk to you."

"Do you want to go inside?" said the chaplain as he took a step toward the door.

Charles looked around. "Well, if it's okay with you, I'd maybe like to talk to you alone."

Oliver noticed a bench outside the door. "Sure thing," he said. "Let's go have a seat."

They plopped down on the wrought-iron bench and Oliver waited for Charles to speak. When he didn't, he asked, "How's your mother doing?"

"Oh, she's fine. A little stir crazy, and her cast itches, but I think she's getting better."

"That's good," Oliver replied. Then he remained quiet. The boy would talk when we was ready.

Charles wasn't sure where to start. He took a deep breath and looked at the man for a long time before he spoke. "People come to talk to you, right?" he asked hesitantly.

"Yes, I talk to a lot of people, Charles."

"Do you tell their business?"

"When people come to me with their problems I keep our conversations confidential. Unless—"

"Unless what?" Charles asked quickly.

"Well, unless someone's safety is involved. If a person is going to hurt themselves or someone else, I have to report that. I don't have a choice. Otherwise, my conversations are private."

Charles considered this and nodded, letting out a deep sigh. He didn't think what he had to say put anyone in danger, so he was safe.

"What's on your mind, son?" Oliver asked gently.

Suddenly Charles was eager to get the whole story out. With the exception of Gracie, he hadn't told anybody about returning Bill Bradford's wallet. Over the next few minutes he told the reverend everything that had happened over the last few days. Oliver listened without commenting until Charles was completely through.

Charles reached inside his back pocket and took out a folded envelope. From inside the envelope he carefully pulled out his stock certificate and handed it to Oliver, who took it, read it, and handed it back.

"Yes, Charles, you definitely own a share of HOA," he confirmed.

"The thing is, this doesn't help us *now*. When I got it Mr. Bradford told me it was worth $45.85. He showed me himself in the newspaper. So every day I'm checking. And every day it's losing money. Now I've only got $41.20. Before you know it, I'll just be holding a piece of paper. I want to get the money for it *today* so I can at least give my mama something."

"I understand what you're thinking, Charles," Oliver said carefully. "Let me try to explain what you have there. Have you ever ridden on a roller coaster?"

"Once last year, at Six Flags. It was awesome!"

"Why?"

"It went up, up, up, then we flew down faster than anything I'd ever been on. And then again it went up, up, up. It was a blast!" Charles laughed just remembering how crazy that ride had been.

Oliver said seriously, "Charles, owning stock is like riding a roller coaster. Sometimes it will go up, up, up, and sometimes it will go down—"

"Down, down," Charles finished for him.

"Yes. Right now it's going down. When you have a stock you have to be willing to hang on tight—even though you might be screaming and hollering—and wait for it to go back up."

"What if it doesn't? I don't want to wait," Charles insisted. "I want to get the money for it *now*."

"Charles, like Mr. Bradford said, having a share in HOA means much more than just having money."

"How do you figure?" Charles asked skeptically.

"Boy, don't you see? You own a piece of the rock!"

"I do?"

"You, Charles Sullivan, own a piece of one of the biggest corporations in America. *You*."

Charles took this information in.

The reverend continued, "Son, you have been handed an *opportunity* here. There aren't too many people I know who own what you own. Most of our people are just standing on the outside looking in. That man let you step in. *You're in*."

"Dang. . . ." Charles was beginning to understand. But that still didn't solve the family's financial problems.

Oliver looked at the youngster. He could tell there was still something bothering him. "Something else on your mind?"

"Well, so, if I keep the stock, then there's this big shareholder meeting next week. And Mr. Bradford said I might learn a lot there. You know, about business and stuff. And, I don't know, maybe it is a good opportunity."

"I feel you," said Oliver. "So you think you should go?"

"Does *everybody* go?" Charles asked, wondering where they could hold a meeting that big.

"Oh, no," Oliver explained. "People from all over the country own stock. But only some of them will go to the shareholders meeting."

Charles studied the letter again."What should I do?" he asked uncertainly.

The reverend looked at the serious boy in front of him and paused before he answered. "Charles, I think you should go."

"I've never been to anything like this before," Charles said uncertainly. "That share Mr. Bradford gave me is becoming a headache."

Oliver put his arm around Charles and laughed. "Why are you stressing, son?"

The boy stared at his feet, not knowing how to answer. All he knew was his stomach was hurting ever since he got that letter. "Charles," he said more seriously.

"Listen to me carefully, because this is real important. You're looking at this all wrong. As you said yourself, this is an *opportunity*. You have to face challenges, not run away from them."

Charles averted his eyes, refusing to look at Oliver.

"Look, Charles, for some reason you *did* return the wallet. And for some reason that man *did* give you that share. Now, you asked for my opinion and I'm giving it to you. Nothing happens without a reason, do you follow me?" He looked at the boy intently. "You're not going to know the reason until you go."

Charles just shrugged, reluctant to admit Oliver might have a point.

"I have an idea," the man persisted. "Go *one* time. If you don't like it you'll never have to go again."

"But what will I tell my mama? She doesn't let me run the streets. She *always* knows where I am," Charles said, starting to worry all over again.

"Charles, I think it's high time you tell your mama and grandma what you've been up to," the reverend advised.

Charles looked up with alarm, but Oliver smiled at him. "You've done nothing wrong. Your mama's going to be *proud* of you. Trust me," he said, trying to reassure the worried boy.

"But, Reverend French, if I keep the stock—if I hang on tight—how am I going to help out Mama?"

The man thought for a long moment. Then he pointed over to his black Continental. "See my ride over there?"

"Yeah."

"I need it cleaned real good, inside and out. You think you could handle a job like that? I'm real picky about Bertha."

Charles snorted. *"Bertha?"*

"She's been a good car to me, son. You think you could treat her right? I pay cash."

"Yeah, I can handle her," Charles said, still chuckling.

Oliver reached out and they shook hands. "All right, Charles, here's ten bucks. Consider it an advance on your labor. I'll pick you up next week and we'll go to one of those car wash places and I'm putting you to work. Deal?"

"Deal, Reverend," Charles said happily. "You got yourself a deal."

The phone rang next to Ramona's bed. Charles had put together a series of extension cords to get it to her from the kitchen, where it usually was. It made her life a lot easier. "It was so nice of Juanita to pay our bill while I was in the hospital," Ramona thought. "They don't have any more money than we do." Ramona knew it was a sacrifice. "I'll make it up to her once the accident settlement comes in," she thought.

The phone rang again as she propped herself to pick it up.

"Hello?" she answered.

"Mrs. Sullivan, it's Mason Smith."

Ramona sat up straighter. "Oh, hello. How are you?"

"Good, thank you." He got straight to the point: "Listen, I just wanted to let you know, we heard back from Bradford's attorney today. They aren't budging. They say you were jaywalking and have no cause."

Ramona's spirits plummeted. So that was it, she thought. The large ball of stress she always felt about money crept into her stomach. "So we're done, then," she said quietly.

"No, not by a long shot. I don't give up easily, Mrs. Sullivan. These are big-city attorneys playing hardball. I spoke with the officer in charge of the scene of the accident. The skid marks suggest that Bradford may have been driving over the speed limit. Not a lot, but enough to make a case that he was being reckless. This guy already has a lot of scandal surrounding him right now. He doesn't need this to go to the press."

"Oh, I wouldn't want to put this in the news or anything," said Ramona. This was a private matter, not something for nosy neighbors to read about in the paper.

Mason grimaced to himself. Of course he had to find a client without nerves of steel. He didn't let his smooth voice betray his thoughts. "I agree. But I think it's sufficient to hint that things do have a way of finding their way to the papers."

Ramona was worried; what would this man do? She wasn't used to this sort of manipulation and risk taking. This was her life he was playing with, not just some card game.

Mason continued. "So I'll go back to them and push a little harder."

"Okay, but please, no press."

"Of course," agreed Mason. "I'll speak with you soon."

Mason already knew he wasn't going to get anywhere with Bradford's attorney unless he had something real to threaten. He picked up the phone and called a friend at the *Tribune*.

"Boverman? Hey, this is Mason Smith. How would you like a good story?" Mason spun his fake-leather chair and looked out on the city. He was going to get his payday if he had to use every last dirty trick in the book.

As Oliver drove the two blocks to the Sullivans' apartment, Charles still had butterflies in his stomach. Lorraine was grumbling about the change in plans. She didn't like mysteries, especially ones where she was kept in the dark. But Oliver had assured her they would still have their picnic in the park—they just had a slight detour.

"Mama, I'm home," Charles announced as he unlocked his door. "We've got company."

Ramona was still nursing her worry over her predicament. Tears had wet her face. From the start she'd tried not to be too optimistic, but thinking that lawyer might win them enough money to cover her bills had taken a big weight off her mind. Now he dropped what seemed like a huge roadblock in front of her. Why had she let herself hope? She was even more discouraged than before. She needed to think. Why did Charles bring company back? Now was not the time! But she couldn't be rude.

"I'll be right there," she called. She dabbed her eyes with a tissue and straightened her dress.

A minute or so later, Ramona wheeled herself out into the living room and put on a smile. She saw her mother and Oliver and felt mildly better. At least it was only them. "Hey, Mama. Hello, Reverend French. This is a nice surprise. How y'all doing?"

Oliver looked at Charles and nodded.

"Mama, I've got something to tell you," Charles began nervously.

Ramona looked from her mother to the chaplain, suddenly worried. "Are you in trouble? What happened, Charles?"

Lorraine rolled her eyes. "Don't ask me. Nobody tells me *anything*. Thought we were going for a picnic," she said pointedly, cutting her eyes at Oliver.

Oliver put his arm around her and said, "Why don't we all sit down. Charles is not in trouble. In fact, far from it."

Ramona raised her eyebrows. At this moment Gracie burst out of her room and said, "What's going on?"

"Sit down, Gracie," Charles said. "You're a part of this, too."

"I didn't do anything, Charles!" Gracie protested, shaking her finger at him. "Don't you try—"

"Shush, Gracie," Ramona admonished her daughter. "Quit your yakking."

Gracie was so shocked that for once she had nothing to say and she sat down without another word.

Little by little, with Oliver's help, Charles told Ramona and Lorraine about finding the wallet, taking it all the way up to the city, and receiving the share of stock. Ramona listened in amazement.

"Charles, you did all *that?*"

"Yes, Mama, I did," he said. "But there's more." He looked over at Oliver.

"Today Charles received a letter inviting him to the annual shareholders meeting next Thursday."

Charles pulled out the letter and handed it to his mother. She read it carefully. "This is a lot to digest," she admitted.

"See, since Charles owns a share he's part owner of HOA," Oliver explained. "He can attend that meeting."

"Mama, can I go?" Charles asked. "Reverend French said he'd drive me."

Ramona sat motionless, leg straight out, holding the letter. Everyone waited for her to say something. "How dare that Bradford man try and bribe my son," she thought. She looked at Charles's expectant face. It was so full of hope—just like hers only a few minutes ago, before Mason Smith had called and said Bradford's attorneys weren't budging.

"Mama?" Charles finally asked, wondering why she looked so sad.

Ramona sighed and slowly shook her head. Her voice was low, almost a whisper. "That man hit me and now I'm laid up here for weeks. Out of work. Stuck in this apartment all day long. Does he call to apologize? Check in on what he did? No. Meanwhile our bills are piling up because I can't get a job. And after all that, he has his big-city lawyers push us around. Do you know they're saying it's my fault I got hit? *My* fault?" Her voice was rising.

Oliver took a deep breath; he saw where this was going.

"Oh, honey," Lorraine said. She tried to put her arm around Ramona to soothe her but Ramona shook it off.

"No, I'm not finished. So, if that wasn't enough, the man makes some nice gesture to my son with a share of stock? *Why?*" By now Ramona's voice was raised. "Nothing good has come from Bill Bradford and nothing good will come of this!"

Everyone looked at Ramona in silence. Charles and Gracie had never seen their mother lose her temper like this before.

"Mama, if you don't want me to go, I won't," Charles said finally, anxious to change the unhappy look on his mother's face.

Ramona's expression gave him her silent answer.

"Now, wait just a minute," Lorraine interjected. "I have something to say." She stood up so everyone could get the full effect. "There is *nothing* wrong with letting Charles go to this meeting. He earned it. There isn't one in a million would have done what he did." She looked proudly at her grandson. "Ain't that right, Mona?"

"Yes, Mama," she agreed slowly. "Most people would have kept that wallet for sure."

"And," Lorraine continued, "the boy could have kept it out of *spite*. That man hit you; he could have said it was payback."

Ramona looked at her mother and tears formed in the corners of her eyes. "Yes."

"But you raised your son *better* than that, Mona. He isn't like these little hoodlums that run the streets."

"You're right, Mama," Ramona said, nodding.

"I'm proud of our boy, Mona. He comes from *good* people. He hasn't got one thing to be ashamed of. Now, I'm not saying that Bradford fellow is a good man or that he should be forgiven. He's done you wrong. But in this world it's not always the good that get rewarded. Your son has an opportunity," she concluded, "and I think we should try to separate one thing from the other."

Ramona wiped her eyes and studied her son sitting so seriously on the couch.

Lorraine looked at Charles. "Charles, do you want to go?" she asked him.

"Yes, Grandma. Just once—for the opportunity." He glanced quickly at Oliver.

Everyone looked to Ramona, hoping she'd changed her mind. But Ramona shook her head. "I'm sorry, Charles. I just don't want that man to have any other way to hurt this family. You cannot go."

Ramona rolled out of the room. The others sat in silence. The reverend reached out a hand to Charles, who got up and walked to his bedroom. Lorraine put a hand on Oliver's shoulder reassuringly. "You did what was right," she whispered.

But Oliver wasn't so sure.

Gracie sat on the stoop outside her apartment building. She tried to hide under the shade of a big tree but couldn't escape the hot air surrounding her. Still, there was no way she was going back into the apartment. No, sir. Everything had been all tense since the fight about Charles going to that meeting. Ramona and Charles barely spoke and despite being on her best behavior, and trying all her best tricks to make them laugh, they both seemed to be lost in their own thoughts. Fine—they didn't have to speak, but that didn't mean she had to stay in there and put up with it.

"What's with Charles, anyway?" she muttered to herself. Why was he so bent out of shape over some meeting with a bunch of suits? It was summer and they should be wasting their time outside, like normal kids. She wiped her brow. It sure was hot.

Laughter up the street caught Gracie's attention. She saw it was Kayden coming out of his apartment building with two other boys. They were all in her class at school. She knew the other boys well enough but had eyes for Kayden alone. She flushed. He was walking right toward her. She sat up and brushed back her hair.

"Hey, Gracie-bell," he said with a smile. Gracie tried to act casual.

"Hey, Kayden. What's up?" Gracie nodded a hey to the other two.

"We're just going to play some ball at the park. You wanna come watch?"

Gracie smiled. She knew she should run upstairs to tell her mama if she did.

Just as she was about to say yes, two other girls walked by. One of them was Harlen Jones. "Ugh," thought Gracie. Harlen was the most beautiful girl in the class. Every guy was in love with her. And there she was flouncing around in some cute skirt. Gracie thought of the wallet again. Why couldn't Charles have kept that money?

All the boys lit up as Harlen and her friend passed. "You guys headed to the park?" Harlen asked sweetly. The boys just nodded their heads. "Pathetic," thought Gracie, and she slouched.

"See you there," said Harlen as she sashayed down the street.

"You coming?" asked Kayden again.

Gracie stared after Harlen. No one would even see her if Harlen was there.

"I'd better go take care of my mama," Gracie said.

"Okay, see you later," Kayden replied with a smile. Gracie gave a weak smile and headed inside.

As Gracie was stomping up the stairs grumbling to herself about the unfairness of it all, she ran smack into Charles coming the other way.

"Where are you going?" she asked. Charles looked like he was up to something again.

"Out," said Charles. "Mama's sleeping but I need you to go watch her for a few."

"Hmmph." Normally she'd interrogate him until he told her what he was doing, but she wasn't in the mood. She let Charles walk by her and stomped the rest of the way up the stairs.

―――――――

Charles was headed to buy himself some new pants. He'd done a lot of thinking. On one hand, Mr. Bradford had done them a terrible wrong. He'd hit his mama. But on the other hand, he seemed to want to make amends. He knew she'd said no, but Charles just couldn't get that meeting out of his head. He didn't want to end up like the other kids around him. He wanted to go to college, provide for his family. Maybe this meeting was a step toward that?

So, for the first time in his life, he was going to lie to his mama and disobey her. He felt terrible about it, but he wanted to go to that meeting.

Charles walked into Goodwill. He had $10 from Reverend French. Surely he could find himself some pants to match his suit jacket. He had to look professional.

Twenty minutes later, he exited with a pair of new slacks that fit him well, and $1.50 left over in his pocket. Maybe he'd buy his mama some of that orange soda she liked so much.

———

That Thursday, Bill Bradford drove home quickly after work and showered. Tonight was the shareholder meeting and he was taking his son. He wanted them both to look good. As he came out of the walk-in closet fixing his tie he called out to his wife, "Do you have Andrew's suit ready?"

Paige replied patiently, "Yes, dear. For the tenth time, I do." She walked up and adjusted his collar. Straightening the tie underneath, she said with a smile, "I think it's so great you want to take him to your meeting. This will be a good experience for him."

Bill smiled with pride as he fixed his hair in the mirror. That Sullivan kid, Charles, had given him the idea. Andrew was definitely old enough to learn about the business. "I thought it was about time he started learning what I do. He's going to take over the business one day."

Paige smiled. She was happy to see her husband making an effort to do more with Andrew.

———

An hour or so later, Bill drove with Andrew toward the office. Andrew sat looking glumly out the window.

He hated wearing a tie and he tried to loosen its grip around his neck. He resented having to go to the meeting. All the guys were headed out to a movie and he had to go to some stuffy office in some stuffy suit. He let out an enormous sigh.

Charles left the apartment immediately after dinner. He gave some lame excuse about going to the library. He didn't know why he'd said it, but it was too late now. He stuffed his suit into his backpack and changed in a McDonald's bathroom near the bus stop downtown. He looked down at his suit and pants, a little annoyed they were wrinkled here and there, but that couldn't be helped. He would rather have a few wrinkles than have someone see him in a suit on the bus and tell his mama.

Charles walked toward the entrance to HOA headquarters with his head held high. He straightened his shoulders and double-checked his pocket for the invitation. Feeling it safely there, he continued toward the entrance, which was absent of protesters this evening. Entering the building, he walked straight to the elevators. No sneaking in today.

Several other people got on and pressed the button for the twenty-sixth floor. No one spoke to him, although they let him get off the elevator first. Charles hung back in the lobby, waiting to follow the crowd toward a large conference room. One by one they approached a man at a desk; he checked their names off a list and handed each person a nametag. As Charles approached the desk, the man smiled at him.

"What can I do for you, sonny? Looking for your father?"

"I'm Charles Sullivan."

"Yes?" the man said, looking at the line forming behind him.

"I should be on your list," Charles said, pointing to the sheaf of papers on the desk.

Reluctantly, the man shuffled through the sheets until he found the right one. Moving his finger slowly down the list of names, he saw it.

"How old are you?" asked the man.

"Fifteen," replied Charles confidently.

"Well, there must be some mistake," the man said dismissively.

Instead of answering, Charles reached into his jacket pocket and produced the folded-up invitation. The man took it, read it, and handed it back.

"Well, that is you. . . ." His voice trailed off with confusion.

Now Charles was becoming impatient. "*Mr. Bradford* invited me."

The man reluctantly gave Charles his tag. Looking past him into the huge room, Charles noticed Bill talking to several people. Not waiting for the man at the desk to change his mind, he walked right past him into the room.

"'Excuse me, Mr. Bradford?'"

Bill looked down and saw Charles standing there. "Well! This is a surprise."

Charles produced the invitation. "You invited me. Remember?"

Bill laughed. "Oh, sure, of course. I'm glad you came."

"That man almost didn't let me in," Charles said. He wanted to make sure Mr. Bradford wanted him to be here.

Bill put his hand on the boy's shoulder. "Welcome," he said. "All set? Why don't you help yourself to some food over there." He pointed to several tables off to the side of the room. "By the way, my son's here, too." He looked around for Andrew. Where was that boy? Andrew could sure use having this kid's enthusiasm rub off on him. He'd complained all the way to the meeting. Bill was more than a little annoyed with him. "Well, as soon as I see him I'll introduce you. Maybe you two should sit together during the meeting."

"Yes, sir."

Bill turned back to the group he'd been speaking to. Taking that as a cue to leave, Charles walked away. He was hungry, so he eagerly went to the buffet. He'd barely eaten any dinner in his rush to get out of the apartment. As he walked around the tables staring at all the food, he watched some of the other attendees to see what they did. He walked behind a woman and grabbed a plate, pondering how many desserts he was allowed to take, when he overheard someone say, under his breath, "This sucks!"

Charles turned around and saw a thin blond boy about his own age with a sullen look on his face, staring unhappily at the food displayed before him. Noticing Charles, he complained, "There's not *one* thing on here I like to eat."

Charles looked more carefully at the selection and frowned. Itty-bitty hot dogs, but no buns in sight. A bowl full of tiny round black things that didn't even resemble food. "What is that?" he asked the boy.

The boy grimaced. "Caviar. It's *so* gross."

"Caviar?"

"Yeah, you know, fish eggs," he explained.

Now it was Charles's turn to grimace. "Fish *eggs*? That's nasty."

"And this," the boy said, pointing, "is pâté. I won't even tell you how they make that. Trust me—it's way gross."

Slowly they walked the length of the table and finally grabbed some rolls and cheese. Charles tried using the rolls as buns for the mini hot dogs, but it didn't taste the same without mustard and relish. At least he had a couple cookies and a brownie. You couldn't screw those up.

He and the boy sat in some chairs near the podium, eating their food.

With his mouth full, the boy said, "I'm Andrew, by the way. What's your name?"

Charles wiped his mouth. "Charles."

"Did your dad drag you here, too?"

"Uh—"

Not waiting for an answer, Andrew reached inside his blazer and produced his iPod. "I came prepared."

Charles noticed that tucked inside the boy's jacket were a set of earphones. A long wire snaked into the inside pocket. He smiled. The kid was smooth. "What are you listening to?"

Andrew broke out into a big smile. "Can you believe they didn't even notice? Parents can be so lame sometimes. Here," he said, fiddling with the controls in his pocket, "listen to this."

Charles put the earphones on and soon was surrounded with the sounds of Lil Wayne. He listened for a moment and handed the earphones back. "Your folks let you listen to this?"

Andrew shook his head. "That's the beauty of the iPod. You can quickly switch over to a Britney Spears song before anyone knows the difference."

Charles chuckled. "You listen to *Britney?*"

Andrew started laughing now, too. "Sometimes, but only her new stuff."

"My mama hardly lets me listen to rap," Charles said matter-of-factly. "Unless it's something without any cussing."

"So what kind of music do you listen to?" asked Andrew curiously.

"Marvin, Smokey, Aretha, the Temptations. You know . . . oldies. My mama loves her some Motown, so that's what we mostly listen to."

Andrew nodded, impressed. "Well, if you ever want to listen to some rap I've got a big collection. A *secret* collection."

Charles laughed. This white boy cracked him up. "His parents probably don't even know what he's up to half the time," he thought.

"What you got?"

Andrew looked around and then said in a low voice, "I've got all of Tupac, Biggie, Juvenile, Dr. Dre, Eminem, 50 Cent. . . ."

"Nice!" Charles exclaimed enviously. "I mean . . . you got a lot of good stuff, sounds like."

Andrew nodded. "Yeah. If you want you can borrow some of it," he offered nonchalantly.

At that point Bill stepped up to the podium to start the meeting. He looked down, glad to see his son had met Charles. Charles straightened in his seat, excited. Andrew slouched and snuck in his earphones. Bill frowned a bit. Why couldn't Andrew be more like that Sullivan boy?

He brought his thoughts back to the business at hand and started the meeting.

―――――――――――

The meeting wore on for more than an hour, but Charles sat quietly without fidgeting. Different speakers got up and talked about various issues. There were charts and graphs. He didn't understand some of what they talked about, but he was still glad he came.

Then there was some open time for questions and answers. Someone in the audience brought up the lay-offs of the housekeeping staff. Charles watched Bill handle their questions. Not everything the people were saying was very nice, but he stood there unflinching. "So Mr. Bradford's in charge," Charles thought, "but he still can get yelled at."

As the meeting was nearing conclusion a woman stood up. "We have a new vacancy for the Policy Advisory Committee," she announced. "As you know, this board advises HOA on directing our workforce and resources. To help maintain its diversity and its independent nature, we periodically invite shareholders to join this committee to represent the broader base of stock own-ers. We have randomly selected one member who is in attendance tonight to serve on the committee. Please check your nametags. If you are number 61 please report to the check-in table to receive further instructions. Thank you."

Charles tried to smother a yawn. He glanced down at his nametag and saw number 19. Getting up out of his chair with the rest of the audience he stretched and waited for his row to file out. He looked for Andrew, but couldn't see him anywhere. He had gotten up almost ten minutes ago claiming he had to go to the bathroom. Charles figured he might have just sneaked out for a few.

His thoughts were interrupted when the speaker got on the microphone again. "Number 61, please report to the check-in table and let us know if you're available to serve on the Policy Advisory Committee. Check your nametags, everybody."

Charles saw some of the people take off their nametags so he did the same. He felt proud to see his name in bold letters, encased in plastic, and wished he could show it to everyone back home—but, of course, they didn't even know he was at this meeting, and his mother had expressly forbidden him from coming. As Charles studied the nametag he frowned. Didn't he have number 19? Suddenly he stopped and turned it around, and then around again. Gripping the tag he rubbed it as if that would change its appearance.

"*I'm* number 61," he whispered. Looking around frantically he saw the room emptying. There were only a few people left. He looked over at the check-in desk where the speaker and the attendant scanned the stragglers. Nametag in hand, he started walking in their direction.

Charles stood without speaking in front of the table. Nobody noticed him until Sheila walked up. "Well, hi, Charles!" she said brightly. "Good to see you."

Relieved to see her familiar smiling face, Charles blurted out, "I'm number sixty-one."

She looked at him with a confused expression while steadily chewing her gum. "Huh?"

He held up his nametag. "They called my number. I'm supposed to be on a committee."

Sheila reached out and took his nametag. She smiled. "Fancy that," she thought. "Good for the kid." Tapping the shoulder of the man who hadn't wanted to let Charles in earlier, she said, "Mr. Stevens, here's your man. Charles Sullivan is number sixty-one."

Frowning at the tag held in front of his face he brushed it aside and addressed Charles. "Is this some kind of a joke?"

Charles wished he'd never come and stifled an impulse to bolt. But something about the man's attitude rubbed him the wrong way and he straightened his back. "They called number sixty-one to be on the committee. That's me. Charles Sullivan. Look on my tag."

Mr. Stevens rubbed his hand over his eyes and sighed. Who the heck was this kid? Sheila stood beside Charles, as if challenging the man to disagree.

Stevens said nothing and walked to another table where another man in a suit was seated. Charles watched as the two conferred. They both gestured toward him, then Stevens walked back over. "You'll need to wait another minute while we look to see if children are even allowed to be on the committee."

"I'm not a child," said Charles defensively. "I'm fifteen."

The man stared down his nose. Sheila could see they were getting nowhere. "Look, I'll go find Mr. Goldstein. He'll know." She winked at Charles and mouthed, "Gum?"

Smiling, he shook his head. She shrugged and tossed her blond hair behind her as she went in search of HOA's attorney. Charles remained standing by the table while the men continued their conversation, ignoring him.

———

Soon Sheila returned, followed by a tall man in his 50s with dark hair, wearing a light-grey suit. "What seems to be the problem?" he asked the two men at the table.

"They've selected a shareholder to serve on the Policy Advisory Committee. And it's this *kid*," Mr. Stevens said irritably. "I know there must be a rule about not having a minor. So let's just clear this up, and he can be on his way."

The tall man reached out and shook Charles's hand. "Ira Goldstein. You must be Charles Sullivan."

"Yes, sir," Charles answered, feeling more relaxed when the man smiled at him.

"Charles, if you'll give me a few minutes I'll look up the age requirements in our company policy. Why don't you wait over there and I'll be back shortly." Ira pointed to a row of chairs against the wall.

Charles nodded and sat down in one of the plush chairs as Sheila pulled up a seat next to him. "He'll get it all straightened out, kiddo."

Charles wrinkled his nose and asked, "What's that smell?"

Popping her gum, Sheila said, "Guess." She blew a big pink bubble, looking at him expectantly.

This lady was a trip for sure. She was always chewing that gum. Ramona had told both her children that it was bad manners to chew gum at school and at church and he was sure he wouldn't be allowed to chew gum in this setting either.

"Watermelon," he answered after a moment.

Sheila opened her mouth in surprise, exposing her white teeth and a big, pink wad of gum. "You're *good*, Charles! Hardly anybody guesses that. You sure you don't want some?" She pulled out an open pack of Big Bubbles.

"Can I have some for later?"

"Oh, sure. Here, take the rest of the pack," she offered generously. "I have a ton of gum at home."

Stuffing it inside his jacket pocket, Charles smiled and thanked her. Maybe he'd give a couple of pieces to Gracie. *Maybe.*

"Okay, folks, I found what we were looking for," Ira Goldstein said, approaching Charles and Sheila. Glancing at the men at the table he said brusquely, "You better listen to this."

Mr. Stevens got up and walked over to the group as Goldstein explained, "I checked the policy, and even made a couple of phone calls and there's nothing in there about an age requirement."

"*Nothing?*" Charles and Mr. Stevens asked in unison, both shocked.

"Charles, welcome to the Policy Advisory Committee," Ira Goldstein said, shaking the boy's hand for the second time that night.

"But—but—that's absurd!" Stevens sputtered.

"Wow, Charles," Sheila said enthusiastically, as if Mr. Stevens weren't already on the verge of having a coronary. "That's *so cool!*"

Mr. Goldstein, attempting to put him at ease, said, "Look, son. Take home the materials and read them over with your folks. Then decide."

Looking into the man's sincere face, Charles asked hesitantly, "I don't *have* to be on the committee?"

"No, of course you don't. But, it might be an experience you'll never get again. Or not anytime soon, anyway," he said, chuckling. He didn't know how the boy had ended up here in the first place, but the whole thing struck him as very funny.

Charles started laughing, too. "You're right about that. Thanks for helping me, Mr. Goldstein."

"My pleasure. Now go talk to Mr. Stevens. And good luck."

Stevens realized it was futile to argue anymore tonight, even though the whole situation was completely ridiculous. *Ludicrous.* Somehow this kid had connections to Bradford and it wasn't worth going against him.

"Take this packet of papers home and read them carefully," he said, shoving a stack into the boy's hands. "You *can* read, can't you?"

Before Charles had a chance to answer, Sheila said hotly, "Oh, come on. Nobody can understand what's in those packets! Give him a break. Just explain it to him, will you?" She blew a big bubble and let it pop loudly for emphasis.

Glaring at her, Stevens explained to Charles briefly what the committee did, and what would be expected of him.

———

Charles walked excitedly toward the elevator and bumped into Andrew and Bill. They got into the elevator together. Charles couldn't contain himself.

"Thank you so much for inviting me tonight, Mr. Bradford."

Bill smiled down at him. "I'm glad you enjoyed it."

Bill glanced down at his son and caught his eye, his silent message to Andrew being, "Why can't you be more like this boy?" Andrew rolled his eyes. What was up with this kid? He couldn't be serious; that meeting was by far the most boring thing he'd been to. A trip to the dentist to have a tooth pulled would have been more fun. Almost.

The elevator reached the lobby and Charles got out. "Well, thanks again," he said as he walked out. Bill watched the kid go. He took in Charles's second-hand suit and backpack. A thought occurred to him and he reached out to stop the doors from closing.

"Hey, Charles. How are you getting home?"

Charles reached into his pocket and pulled out a bus pass. "City bus."

"You sure you don't need a ride?"

"No, sir, I'm good," said Charles as he turned to walk out.

Bill and Andrew watched the doors close in front of them and took the elevator down to the parking garage. Bill wondered to himself if his son had ever even ridden a bus.

Charles watched the lights go by in the darkness outside, feeling safe inside the air-conditioned bus. He leaned back, listening to the quiet hum of the engine. The bus was almost empty. He smiled to himself and looked at his watch. It was ten o'clock. He sat up straight. He was late. Then he looked down. He was still in his suit! He slapped his hand to his forehead. How could he have been so stupid? Someone was going to see him for sure. And the bus was almost at his stop. He had to think of something, and quick.

The bus pulled up to the stop. Outside he saw the face of Reverend French staring at him. The man's face was expressionless but Charles knew he was waiting for him. Too late, thought Charles to himself.

Oliver watched as Charles got off the bus. He looked at Charles's suit and tie but asked no questions. "You're mama's been worried sick about you, son," he said, and then turned without another word toward the apartment building.

10

Oliver walked slowly up the stairs in front of Charles. Charles didn't mind the reverend's slow pace. He was in no mood to face his mother.

When they got to the apartment, Oliver knocked loudly on the door. Charles shuddered, listening to the loud voices inside; then, realizing that no one was coming to answer, he dug out his keys and opened the door himself.

An unexpected scene greeted them. Charles had rarely seen his mama yell, but she surely was yelling now. "You better answer me, Gracie! Where did you get that skirt?" Her hands were clenched around the arms of her wheelchair and you could tell that—cast or no cast— she was ready to jump up out of the chair.

Gracie stood whimpering with her head down while Aunt Etta stared at her, holding a short ruffled skirt— the kind Ramona would never let her daughter wear. Not until she moved out of the house, and then she'd *still* have something to say about it. Lorraine was sitting on the couch, looking from Ramona to Gracie to Aunt Etta.

Gracie sank to the floor on her knees and buried her face in her hands and began sobbing. "You better be praying, Gracie," Ramona said matter-of-factly, "because all that crying isn't going to help you."

Sobbing louder, Gracie finally said, "I—I—I'm so—sorry . . . I'm *sorry*, Mama. . . ."

"Quit crying and stand up. I'm not going to ask you again. Where did you get that skirt?" There was no trace of sympathy in Ramona's voice.

Slowly, Gracie got up and wiped the snot and tears from her face. "I stole it."

Charles thought for a moment about backing into the hall, but his mother saw him out of the corner of her eye. Without breaking eye contact with Gracie she snapped, "I'll be with *you* in a second, Charles."

Charles slunk over to a chair and sat. Oliver hovered in the doorway.

"Why would you steal? I know we don't have much, but I didn't raise my daughter to be a thief."

"I'm sorry, Mama," said Gracie, with her head hung low. "I was just . . . It's just, Harlen and all those pretty girls. And I just wanted. I—" Gracie realized how stupid her excuses sounded now. What was she thinking? She hadn't gone to steal the skirt. But then, she'd seen the adorable thing and she thought about Kayden looking at her the way he and his friends looked at Harlen. It didn't make sense now.

Ramona understood, but it did nothing to soothe her anger. Her head was reeling. This wasn't the daughter she knew.

"I'm just so disappointed in you." She was silent for a moment and then said, "Tomorrow morning you're going back to that store and you will return that skirt."

"But, Mama, they might arrest me," said Gracie. Suddenly she realized that something even worse than her mother's anger could happen.

Ramona paused. It would serve Gracie right if she got in trouble. But she knew the store owner, and she was sure they would let Gracie go so long as she returned it. She was so embarrassed.

Then she remembered Charles.

"And you!" she said, turning her gaze on him. "Just where have you been?"

"I was, um—" Charles fumbled.

"The library? Because I'll tell you what, the library closed hours ago. Do you know that the reverend, your aunt, and your grandmother have been combing the streets looking for you? Just where have you been! And don't lie—I've had enough lying for one evening."

Ramona waited for her son to speak.

"I was at the shareholders meeting," he replied, looking down at the floor.

Ramona stared at him. "After I forbade you to go?"

"Yes, Mama," said Charles, not looking up. She looked at his clothes.

"Are those new pants? Did you steal those, too?"

This made Charles look up. He may have lied but he wasn't a thief. "No, ma'am," he said. "I got them from Goodwill with the ten dollars Reverend French gave me to wash Bertha."

"Bertha?"

"My car," Oliver interjected.

"Well, then, you're one step ahead of your sister—which isn't saying much. Why would you lie to me and disobey me?"

"Because I wanted to go, Mama. And I got put on a committee. They meet every couple of weeks."

Charles pulled out his paperwork to show it off. "See? And Mr. Bradford—"

He stopped. He could see that his mother didn't want to hear any more. She turned her head away. Charles dropped the papers on the floor, defeated.

Aunt Etta shook her head. "That man has surely been bad luck for this family," she said solemnly. "He just about *killed* and crippled Ramona. He's taking away my job. *And* all my health benefits. And now he encourages Charles to sneak out of the house at all hours. He's destroying this family. There's nothing good coming from Mr. Bill Bradford and the sooner you stop messing with him, the better." She folded her arms, resting her case.

Oliver cleared his throat, unsure of how much to interject in this situation. He bent down and picked up the papers to take a look.

Etta continued, "That man is bad news. I'm telling you. Ramona, if I was you I wouldn't let Charles have any more to do with him. He is *bad*. I'm telling you!"

Lorraine had had enough of her sister's preaching. "It isn't up to you, girl. And it's none of your business, either."

"What?" Etta looked at her, outraged.

"Just what I said. Stay out of it." Etta always could get on Lorraine's last nerve, going back to when they were children. Being ten years older, Etta had never taken her seriously.

Oliver cleared his throat again. Five pair of eyes turned toward him. "Uh, why don't we all take a moment to cool off," he began. He held up the paperwork. "This committee Charles has been elected to advises the chief executive officer of HOA. And do you know what about? How the company deals with its workers. Etta, you're talking about how you're going to lose your job. Maybe there's a real opportunity here for Charles to have some say in that."

Charles beamed at Oliver. He hadn't even thought of that.

Etta scoffed. "Yeah, Bradford's going to listen to some kid. There's nothing to talk about, Reverend. And if you don't mind my saying so. . . ." She paused, glaring at Lorraine. "It isn't *your* place to tell this family what to do."

Lorraine jumped up. "Oh, no, you don't. Don't you talk to him like that, Etta! Show some respect."

Oliver put his hand on her shoulder to calm her down, but it had the opposite effect. Shrugging him off, Lorraine said, "You don't *know* Etta, Oliver. She's always been a—"

Etta yelled back, standing up. "You're the one who—"

"Enough," shouted Ramona, loud enough to make them both stop. Etta and Lorraine sat back down, shamed. "This is my house and these are my children. If anyone gets to have an opinion here, it's me."

"I'm sorry, Ramona," Oliver said, crouching next to her wheelchair. "It's none of my business. And I shouldn't have encouraged Charles to attend the meeting in the first place. It seems to have caused some unnecessary problems," he said wearily.

Ramona shook her head helplessly. "I don't know what to think. I'm worn out from all this stress." She looked from Charles to Gracie. Her disappointment was all over her face. Finally she spoke: "I'm going to bed." And she slowly wheeled herself into her bedroom and shut the door without bidding anyone good night.

———

Ramona struggled to get out of her wheelchair and into bed, and as she lay there she finally heard everyone leave. Then, moments later, she heard her two kids close their bedroom doors. She stared at the ceiling above. The fan spun 'round and 'round. She watched the shadows from the streetlights outside, bouncing with each rotation of the fan. Where had she gone wrong? She had taught her children to be honest. More than anything, she was disappointed in herself. She couldn't even make sure they'd have a roof over their heads. If that lawyer didn't come through, they'd have no way to pay their bills. Even if he did, would it be fast enough to make sure their water didn't get shut off and that they had food on the table? She cursed her leg. She felt trapped. She looked at her bedside table at the picture of her late husband. She missed him so much. He'd always known what to do.

"I'm even letting him down," she thought.

And then she began to cry, weeping silently in the dark.

Lorraine was worried about Ramona. She wasn't eating much and had been very quiet since the big blowup a week earlier. The kids had been on their best behavior trying to make their mama happy, but there was no question Ramona was depressed. The hospital bills had come and the numbers were in the thousands. Lorraine worried. "How am I going to help my daughter? I don't have that kind of money." And that sneaky lawyer, Mason Smith, didn't seem to be making any progress. No, he wasn't going to help them, either. She picked up the phone and called Oliver.

A week later, Lorraine had Ramona loaded into Oliver's pride and joy: Bertha, a very long, very large black 1970 Lincoln Continental. It took some prodding but she'd finally gotten Ramona to put on a dress and agree to an outing. Ramona looked disinterestedly out the window. From the back seat, she strained forward and tapped her mother on her shoulder. "Mama, just where are we going?"

Lorraine answered blithely, "Oh, we're just going to make a stop by the church. I've told Oliver so much about it."

This made no sense to Ramona. Why did he have to see it *now*? She sighed. She'd only agreed to come to get her mother to be quiet. She could be persistent when she wanted to. She settled back with her shoulders resting against the window so her cast could lie across the seat. It was very uncomfortable, but she wasn't complaining.

As they pulled up to the church Ramona looked out the window and her mouth dropped open in surprise. "What—?"

Lorraine and Oliver exchanged glances, and Lorraine turned around so she could see Ramona's reaction.

"Mama?" Ramona said, staring out the window.

A big banner was draped across the church: *We Love You, Ramona!* The church doors were open and people dressed in their Sunday best stood on the steps, waving. She could hear music playing. There were balloons and streamers.

"How did you—? I mean, who . . . I just can't believe it." Ramona couldn't find the right words to express herself. Tears formed and slowly rolled down her high cheekbones and dripped onto her new dress.

"Don't start, Mona," Lorraine said, "or I'm going to start, and I'm looking too cute today to have mascara running all down my face. And baby, this was Oliver's idea," she added proudly. "He wanted to gather up all your friends and family to show you how much you are loved."

"And that no one has to fight alone," Oliver continued. "Your mother was worried about you," he said, looking to Lorraine fondly.

Suddenly Gracie and Charles were next to the car, eager to see their mama smiling again. Oliver got out and opened the trunk to pull out Ramona's wheelchair, then helped her out of the car. Lorraine took one last peek in the mirror and straightened her pink hat with daisies. *You still got it going on, girl,* she thought. *You sure do. Even if you are a grandma!*

"Are you surprised?" asked Gracie.

"Why are you crying?" Charles asked. "Mama, say something." Gracie and Charles had had a hard time concealing the plans they'd been making all week, and now they were anxious to get Ramona's reaction. They hadn't expected tears.

Finally she blew her nose and smiled. "This is the nicest thing anybody's ever done for me."

As Oliver wheeled Ramona up the ramp to the church she was greeted by members of the congregation and friends. Many of them cried when they saw her. It was a miracle that she was back safe and sound after a car accident, with only a cast to show for her ordeal.

"Hey, girl! We *missed* you!"

"Mona, welcome back, sugar."

"What's up, girlfriend?"

"I been praying for you, child. The Lord's watching over you."

"Oooh, baby, you *still* looking good," said a man over to one side. Ramona smiled, greeting Jamal, her co-worker and friend.

"Jamal, stop," she said, laughing, as she hugged the young man tightly. "You miss me?"

"We're losing customers, I can tell you that, girl. Nobody can serve them up like Mona," Jamal said half-jokingly. It was true that many customers came to the diner because of Ramona. Some of them had stopped coming around since her accident.

Ramona frowned. It would be weeks before she'd be able to stand for hours, serving customers. But she didn't want to think about being unemployed now, not with a party going on. Smiling up at Jamal she said, "It sure is good to be out of the house. I almost started missing *you*."

"Yeah, yeah," Jamal said. "Let's get you inside, out of this heat. Wait 'til you see what we got going on in here."

Inside the church the lower level had been transformed into a carnival atmosphere. In the kitchen they were selling good old-fashioned Southern-style comfort food: fried chicken, collard greens, black-eyed peas, corn bread, and peach cobbler, plus all the sweet tea you could drink.

"Mmm mmm! Smells like fried chicken, Jamal," Ramona said, eyeing the food.

"You'll get some, but I'm going to make you wait a little longer, Mona. Look over here," he said, wheeling her by a crowded table with a big sign: *Raffle Tickets $2.00!*

"What are they raffling off, Jamal?" Ramona wondered.

"Take a look, take a look." It was a basketball signed by all the Atlanta Hawks.

"Where'd they find that?" Ramona asked. "That's got to be worth a lot of money."

"Oh, somebody just donated it for a good cause," Jamal answered cryptically.

Ramona looked at him. "Jamal. What's going on here? Why is everyone trying to raise money? I don't get it."

Jamal shifted uncomfortably on his feet. He thought Lorraine would have told her, but she was nowhere in sight. "Girl, this is all for you. We knew it'd be awhile before you're back on your feet again, so, you know. . . ."

"Jamal, everybody is raising money for *me*?"

"Yeah, Mona. All of us wanted to help you. You're always there for us. Now we're here for you. That's just how it goes."

She was stunned. "Whose basketball is that?"

Jamal cleared his throat. "It's D'Andre's. He donated it."

"*D'Andre?*"

"You remember my little brother. He wanted to help out."

Tears welled up in Ramona's eyes. D'Andre was the Atlanta Hawks' number one fan, for sure. He was, among other things, a high-school dropout and had been in jail a number of times since Ramona had known him. Still, she knew that no matter what D'Andre did, Jamal was always there for him and always had something positive to say about him.

"Wow. I can't believe D'Andre *donated* his basketball," Ramona whispered.

"He's got a big heart, Mona. I've been telling you. As soon as I told him about your accident he wanted to do something." What Jamal didn't tell her is that D'Andre had been so upset that he had offered to find the guy and—well, never mind. The important thing was Jamal had talked him out of it. It was the thought that counted, right? Surprisingly, though, it *was* D'Andre's idea to raffle off his basketball. Sometimes his little brother surprised him.

"Well, let me show you something else. This one was Charles's idea." Jamal wheeled her to the center of the room. Propped up on a table was a hand-painted sign that said simply, *Sign your name for $1.00.*

"Huh? I don't get it. Sign your name for what?"

"Mona, Mona . . . you're sitting on a money maker, and you don't even know it," Jamal teased. "Everyone loves to sign a cast, right? Well, your brilliant son had the idea of making people pay for it! The kid's a marketing genius."

Soon a line formed, markers of all colors were handed out, and people were willing to pay extra if they could draw a picture by their name. Gracie stood by with a big pickle jar, collecting the money.

"Hey, Mama, leave some room for me! I want to sign your cast, too," Gracie said, watching as signatures filled up the cast.

"You have to pay like everybody else," Charles warned.

"I do not!" Gracie whined. "Tell him, Mama."

Ramona dropped her smile and looked at her daughter. Gracie saw that look and she halted mid-sentence. She knew when to stop.

"Gracie, Charles. Come sign my cast," Ramona said, averting more bickering. "You two have been working so hard, you can do it for free."

Gracie stuck her tongue out at Charles as she grabbed a purple marker. Carefully she wrote out her name and drew a flower and a bee by it. Charles grabbed a black marker and printed CHARLES SULLIVAN I.

Ramona looked down and chuckled. "The First, huh? Since when are you Charles *the First*?"

Charles just shrugged. "I don't know. I *am* the first, right?"

"Yes, sugar, you are. And you know you're my number one son, right?"

"Sure do, Mama," Charles said. It had been a while since he'd seen her smile.

"And I'm your number one daughter, right, Mama?" Gracie added quickly.

"You know it," Ramona agreed. She pulled them both into a big bear hug.

Lorraine made the rounds thanking everyone for coming, and for their contributions. She had Oliver do the thanking with her so that she could quietly show him off to anyone who didn't know him yet. She was so proud to be seen with him. Not only was he respectable, but he was also *very* handsome and charming. Best of all, the other single ladies looked positively sick with envy when they saw her strolling around with him, arm in arm. There was nothing like the satisfaction of putting some folks in their place. *Especially* that old gossip, Miriam. She—but Lorraine made herself stop that train of thought. Not in church, not on a Sunday. Plenty of time to think those thoughts tomorrow.

"Oliver, this was such a wonderful idea. It couldn't have turned out better," Lorraine said sincerely. When she had broken down last week and told him how worried she was about Ramona, he said he would pray on it and figure out a way to help her. Actually, just the way he looked at her with his warm brown eyes while she poured out her worries had comforted her immensely. The very next day he told her of his idea. Not only that, he helped her call people to get it organized quickly. He was there when she and her family needed help the most.

"It couldn't have worked without your congregation, Lorraine. They made it all happen. And, of course, it couldn't have happened at all without help from above," Oliver said humbly.

"Amen," Lorraine agreed. "Amen!"

As they walked around looking for Ramona and the kids they saw activities for everyone. Card games, bingo, darts, face painting. Lorraine teared up in spite of herself, seeing the parish enthusiastically reaching out to help her baby.

She walked over to Ramona, who had a line nearby of people waiting to sign her cast.

"Hey, baby," Lorraine called. "You having fun, Mona?"

"Oh, Mama, I still can't believe it. And, Oliver." Ramona had to stop and swallow. "I really don't know what to say. It's . . . it's. . . ."

"Mama! Why are you crying again?" Gracie asked, reaching out to wipe a tear that was rolling down her mother's face.

"Oh, Gracie, you know when something's just so good it *hurts?* That's why I'm crying."

Charles sat off to one side. He smiled to see how everyone was coming out to help his mama. He looked at his grandmother, smiling with Reverend French. He hadn't seen her so happy in years. Singing with some friends off to another side, even Gracie was smiling.

Charles was so distracted, he didn't notice his mother roll up behind him.

"Hey, sugar," she said.

"Hey, Mama, I didn't see you."

"I just want you to know how proud of you I am," she said, as tears welled up in her eyes.

Charles reached out to silence her. "Don't cry, Mama."

"No, hear me out. Through everything that's happened these last few weeks, you've shown nothing but character. Your daddy would've been proud of you. I'm proud of you. You were brave about that shareholder meeting, even if I didn't see it that way at first, and you did what you thought was best."

"Thanks, Mama," he said humbly.

"So I want you to know, I think you should also go to that policy committee meeting."

Charles sat up straight. "Really?"

"Oliver was right. Maybe someone as good as you can make a difference in this world. I'd be failing you if I tried to get in your way."

Charles hugged his mother tight. "Thank you, Mama," he said.

———

They were interrupted by a group of young men who entered the room. They were dressed like a gang, all alike, in baggy blue jeans and big, bright-blue-and-white Tommy Hilfiger shirts, with baseball caps turned backward and sideways. There was lots of gold jewelry in the form of chains, earrings, and gold teeth. The noisy room became quiet except for a few murmurs. Everyone knew who these guys were, and no one knew what to do.

"Hey, Jamal, isn't that D'Andre?" Ramona tugged at her friend's sleeve.

"Yeah, but I don't know what he thinks he's—"

"Wheel me over there," Ramona said.

"D'Andre," she said, reaching out for his hand, "it sure is good to see you."

"What's up, Mona," he said, remembering the last time he had seen her was when she came with Jamal to visit him in jail.

"How am I ever going to thank you? You sure do know how to make a girl's day. You know that, don't you?" Ramona tilted her head up at him and smiled broadly.

"Aw, just wanted to let you know we got your back. You know how it goes," he said awkwardly.

"I do. I do know how it goes. You did a beautiful thing, giving away your prized possession. I'm not going to forget it, either. Now introduce me to your partners," she said, looking at the group of young men.

"This is Mona, y'all. Uh, this is Teenie, Tyrone, Bryce, and Jay-Jay."

"Pleased to meet you," Mona said, shaking everyone's hand. "Y'all go on and fix yourselves a plate. We got plenty of good food."

"We came to perform."

Seeing Ramona's puzzled look, D'Andre continued, "See, we know y'all are trying to raise money, right?"

She nodded, confused.

"So, we thought we'd perform and people could just donate money if they liked what they heard."

Jamal interrupted his younger brother. "D'Andre, that's cool and all, but this is a *church*. You feel me?"

Ignoring his brother, D'Andre said to Ramona, "Introduce me to your pastor. I want to talk to him."

"C'mon, Jamal," Ramona said. "Wheel me around so we can find Pastor Davis."

As they left Pastor and Mrs. Davis talking with D'Andre and his friends, Jamal said worriedly, "Mona, I've heard them rap. This won't fly in a church! I know D'Andre means well, but—"

"Jamal, quit fussing," Ramona scolded.

As they sat eating with Gracie and Charles, Pastor Davis took a microphone onto the stage and welcomed everyone before leading them in a prayer. There was not a dry eye in the house when he was through. Then he said, "We have a surprise in store for us this afternoon. These young men have offered to perform for us today. If you like what you hear, then please make a donation for our sister and friend, Ramona Sullivan."

Everyone stared at the pastor like he'd lost his mind. Didn't he know who these dudes were? Every one of them had done time. It was a miracle they were even out of jail. Who knew when they might have found time to rehearse in between court appearances and probation appointments!

Thoughts like these were interrupted when D'Andre took the mike and coughed nervously. For all his talk of becoming a big rap star, he was terrified of crowds. Especially this one. He was met with skeptical stares and folded arms—not the adoring, scantily clad women he had dreamed of. "Thank you all for coming today. We're here because we love Ramona and we want to help her out."

Slight applause.

"We're going to perform some songs we think y'all might like. Oh, and Mrs. Davis is going to accompany us on the piano. So . . . enjoy," he finished.

More worried glances. *Mrs. Davis?* The pastor's wife had no idea who she was dealing with, apparently.

The five men got in formation, three in back, and two in front. Heads bowed, legs spread, arms crossed in front of their chests, hands on shoulders. D'Andre nodded to Mrs. Davis, and her music filled the room. The men lifted their heads and spread out their arms as their strong voices blended together into the sweet sounds of "Amazing Grace." Soon the whole room started humming and singing along. Doubting glances gave way to appreciative murmurs. Pastor Davis bowed his head and smiled with wonder. When it was all over, D'Andre and the others looked at the stunned crowd.

No reaction.

Then—thunderous applause, people on their feet, hands waving in the air. Ramona and Jamal clapping loudest of all.

12

Later that Sunday evening, on television screens across Atlanta, a newscaster announced a breaking story and then cut live to the outside of a fancy restaurant. "Hospitals of America CEO Bill Bradford has been dining tonight with board chairman Robert Strom and his wife," said a pretty young reporter. The Bradfords emerged casually through the front doors, obviously not expecting an ambush, and the journalist hurriedly reported, "Bradford is just now leaving the restaurant with his wife and son." Followed by her cameraman, she ran up to Bill and thrust her microphone into his face. "Mr. Bradford, are the Medicare allegations true?"

Surprised and unsmiling, looking down at the ground, Bill tried to step around the eager reporter, but she persisted. "Mr. Bradford, we've been hearing reports that Hospitals of America has been charged with Medicare fraud. Can you tell us anything about that?" She had to hurry to keep pace with him.

It was obvious, even on television, that Bill was angry—his face was red and his mouth was set grimly. "No comment," he said abruptly, dodging her.

"Are the allegations true, then?" she persisted, glancing from him to the camera.

Bill opened his mouth to respond, but then shook his head without answering. He breathed deeply and reminded himself he was on TV. More than anything he wanted to push this reporter out of the way. *Hard.* Paige and Andrew looked worriedly at the camera as they followed Bill to their waiting car.

"Ma'am," the reporter called out to Paige, "can you tell us any—"

Bill gripped Paige's arm and pushed her forward into the waiting car while Andrew ran around the other side and climbed in. "Leave my family out of this!"

He got in and barked at the driver out of earshot of the reporter and her crew. "Drive!"

The car sped off while the reporter faced the camera once again. With a serious look on her face, she said earnestly, "No comment from Bill Bradford, CEO of Hospitals of America. The allegations are very serious, accusing HOA of overbilling and fraud. If true, the fines could be enormous for this company, not to mention the implications for Mr. Bradford himself. This comes only weeks after housekeeping staff began picketing to keep their jobs."

In the back seat of the car, Bill watched the live television report. "Everybody's watching this. I can't believe it." He swore under his breath. Paige winced at her husband's profanity, but decided to ignore it.

The TV showed the Bradfords speeding away in their car. Bill shook his head angrily as the pretty young reporter finished her broadcast, condemning him with her words.

"I cannot believe this," he repeated furiously, as he clicked the TV off.

The ride home was tense for the Bradford family. Paige and Andrew knew better than to speak and they rode the whole way in silence. After he'd dismissed their driver and went into the house, Bill headed straight for the family room and turned on the large flat-screen TV to catch the news.

Still not speaking to one another, they took their familiar spots on the sofa and chairs and watched in horrified fascination as Bill's face appeared on the screen, soon to be followed by Paige and Andrew.

"I look like a geek," Andrew muttered under his breath, unhappy with his first television appearance. "I hope nobody's watching this."

Paige was full of questions, but wisely waited for Bill to fill her in. She had no idea if he was aware of the fraud or not—or if the allegations were even true. Andrew slouched on the sofa and looked at his father with worry. He was dying to ask his dad what it was all about.

"Is it true?" he blurted.

Paige looked at her son. He had more courage than she did.

Bill paused a beat and stared at Andrew, who looked genuinely concerned. "Yes," he said. He folded his hands and spoke, slowly at first, but then more conversationally. "It turns out one of our branches has been committing fraud. We were notified a while ago and we've been working with the government to fix the problem. The man in charge has been let go and we're cleaning the branch up. We're paying fines. We'd been working behind the scenes to keep this quiet and get it taken care of. It certainly wasn't our policy, but that doesn't matter. We've been under a microscope from all this housekeeping nonsense. Someone must have tipped off the press, but the information wasn't hard to find."

Andrew studied his father. For the first time, he thought he looked worn down. Maybe even a little old.

"Are you going to lose your job?" he asked.

Bill looked to Paige. How should he answer the question? He didn't want to worry his son. "I don't think so," he lied. He wasn't so sure. With this much heat on the company, people needed someone to blame—and he was the CEO. It didn't matter if it was some crooked manager in another state who committed the fraud. Ultimately he was responsible.

He stood up and turned to leave the room. "I need to go make some phone calls," he said. Then he paused. "Son, remember that cruise I scheduled for our vacation?"

Andrew nodded.

"I'm sorry, Andrew, but with all this . . . this *stuff* . . . happening right now, it just won't be possible. The timing, you know?"

Andrew could barely believe this bit of good news. Now he could go to soccer camp.

Bill put his hand on his son's shoulder. "I'm sorry. I ruined your birthday . . . and this was supposed to make up for it."

"Sure, Dad," Andrew managed to say. He tried to look disappointed. He figured that smiling would be totally inappropriate considering the evening they'd had. At least now he didn't have to tell his dad he didn't want to go after all.

"Thanks, son," Bill said gratefully. "You're a sport."

Bill headed to his office and closed the door.

13

Charles was annoyed. After Gracie's stealing incident, Oliver had given her the job of washing Bertha along with her brother. While Charles didn't mind splitting the money with Gracie, he did mind her whining.

"It's hot," she complained. "Can't you help me?" They had split up their duties before they started, and now Gracie was drying off the car.

"No, Gracie. I wash and scrub Bertha, and all you have to do is dry her." He looked at the hood. Spots were forming because she was drying too slowly. Charles glanced to see if Oliver noticed that his sister was slacking off. He was reading his paper in the shade on the other side of the car-wash parking lot, oblivious to their goings on. Gracie continued wiping down the car, but slowly.

"Girl, you're doing less than half the work, and all the whining," Charles huffed as he grabbed a towel to help her. "You're going so slow we'll have to wash the car again."

Oliver drove them back from the car wash. "Bertha sure looks mighty fine today," he said. "Do you want me to take you home or to your grandma's?"

Before Charles could answer, Gracie said, "Could you drop us off at the mall?"

"The mall?" asked Oliver.

"Yeah," said Gracie, "I've been saving up. I wanted . . ." She trailed off. Charles guessed she wanted to buy a skirt. But that topic was still a little sensitive.

"Okay, but I have to head off to the hospital to talk to a few people. Charles, will you two be okay?"

Charles frowned. If washing a car with Gracie was bad, shopping with Gracie was going to be a whole lot worse. Still, he couldn't just let her run around the mall by herself.

"Yes, sir."

"Okay, then."

Gracie wiggled with excitement.

A few minutes later the reverend dropped them off in front of the mall. As they got out he reminded them, "Now, don't be too late. I don't want your mother to worry."

Charles held up a quarter. "I'll call her, don't worry."

Oliver smiled and pulled away. Gracie wasted no time walking toward the mall entrance. Charles rushed to catch up.

Paige Bradford pulled the Range Rover into the mall parking lot. Andrew was texting his friends madly and didn't seem to notice they'd arrived. Paige unbuckled her seat belt and grabbed her purse. "Andrew, let's go," she said, breaking his concentration.

"Oh, sorry, Mom," he said, getting out of the car.

"We should be able to get all your new workout clothes for camp here. Hard to believe you've outgrown everything from last year."

"I need some new cleats, too," he reminded her.

Paige looked him up and down. "And maybe some new clothes in general."

Andrew groaned. What was supposed to be a quick trip to the mall was about to become a several-hour process during which his mother would make him try on tons of shirts and pants. He knew the mall had been a mistake. They should have gone to the sporting-goods store like he'd originally suggested. He kicked himself for the tactical error.

Walking through the unfamiliar shopping mall, Charles quickly felt out of place. There was nothing but rich folks here. A few people looked twice at Charles and Gracie—his pants were still a little wet from the car wash—but for the most part they ignored them.

Over the course of what felt like days to Charles, Gracie dragged him through several stores. She tried on at least ten things at every shop, making him wait outside the dressing rooms, first to guard the door and then to give his opinions. She only had a certain amount of money to spend, she said, and she wanted to make sure she spent it well.

―――――――

When they arrived at the fifth store, Charles put his foot down. "I'll wait out near the water fountain while you do your one-woman fashion show," he told her. "Don't take forever!" Gracie shrugged and went inside.

Charles sat down on a bench and sighed. He leaned his head back and noticed a kid next to him, listening to an iPod. Charles wished for a moment that he had one. He looked again at the kid and suddenly recognized him—it was the guy from the shareholders meeting. "What was his name?" he thought. "Oh, yeah: Andrew."

Charles tapped the boy's shoulder. Andrew took off his earphones.

"Hey, man," said Charles, "Remember me? From the shareholders meeting?"

It only took Andrew a second to remember and then he said, "Oh, yeah—Motown! How you doing?"

"Not bad," said Charles, smiling. He gestured toward the store. "Just waiting for my sister to finish her shopping. I swear we've been to a million stores already."

Andrew laughed. "Tell me about it. I'm with my mom." He pointed to the bags in front of him. Charles inhaled. Wow, Andrew sure did have a lot of shopping. "I just needed some shoes and suddenly we're buying a new wardrobe. Finally I put my foot down."

"Me, too," said Charles.

Andrew handed Charles an earphone. "Wanna listen?"

"Sure."

The two boys sat for a while, listening to Andrew's music. They laughed as they listened to Tupac, Eminem, and 50 Cent. Every once in a while Charles would look at Andrew to see his reaction to the lyrics. Andrew mouthed all the words and Charles shook his head. Crazy kid didn't even know what half this stuff was really about. Here he was, rapping about living on the streets, running from the cops—and it was all just words to him.

Then Charles remembered there were some other things Andrew might know, being Bill Bradford's son. Out of the blue he asked, "You ever been on the Policy Advisory Committee?"

Andrew took off his earphone and looked at Charles quizzically. *"What?"*

"You know, for HOA," Charles said. "The Policy Advisory Committee."

"I don't even know what you're talking about," Andrew said.

"Remember how they picked a number right before the meeting ended?" Charles persisted, feeling frustrated. "And they picked a shareholder to serve on that committee?"

"I couldn't pay attention in that meeting," Andrew admitted sheepishly. "I think I was listening to my music, to tell you the truth."

"Oh." Charles was obviously disappointed. Andrew was no help.

"But my mom would know," Andrew offered, seeing Charles's expression.

"She would?"

"Yeah. Ask her when she comes out." Andrew put his earphone back in. Suddenly Charles heard the low bass voice of Al Green. He turned and looked at Andrew.

"What can I say, you inspired me to try something new," he laughed.

Charles smiled. This kid was all right.

A few moments later, Paige walked out of the store carrying two more shopping bags. "These people do spend a lot of money," Charles thought to himself.

———————————

Charles and Andrew both got up. "Hey, Mom. This is Charles." Then Andrew realized he didn't know his last name.

Charles helped him out: "Charles Sullivan," and he held out his hand to Paige. "Hello, ma'am."

"Nice to meet you, Charles. I'm Paige." She shook Charles's hand, and he waited to see if his last name registered with her at all.

"I met Charles at the shareholder meeting the other week."

"Oh, is your father on the board?" asked Paige.

"No, ma'am. I'm a shareholder. I have one share of stock," he said proudly. "Your husband gave it to me."

Paige looked more closely at Charles, reassessing him. She noticed his clothes. This boy didn't dress like he had a lot of money. And he'd attended a shareholder meeting on his own? She wondered why her husband had given the boy stock.

"How do you know my husband?" she asked cheerfully.

Charles hesitated. He didn't want to bring this up. As luck would have it, his sister interrupted, marching out of the store with a bag.

"I found the perfect outfit!" she announced to him triumphantly. Then she noticed the other two people standing with Charles.

"Hi, I'm Gracie," she said. But as she shook their hands and got a better look at their faces, she realized who they were—she'd seen them on television the other night. They were the Bradfords. Bill Bradford hurt her mama. Gracie scowled.

Charles saw her expression and tried to calm the situation before something happened. "Well, we'd best be going," he said.

Gracie looked over at all the bags Paige and Andrew were holding, and then down to her single small one.

Charles grabbed Gracie's hand. "Come on, we're going to miss our bus."

Paige looked at the two kids and Gracie's little bag. "That poor girl probably saved up for weeks for that little purchase," she thought, remembering what it was like. Paige herself had grown up poor, and not so long ago she'd been working two jobs to put herself through college. Lucky for her, she'd met Bill, and her life had changed for the better. Only her hard work had gotten the society snobs to forget her humble upbringing. And she knew they still probably judged her behind closed doors, while publicly accepting her husband's checks for their charities. She suddenly felt burdened by all her bags. "I have to do something," she thought. But she knew they probably wouldn't take money.

"I have a better idea, Charles," Paige said brightly. "Why don't I drive you home!"

Charles froze. "Oh, that's not necessary."

"Besides," Gracie quipped, "I wouldn't feel safe with a Bradford driving us."

Charles glared daggers at her but the comment seemed to go over Paige's head. Not getting Gracie's meaning, she continued, "No, really, I insist. Save your bus money." Paige looked determined. "Andrew, help me with these bags," she said, and without further ado she headed for the exit.

Charles had no choice but to follow her and Andrew to the car. He dragged Gracie along despite her protests. As he pulled her by the hand, he whispered, "Now, don't you say anything."

Gracie scowled and whispered back, "Traitor," as they approached the Range Rover.

"*This* is their car?" Charles thought. "And she wants to take it into *our* hood?" He had to talk her out of it—but she was already behind the wheel, starting the engine. Gracie rolled her eyes as Charles pushed her into the front seat.

Andrew looked at Charles's expression as he got into the car. "Hey, don't worry. It's no problem to take you home. I mean, she wouldn't offer if she didn't mean it. Really."

Charles didn't know what to say. No way could Paige and Andrew come to his neighborhood. He wondered if he could give them the wrong address.

"C'mon, Charles," Andrew said from the back. "Ride back here with me. Mom can be our chauffeur!"

"Very funny, Andrew," Paige said good-naturedly.

Charles slowly climbed into the huge car and sat gingerly on the tan leather seat. Andrew pointed to the seat belt. As if in a trance, Charles buckled himself in as Paige maneuvered her way out of the parking lot. "Okay, tell me where you live, Charles."

"Mrs. Bradford," Charles said. "This isn't . . . I mean, you don't have to—" He struggled. He had to find a way to make sure they didn't go to his apartment. Or meet his mother, he thought with renewed panic.

"Charles, it is absolutely no problem to take you home! Goodness. Now please, just tell me where you live, okay?"

Before he could stop her, Gracie gave her the address. He lowered his head. Maybe she'd realize where that was and take it all back. He waited for her to slam on the brakes and screech to a halt. Instead she said, "So, let's see. If I go down here. . . ." She trailed off as she figured out the route in her head. "Oh, I think I know where that is. You'll have to help me when we get closer, okay?"

"Sure," Charles mumbled, trying to figure out how to avoid disaster. It looked like they were all headed straight for it and there was nothing he could do. He looked outside at the setting sun and suddenly remembered he'd forgotten to call his mother. Now he would be in even more trouble.

14

Ramona sat in the quiet apartment with the TV on mute and wondered where her kids were. It had been hours since they'd gone to help Oliver wash his car. She trusted the reverend—no question there—and she knew they'd be safe with him. Still, it was getting late. The silence felt particularly gloomy today. She felt alone.

Ramona had tried to keep up a good attitude, but after weeks of being cooped up in the small apartment she was ready to scream. It gave her too much time to think and worry. Even though she and her family blamed Bill Bradford for the car accident, she knew that she had walked out into the street without looking first. They *both* should have been paying more attention. Nobody had said to her, "Well, you shouldn't have been talking so much that afternoon, Mona," but it was true: she had been talking and looking *behind* her to see if the kids were listening.

Where was Charles? She felt so helpless stuck in the wheelchair.

Suddenly she heard footsteps and voices in the stairwell. Sounded like Charles and . . . she couldn't make out who else. Ramona wheeled her chair in front of the door, wiped her face, and decided that she wouldn't reprimand the kids too much as long as they were safe.

———————

As Paige neared Charles's neighborhood she realized she had made a mistake. A very *big* mistake. Suddenly she wished for a less conspicuous car. Suddenly she felt showy and out of place. It couldn't be helped, but now she knew why Charles had tried to dissuade her. If Bill ever found out . . . well, he must *never* find out. That was that. She would have to impress upon Andrew that this was their little . . . adventure, and Dad just didn't need to know about it. . . . Ever.

Andrew, however, had his head practically hanging out the window trying to see everything, until Paige abruptly rolled all four tinted windows up and locked the doors. "Mom, why'd you do that?" Andrew complained. He had never seen anything like this place. It was so cool—just like some of the stuff he saw on MTV.

Paige glanced nervously in the rearview mirror, not wanting to offend Charles, but Charles answered for her. "This isn't a place to be playing tourist, Andrew," he said quietly. The kid acted like he never got out of the house. "Probably spending too much time at the country club," Charles thought.

Andrew looked at Charles. "Whatever. It's just . . . interesting to me. Where I live there's nothing. I mean, just houses and trees and stuff. But this. . . ." This was real life, he thought, looking at the streets and the people.

This neighborhood was *loud*. He could hear music blaring. Graffiti covered the apartments and businesses. People were everywhere. This was nothing like his silent neighborhood with huge houses set far apart from one another, separated by great expanses of carefully tended lawn.

Charles could see Paige's face tighten up as she asked, "How much farther is your apartment?"

He again thought of trying to lie, but Gracie chimed in smugly, "Turn left at the next light, go two blocks, and turn right. We're almost there." Watching her brother squirm gave her pleasure. "Why doesn't he want Paige to know where we live?" she wondered, her curiosity piqued. She wanted to see how this all played out.

All of a sudden a cop on a motorcycle turned on his strobe lights and squawked his siren, pulling up behind them. Paige checked her speedometer and saw that she was going the speed limit. Nervously she signaled and pulled the big car to a stop at the curb.

The officer got off his bike and swaggered up. Paige rolled down the window. She fumbled with her purse to find her driver's license. As the man in the helmet peered into the car, he looked in undisguised surprise at Paige. She looked up anxiously, as this was only the second time in her life that she'd been pulled over.

"Ma'am," he said curtly, "I need to see your driver's license and registration."

Paige handed him the documents and watched as he read them. "You're Paige Bradford?" He looked carefully at her photo and then at her face.

"Yes."

Reluctant to admit he'd made a mistake, he looked closely at her driver's license again. "Aren't you a long way from home?" he asked, narrowing his eyes.

Paige lost her nervousness as anger took over. "I beg your pardon, officer?" she said in her best Junior League voice, staring at him with cold, blue eyes.

The cop shook his head. "Sorry, ma'am, it's just this neighborhood isn't the safest. We don't see nice cars like yours around here very often." He handed back her papers. "Are you lost?"

"Thank you. We aren't lost," she said. "I was just driving my son's friend home."

The officer peered into the back of the car to confirm there were kids inside. Feeling like she was telling the truth, he stood back.

"If you don't mind, officer, we'll be on our way."

"No problem, ma'am," he said. "Have a nice day." He walked back to his motorcycle.

With that Paige rolled up the window and pulled back out onto the street. "The nerve of him," she fumed to herself. "He pulled me over for *nothing!*"

Charles knew why he'd pulled her over, but kept it to himself. A big Range Rover with tinted windows could mean only one thing: nobody drove a car like that around here unless they were dealing drugs. "Cops are pulling brothers over all the time, just because," he thought. "They don't have to have a good reason."

Paige slowed down in front of the apartment building. To her eyes, used to everything being shiny and new, the place appeared to be falling apart. "Those children live here?" she thought, looking at the broken windows on the first floor, and the weeds growing out of the sidewalk.

Charles unbuckled his seat belt. "You can just drop us off at the curb," he said.

"Oh," said Paige, not knowing quite what to do.

"Thanks for the ride and all. I appreciate it," Charles said, trying one more time to get Paige and Andrew out of his neighborhood.

She made a decision. "I can't just drop you off, Charles. We'll park and walk you to your front door. Just to be sure you get home safe." She backed her car so she could parallel park in an open spot in front.

"Really, it's no problem," Charles assured her quickly. "We're perfectly safe. Right, Gracie?" He looked to his sister for support. No telling what kind of mood Mama was in, especially with them being gone this long.

"That's very nice of you to walk us in, Mrs. Bradford," Gracie said sweetly. It might be fun to see this woman's reaction to where they lived. She already looked like she'd eaten something sour—like it was all she could do not to lock all the doors and tear out of there.

Paige bravely turned off the engine and forced a smile. "Great. I'd like to meet your mother."

Gracie saw an opportunity to close the deal. "I think she'd love that, too." She smiled wickedly at Charles.

Paige opened her door and motioned for Andrew to get out. "We won't stay long, Charles," she said, sensitive to his reluctance.

Charles looked worriedly up and down the street. He wondered how long the car could stay parked here without someone messing with it. Five minutes, maybe? Well, he'd tried to tell her, but she didn't want to listen. Nothing he could do now, except take them upstairs to meet Mama.

Walking up the flights of stairs, Paige tried not to breathe. The odor was overpowering. Charles acted surprised when she asked about the elevator. "Elevator?" he said, wrinkling his forehead. "That thing never worked. We have to use the stairs."

Andrew didn't like this part of the adventure and he gave his mom a look that clearly said, "I want to go home!" But Paige felt obligated to meet Charles's mother now. Something made her want to help these two children. She couldn't quite put her finger on it. She was uncomfortable, for sure, but she wasn't about to criticize how other people lived. Ignoring her son's look, she smiled and pretended everything was all right—as if they did this every day.

When they reached the third floor, Charles knocked on the door to give his mother some notice that he was there, then took the keys from around his neck and opened the three locks. Pushing the door open a crack, he said, cautiously, "Mama? We're home."

Waiting for some response before he invited Paige and Andrew in, he stood at the doorway uncertainly. "Charles? Do you have Gracie with you?" Ramona called from the living room.

"Yes. I've got company." He took as long as he could with the door.

"Come in. Who've you got with you?"

Gesturing for Paige and Andrew to follow him, Charles walked into the living room.

Ramona rolled around the corner and looked at her son sternly, hiding the utter relief she felt. "You and your sister had me scared to death. Where've you been?"

"Sorry, Mama. I told Reverend French we'd call but I forgot."

Charles turned to introduce Paige and Andrew, but before he could, Ramona was looking past him with surprise. That blond woman . . . that skinny boy, about her son's age . . . Ramona's mouth popped open as she realized who they were. This was Bill Bradford's wife and son. She'd seen them on the news.

She stared at Charles. What was he doing, bringing them here?

Paige stepped forward after an awkward moment and said, "Hi! You must be Charles's mother. It's so nice to meet you." She held her hand out and waited for Ramona to take it. Instead Ramona stared at her and then at Charles.

Charles could see right off that this had been a mistake. "Mama," he said. "This is Paige . . . and Andrew . . . Bradford."

Ramona set her mouth and stiffly shook Paige's hand. This woman was looking at her with absolutely no idea at all who she was. Unsure of what to do, she said politely, "I'm Mrs. Sullivan." And then, realizing that they were all just standing there, she added, "Would you care to sit down?"

Paige looked at the tattered old couch. She gently pushed Andrew and took a seat, sinking in and then awkwardly falling back. She recovered and rested firmly on the edge, with an uncomfortable small laugh.

Then they sat for a moment in silence until Paige finally spoke.

"So, my son met Charles a couple weeks ago at the HOA shareholder meeting. I am really impressed that Charles went all on his own."

Ramona continued to watch her cautiously, so Paige kept chatting. "It's never too early to learn about how the world works, is it?" As if she'd just noticed Ramona was in a wheelchair, she exclaimed, "Goodness! That's some cast you have on your leg, Mrs. Sullivan."

Ramona and Charles exchanged glances. Clearly this woman had no clue. Charles just gave his mother a look like a rabbit in a trap. Ramona answered carefully, "Please, you can call me Ramona. I was in an accident a few weeks ago."

Andrew, feeling more relaxed and therefore curious, said, "Wow. That must have been something. What happened?"

Gracie jumped in: "She was in a car accident."

"Really?" asked Andrew. He looked ready to ask another one when Paige elbowed his side to keep him from being too nosy. He didn't take the hint. "Ow! Mom, watch your elbow!"

Paige's face reddened and she said, "Well, I'm sure it must be difficult being in here all day with no elevator."

Ramona nodded in agreement. "It sure is. I'll be happy to get this thing off."

Another silence fell. Ramona smiled a careful smile.

Paige waited for Ramona to say more and thought maybe she didn't want to talk about her leg anymore. She decided to change the subject. "I'm curious, how do you know my husband? Charles said he gave him a share of stock."

Ramona stared at her, puzzled. This woman really didn't know who they were. Gracie, who'd been watching everything, couldn't take it anymore. She hated all this dancing around the issue. If her mama wasn't going to say it, she would. "Charles gave him back his wallet after he lost it."

Paige looked puzzled. "He never said anything about losing his wallet," she said, more to herself than anyone else.

"It fell out of his pocket right after the accident," Gracie continued, staring into Paige's eyes. Her meaning was clear. She saw the realization slowly come over Paige, who looked at Charles and then at Ramona.

Charles looked at Gracie, silently begging her to be quiet. But she continued: "Your husband hit my mama on a Sunday a few weeks ago. We were just coming out of church and. . . ." Gracie couldn't finish. Half of her wanted to smack this pretty rich lady and the other half wanted to cry, remembering how it had all happened.

"Andrew's birthday," Paige remembered slowly. "He was in such a state. He did tell me about the accident, but I never dreamed our paths would cross. Oh, my . . . I'm so sorry," she said helplessly, her eyes filling with tears. "I don't even know what to say."

"My *dad* hit you? With his car?" Andrew said, not quite believing what he was hearing. He suddenly looked at Charles as if he were a stranger. "I don't get it. Why were you at the shareholders meeting, then?"

Charles wiped his eyes, let out a deep breath, and collected himself. "Well, I guess I better start from the beginning. After they took my mama away in the ambulance. . . ."

For the next half hour, Paige listened to them tell their story. She sat on the couch in shock after hearing everything Charles had to say. Finally Andrew broke the uncomfortable silence by asking, "You mean you went all the way to my dad's office just to return his *wallet?*" The blond boy shook his head in bewilderment, thinking of his friend Kevin, who recently bragged about a wallet he'd found, and spent the money that same day. At the time, Andrew had listened to him enviously, wishing he'd been the one to find it—even though all he had to do was ask his parents for money and they would give it to him.

Paige looked around the sparsely furnished apartment with its worn sofa and chairs. Her eyes welled up with tears again. Embarrassed, she wiped them away. "So, did Bill ever . . . you know . . . did he ever *help* you or anything?" she asked awkwardly.

Ramona stared at her coolly and remained silent.

"Mama has a lawyer," said Gracie. "But he says that *your* lawyer says it's Mama's fault and so they won't pay for anything."

"Gracie!" said Ramona reproachfully. "It is not Mrs. Bradford's fault. Now if you can't keep your mouth shut, I'll have to ask you to leave. Do you understand?"

Gracie put her head down. "Yes, Mama."

"You could've kept that money and no one would have blamed you!" Andrew burst out.

Charles looked at Andrew curiously. "We weren't raised like that," he explained.

Andrew's face reddened and he stole a glance at his mother. Paige looked at the family before her. They were so full of goodness and pride. She ached to think that somehow, in a roundabout way, she was responsible for their recent troubles.

Ramona shifted in her wheelchair and looked questioningly at the Bradfords. "Tell me, Paige, Andrew: Why did you come here today?"

Paige sniffed her nose and fished in her purse for a tissue. She paused. "I don't know, really. I just wanted to give Charles and Gracie a ride home. So they could save their bus money," she said.

"A ride home from where?" Ramona interrupted, staring pointedly at her son.

Before Paige could answer, Charles said, "Reverend French dropped us off at the mall so Gracie could spend her car-washing money."

Ramona sighed and gave Gracie a look that meant, "I'll deal with *you* later."

Paige looked from Ramona to Charles and wiped her nose. "It was no problem! Really—I did insist." She looked around. "Ramona, is there anything I can do? Anything at all?"

Ramona saw the sense of guilt all over Paige's face. "Thank you, but no. We'll be all right."

"But your hospital bills, they must be astounding, and. . . ."

Gracie looked up. Maybe this was the break their mama needed. But Ramona shook her head and this time she said, more forcefully, "Thank you, but no."

Paige's face reddened as she realized that she'd offended her. She looked at Ramona closely. She knew that pride. She remembered when she'd eaten cheap noodles in those long stretches between paychecks because she couldn't afford anything more. Paige bowed her head. She wished that she could be half as brave as this woman. She cleared her throat, and said, "We really had better be going. It's getting late."

"But, Mom," Andrew protested. Wasn't his mom going to help the Sullivans? After what his dad had done?

Paige ignored him and stood up and shook Ramona's hand. "It was a pleasure to meet you, Mrs. Sullivan. I mean, Ramona," she said sincerely.

Ramona held her hand firmly and said in return, "It's a pleasure to meet you, too, Paige."

"Charles, walk the Bradfords downstairs," she said, eager to bring this visit to a close. Then, to Paige and Andrew: "Be careful getting home."

The trio walked silently down the flights of stairs. Charles was only too happy to have this encounter over with. He guessed it went as well as it could have, all things considered. As least there were no fists thrown. He hoped the Bradfords' car would still be in one piece waiting for them at the curb.

Paige followed Charles numbly. She wondered how— or if—she would talk to Bill about the Sullivans. As they reached the outside of the building she looked up at their apartment, wishing there was something she could do.

Luckily, the car was intact. Charles thanked heaven for the little miracle. Paige hugged Charles a little too long but he let her. The lady seemed really upset. Andrew and Charles bumped fists and Andrew went to get into the car. Then he turned around. "Hey, man, I'm sorry that happened to your mom."

Charles nodded in appreciation. He watched the two get solemnly in the car and drive away.

Paige and Andrew went home silently, each lost in their own thoughts. Gripping the wheel tightly, Paige almost forgot to make the right exit and remembered just at the last second, gunning her big car over three lanes of traffic with screeching tires.

"Mom!" Andrew yelled, alarmed. "What are you—"

"Sorry," Paige gasped. "I didn't see it." Checking nervously in her rearview mirror she saw an angry driver raising his fist at her as he blared his horn. She checked her speedometer and watched the impatient driver pass on her left, this time with his middle finger raised in the freeway salute. Paige stopped herself from saluting him back.

"Mom?" Andrew asked cautiously. "Are you okay?"

Sighing deeply, Paige shook her head. "No. I just can't believe your father." She stopped, feeling disloyal, not wanting to share these thoughts with Andrew.

"I can't believe he hit her. And didn't even help her!" Andrew echoed his mother's thoughts.

Paige remembered all too well the day it happened, the ruined birthday party . . . but Bill had assured her that it had all been settled. Morrie had taken care of everything, hadn't he? The more she thought about it, the angrier she became. The thought of Ramona stuck in that old apartment building without an elevator . . . her pride in refusing Paige's help. Paige swallowed hard. She wasn't used to feeling rage, but that was exactly what she was feeling now.

She pulled the Range Rover expertly into the driveway, pressing on the remote to open the garage door. Guiding the car in, she was relieved to see that Bill's Jaguar wasn't there yet. Andrew followed his mom inside the house, silently watching her as she dumped the shopping bags on the dining-room table.

Restlessly she walked into the kitchen, opened the refrigerator, and then slammed it shut. "I don't feel like cooking tonight," she muttered. Then, as she noticed Andrew hovering in the doorway, her shoulders sagged and she shook her head in apology. "I'm exhausted, Andrew. How about we order a pizza?"

Normally Andrew would have been thrilled at the idea of pizza, but all he said was, "Sure, Mom." Paige stood staring out the kitchen window until Andrew cleared his throat. Turning around, she frowned at him.

"Uh, are you going to order it?" he asked cautiously.

"Bring me the phone book," she answered wearily. "Actually, why don't you just order it? Get whatever you'd like; I'm not hungry." Paige left the kitchen without waiting for an answer. Carrying the packages from the table, she slowly headed upstairs.

Bill Bradford pulled his sleek car into the garage next to the Range Rover and turned off the engine. It had been a grueling day with reporters constantly calling, wanting to speak to him about the Medicare fraud. Not to mention the TV camera crews who had been there all day, hoping to get a glimpse of the CEO and a few minutes of question-and-answer. Instead they'd had to content themselves with interviewing the marchers outside the building. Several people had given the public an earful about HOA's plan to outsource, and the newscasters had listened to them sympathetically.

Bill had felt like an escape artist, sneaking out the building's back loading dock and eluding the media. But he had done it, and thank God he was home. All he wanted now was to relax with his family and eat. "I wonder what Paige is serving tonight?" he thought hungrily.

Walking into the house, he sniffed for clues about dinner. "Roast beef and potatoes," he hoped—but the house didn't smell like anything.

"Paige? Andrew? I'm home!"

No one answered, although he could hear the television blaring in the family room. Making his way past the darkened kitchen and dining room, he found Andrew sitting by himself in front of the TV with an enormous pizza in front of him.

Bill was confused and a little irritated. "Son? What are you doing?"

Andrew jumped and stopped eating his pizza mid-bite. "Uh, hi, Dad," he said, without offering any further explanation. He picked up his pizza, turning his attention back to the television.

"Andrew," Bill said sharply, causing the boy to stop eating again. "Where's your mother?"

Before answering, Andrew took a swig of soda straight from the can, then motioned with his head. "Upstairs."

Frowning, Bill headed up the stairs. "Paige? Paige! I'm home." Stomping noisily, he wondered what was going on. He couldn't remember ever coming home and not having a good dinner waiting. He was hungry, he'd had a rotten day; where was Paige? He forced himself to breathe deeply, and called out for her one more time: "Paige?"

Entering their bedroom, he saw her sitting up in bed with her nose buried in a book. She didn't even glance at him.

"Paige? Honey, are you okay? Are you sick?" Bill softened his voice as he sat on the edge of the bed. "Didn't you hear me calling you? Paige?"

Glancing at him briefly, she said, "I'm reading."

"Paige, what's gotten into you?" he asked, staring at her.

She ignored him until he roughly grabbed the book from her hands. "What are you—" she protested, sitting up and reaching for her novel.

"Paige, what's going on? What is the matter with you?" Bill demanded, holding the book out of reach. "Don't ignore me when I'm talking to you."

Paige trembled as she pulled the covers tightly around her shoulders. She stared at him coldly, and a tear made its way slowly down the side of her face. She made no move to wipe it.

Bill looked at her, bewildered. "What did I do?" he asked. "You're obviously mad at me, but how can I defend myself if I don't know what I did?"

She sat up straighter in bed. "How could you not let me know about the sorry state of the woman you hit?" she asked accusingly.

"What are you talking about?"

"I've never felt so embarrassed or as ashamed as I was today. That woman, the one you hit, well, we met her today. You should see her, Bill, with her big, huge cast. And she's stuck in a tiny apartment all day. And she says your fancy attorney won't pay for her medical bills."

"Okay, please slow down." Bill tried to be calm. "How on Earth—?"

"We ran into Charles Sullivan today at the mall. The boy you gave the share to. I felt sorry for him for some reason and so I drove him and his sister home."

"Paige, you went to that part of town alone?"

"Yes, to that part of town," she said with a sneer. "Don't forget I was born not too far from 'that part of town' in the city I grew up in. I know you like to forget that, with all your rich friends."

"Now, wait a minute," said Bill. "When have I ever criticized where you came from? Regardless, it's not safe. Don't you know anything?"

Leveling her gaze at him, Paige said quietly, "No, apparently I don't know anything, Bill. Apparently I don't even know my own husband. What happened to that idealistic man I married? Who are you? I can't believe you wouldn't try to help that poor woman!"

Bill gave her a withering look. "How would that look in court, huh? If I gave that woman any money that's as good as saying I'm guilty. And for crying out loud, Paige, *she* walked out in front of *me*. Did you forget that? Or did she fail to mention that little fact?"

Fuming, Paige said, through clenched teeth, "What difference does that make? You *hit* her and now she's stuck in a wheelchair for Lord knows how long. Stuck in a building without an elevator. She can't work. She can't do anything! How can you be so heartless? And then her *son* had enough integrity to return your wallet when he and his family could have really used that money!"

Bill tried to protest but she ignored him.

"Look around, Bill. Don't we have enough money? I mean, isn't that what we pay insurance for? Can't *they* pay her, if you won't?"

"You're naive, Paige. You stay at home and talk to your girlfriends all day. You're not out in the real world, like I am. What do you know about real life?" Bill asked her harshly. "How dare you judge me? How dare you?"

Paige slid out of bed and stood up, trembling, her face drained of color. "Is that what you think of me? Someone who does *nothing* all day? Is it, Bill?"

Bill sensed too late that he had crossed a line. "Sit down, Paige. Let's discuss this calmly. Look, I didn't mean to make it sound like that. It's just—you're judging me and you don't know all the facts. Just sit down, okay?" he coaxed.

As if he hadn't even spoken, Paige continued, "You think I talk to my girlfriends all day? You think my life isn't important? You think I'm stupid—don't you?"

"No, honey. Paige, listen," Bill said, fumbling for words, wondering how they'd gotten into such dangerous territory.

"Did you ever take me seriously, Bill? I thought you respected me. I thought we were a team. I thought—"

"Paige, I—"

"I wanted to be a nurse," Paige reminded him. "Remember? I was going to go to nursing school, but then I met you, and—"

"Paige," Bill interrupted her. "What does this have to do with anything? Why are we arguing over something so . . . so unimportant? Let's go downstairs and eat dinner, okay?"

"*Unimportant?*"

"Well, maybe that wasn't the best choice of words, but—"

"*Unimportant.*"

"Shhh . . . you're getting hysterical," Bill admonished her. "Stop it, Paige. Quit overreacting!" He unsuccessfully tried to calm his wife down.

"*Overreacting?* Is that what you think I'm doing? *Overreacting?*" Paige's words spilled out passionately. "Do you have any idea how it felt to meet that family living in poverty—seeing that woman in a *wheelchair*, unable to work—knowing that my husband, *my* husband, was the one who put her there? Do you have any idea how humiliating that was? And do you know what the *worst* of it was?" She continued without waiting for a response. "When I offered to help her, she refused my help. She didn't want anything from me. Can you imagine how low I felt? Can you imagine how your son felt? Can you?"

Bill stared at his wife, not knowing how to defend himself. How could his lovely wife be looking at him with such disdain in her eyes?

"What do you want me to do?" he whispered, desperate to get that look off her face.

Paige just shook her head sadly, staring at her husband standing there helplessly. "If you have to ask that . . . well, that's the whole problem right there, isn't it?"

"Now listen, Paige," he said, reaching out to her.

"No," she said finally. "There's nothing you can say to defend yourself. *Nothing*." And with that she turned off the small lamp, turning her back to Bill, shutting him out, waiting for him to leave the room.

After heading slowly back down the stairs, Bill sat wordlessly next to his son. He took a slice of the now-cool pizza and hungrily devoured it in a few bites. Andrew glanced at him, but kept his attention on the TV.

"What are you watching?" Bill finally asked, with his mouth full, staring at the gunfire on the screen.

Andrew shrugged. "I dunno. Just some movie."

"Well, I don't think your mother would want you to be watching this, Andrew," Bill said, reaching for the remote. "Did she say you could watch it?"

Again, Andrew shrugged, and he slouched further down into the couch. "I dunno."

"Andrew!" Bill bellowed as he stood up. "What is going on around here?" He shut off the TV with an angry click of the remote. "I said turn it off. I'm your father."

Andrew carefully put his half-eaten slice of pizza back in the box and wiped his hands on his jeans, staring back at his father without offering an explanation.

Bill pointed his finger at his son threateningly and said in a low voice, "Now tell me what's going on!"

Andrew tensed at his father's words and stood to look him in the face. Bill flinched at the anger in the boy's eyes and stepped back a bit. Andrew went to speak but decided better of it and silently stormed out of the room.

Mason Smith smiled smugly. He had the Bradford case in the bag. He'd made sure that Bradford's lawyer heard, in a roundabout way, that he was the one who leaked the Medicare news to the *Tribune* and from there to the rest of the media. Now they knew he could play hardball. He was less than subtle with his threat to also bring the car accident to light. Bradford would never recover from that sort of press.

Mason had asked for a nice, quiet, million-dollar settlement—and he felt confident he'd get close to that.

He had a nagging feeling in the back of his mind, though. Mrs. Sullivan had been short with him. You'd think she'd be happy. She asked him to take whatever settlement the other lawyer offered and be done with it. She just wanted enough to pay her bills. Only after much prodding did she agree to let him talk to Bradford's attorney one more time. He was going to make it worth it.

15

Bill Bradford was out of breath and sweating. He was on his usual morning jog but it wasn't making him feel any better. Paige still wasn't talking to him. Andrew barely was. He'd been up all night thinking about things—remembering his wife's stinging words.

"Was I young and optimistic once?" he asked himself. He could barely remember that person. Life had made him cynical. "I just assumed that kid had stolen my wallet."

Last night made Bill realize how much Paige's approval mattered to him. "And Andrew's, too," he mused. He was so used to being their hero, he didn't realize he could fail them.

His mind wandered to the company and then naturally to his father. "What would he think of everything that's going on? Would he be disappointed?" The company was more profitable than ever, but something made Bill feel like the answer was yes—his father *would* be disappointed.

He ran harder, pushing himself until his chest hurt. "Just to the top of the hill," he decided. His legs burned but he pushed on until he reached the top. Then he slowed down, noticing his surroundings.

His leg cramped up and he took a moment to stretch it out. "When did everything start going wrong?" he wondered. "It all comes back to the car accident." Or maybe it was some time before that. He stretched his other side and looked out onto the lake. "I'm going to call Morrie as soon as I get into the office, and have him fix everything. Paige was right: that's what insurance is for. I pay them enough, and it should take nothing to settle this."

He felt a weight lift off of him. He felt, for the first time in a while, like he was doing the right thing. Suddenly the world was silent and he saw nothing but the blue sky overhead, heard only the breeze in the trees and the ducks quietly splashing in the cool morning light. He wondered if he'd ever even noticed how beautiful it all was. Feeling lighter, he headed home.

When Bill returned, the house was still quiet. He got ready for work in silence and skipped breakfast, then headed out, grateful for the early morning's light traffic as he drove to the office. Pulling into his parking space, he straightened his shoulders and strode confidently into HOA headquarters. A few years ago, it was not unusual for him to arrive before eight a.m., but he hadn't been in so early lately. He was pleasantly surprised to see several employees already there. He was feeling good and decided he'd brave the break-room coffee and try to mingle with his employees. Eager to see friendly faces and grab a bite to eat, he headed for the kitchen, where he could hear people talking.

". . . fraud, can you believe that?"

"You know darn well he did it, or at least *knew* about it."

"This company sure isn't what it used to be. William Bradford would never have gotten us into this mess. He never forgot where he came from. The company was built on family, not on stock options. He was one of us."

"And he never compromised his integrity. He was about the most honest guy around."

Bill stood outside the door to the break room. He couldn't move. He wanted to turn back to his office, but found himself frozen there. The smile he'd come in with suddenly turned to a look of pain.

"First it's the housekeeping staff because they cost too much," said one man. "It won't be too long before we're all getting fired in favor of younger and cheaper workers. God forbid an American company today should have any loyalty."

"The days of the retirement party and a gold watch are gone," said another man as he came around the corner with his office mate. They both stopped abruptly when they saw Bill standing there.

Awkwardly one of them blurted, "Good morning, Mr. Bradford."

Bill nodded at the men and they both turned away, red-faced. He continued into the break room. He wasn't going to let them know what he did or didn't hear.

Inside the kitchen, one office worker nudged another and they looked up with a start. "Oh! Good morning, Mr. Bradford."

All other conversation had stopped and there was an uncomfortable silence.

"Mr. Bradford, can I get you a donut and coffee?" asked an older woman who had been with HOA for years. She looked nervously at her boss.

Bill swallowed and looked at the room full of people— who were looking everywhere but at him. Even though his stomach was rumbling, he wasn't sure he was hungry anymore. "Thank you, that would be great."

She handed him a glazed old-fashioned donut and a cup of coffee. "Thank you, Mildred," he said, and turned on his toes back toward his office.

As he walked away he heard a whispered, "Do you think he heard us?"

Bill's upper lip trembled. He always thought he'd known who he was. He thought everyone saw him as he saw himself—a smart businessman with a loving family; a man just like his father. He'd assumed his employees loved and trusted them just like he knew they'd loved and trusted his father.

Suddenly he realized he might have it all wrong.

Bill half-heartedly returned some emails and made calls to Europe until finally his desk clock read "9:00

a.m." He called Morrie, whose assistant answered the phone. "Oh, hello, Mr. Bradford."

"Hey, Bernice. Is Morrie in?"

"I'm sorry, he's not in today, Mr. Bradford. He's on his annual wedding-anniversary trip to the Keys. He's been hard to reach but I can let him know you called, if he checks in."

"Sure. Fine," Bill said, trying not to sound disappointed.

"Otherwise, he's back on Thursday. Will that be all right?"

"Yes, that's good. Thanks, Bernice," he said and hung up.

Bill was frustrated. He wanted to do something. He looked at his calendar. "Today is Tuesday." Then he noticed something: "The Policy Advisory Committee meeting is tomorrow." They were going to discuss the Medicare fraud claims, among other things. "Might be a good idea for me to attend that meeting, unannounced," he thought. Then he remembered Charles was on the committee.

Bill called Gladys into his office. "Do you still have the address for that kid, Charles Sullivan?"

"I should have it, sir."

"I want you to have a driver pick him up tomorrow for the Policy Committee meeting. I'm going, too, but I'll drive myself."

Gladys nodded and walked out. As she shut the door she wondered if Mr. Bradford was okay. He was acting so strange lately. But, then again, no more or less than anyone else. She put it quickly out of her head and went to call the car service.

———————

The next day, Charles nervously adjusted his tie in the mirror one last time as Gracie knocked on the bathroom door impatiently. "Get out of there! I have to pee! *Bad!*"

Charles ignored her and hopped up onto the rim of the tub, peering at his suit—the same one he'd worn to the shareholders meeting. It would have to do. He was so excited about the committee meeting that he didn't even feel annoyed by Gracie, who had been pestering him all morning. Despite warnings from Ramona, she managed to work in some whining when she thought their mother wasn't listening.

"Get away from that door, girl!" Ramona chastised her youngest child. "What did I tell you about hollering all the time?"

"Sorry, Mama," Gracie mumbled. "But I have to pee."

"He'll be out in a minute," Ramona said, softening her tone. "This is a big day for Charles."

Gracie rolled her eyes and slumped dramatically against the wall. Finally, Charles emerged and said, "How do I look?"

"You look real handsome, son. You look fine. And I mean *fine!*"

Charles laughed. "Thanks, Mama."

———————————

Oliver and Lorraine pulled up to the Sullivans' old, three-story apartment building. "Now, I hope you don't get your feelings hurt if Charles doesn't like it," he said gently.

Lorraine looked at him levelly. "Oh, I'm not worried about that," she said confidently. "He'll like it."

Oliver cleared his throat. "Okay, let's go on up, then. We don't have too much time before I have to take him downtown."

"I just want my grandson to show up in style," Lorraine explained. "You with me, Oliver?"

He smiled at the pretty woman beside him. "I'm with you. Let's give Charles his surprise."

Up on the third floor, Oliver knocked on the door and it was immediately opened by Gracie, who had been waiting anxiously for them to arrive.

"Give me some love, girl," Lorraine said, embracing her granddaughter.

"Grandma, what'd you bring me?" Gracie said, greedily eyeing the big box.

"Nothing for you this time," Lorraine said bluntly. "Go find Charles."

Pouting, Gracie banged on the bathroom door. "Charles! Grandma and Reverend French are here!"

She flounced over to the couch, determined not to miss anything. Ramona wheeled herself out of the kitchen. "Hey, Mama. Hey, Oliver. You ready to take my son to his meeting?"

Ramona was more nervous than Charles, but she was trying to hide it. Most of all, however, she was real proud of her son. She hoped he would have a good time this evening.

Finally Charles emerged from the bathroom wearing his suit. "You ready to go, Reverend French?" He was clearly excited and eager to leave.

Lorraine handed him the box. "Hi to you, too, Charles," she teased him. "You look good, but I brought you something that's going to make you look even better. Now go try it on."

"Aww, Grandma. . . ." He took the box reluctantly. The last thing he wanted to do was change clothes, but he couldn't hurt her feelings. "Thanks," he continued, and he disappeared into his bedroom.

Charles opened the box and took out a tie, a shirt, slacks, a blazer, and even socks. Grandma went all out! "But why is everything the same color?" he wondered with dismay. He'd better put it on and show everyone and then think of a reason not to wear it tonight.

Pulling on the blazer, he had to admit it all fit, at least. Grandma always was good about knowing his size. He looked at himself in the mirror and took a deep breath. He barely recognized himself. "I look good," he thought, "like a grown man." He smiled with pride. Grandma knew what she was doing. The slate-blue suit with the matching shirt and tie looked good against his chocolate complexion. He looked older. It was like getting a glimpse into the future. Opening his bedroom door, he joined the others in the living room, eager for his family's reaction.

Oliver whistled with approval. "Looking *good,* little man."

"Let's see, turn around," said Lorraine, wanting to see him from all angles. "Mmm, mmm, *mmm.* You got that right," she said proudly.

Charles knew Gracie would be the hardest to please. She frowned, as she looked him up and down. "That suit's tight," she admitted finally. "But why is everything one color?"

Lorraine scowled at her. "That's the new look. That one fellow wears it every night. You know, that newscaster on Channel 5. The *handsome* one." Oliver raised an eyebrow at Lorraine, pretending to act threatened.

But Ramona hadn't spoken yet. Charles looked to her for her reaction. She pursed her lips, and finally she said in a choked whisper, "You look mighty handsome. You sure do remind me of your daddy."

Now *that* was the best compliment of all. Charles smiled broadly, showing both his dimples.

"Thanks, Grandma. I like it," he said sincerely.

Gracie glanced out the window and saw a gleaming white town car waiting down at the curb. "Hey, Mama! Check this out!"

Ramona wheeled over to the window and positioned her chair sideways and craned her neck so she could see out. "My, oh my," she exclaimed. "Would you look at that? I wonder who that's for?"

Gracie knocked on the bathroom door. "Charles! Come check this out! You're not gonna believe your eyes."

Charles came out of the bathroom. He ignored Gracie and walked over to Oliver. "You ready to go?"

But the reverend didn't answer. He was looking out the window, too. He squinted his eyes at the license plate. Did it say HOA? He couldn't be sure.

Charles kept moving forward and, hugging Ramona tightly, he said, "I'll see you later, Mama. Love you."

"Love you, too, Charles," Ramona said. "But honey, I think you'd better take a look outside. That may be for you."

Charles looked down in awe.

"I'll go with him," said Oliver. Ramona nodded. She heard Charles already moving down the stairs two steps at a time.

Jimmy, the town car's driver, waited nervously in front of the rundown apartment building. He had circled the block twice and made sure his doors were all locked before deciding that this really was where Charles Sullivan lived. He had no idea what to expect—no idea who his passenger was going to be. From the looks of the neighborhood it was safe to assume Charles was a brother like himself. But why was he going to the HOA Policy Advisory Committee meeting? That didn't make any sense. Jimmy hoped it wasn't some type of a criminal set-up. He was through with all that foolishness years ago, but his suspicious nature remained.

Lots of folks stopped by to admire the town car. A little hoodlum made an attempt to touch it until Jimmy rolled down his window. All it took was a direct look in the eye for the boy to know he was a serious man. "I may have moved out of the hood," Jimmy thought, "but I still know how to give the cold stare." He watched the other passersby out of the corner of his eye, but gave no indication that he even noticed them.

With the window rolled down to get some air, he heard, "Hey, Pops, what are you doing here? This ain't no place for a fancy car. You lost, man?" A young man clowned around in front of several others.

"Naw, man, that limo's for *me*," one of his friends answered. "I told you I had a good week, but you didn't want to believe me."

"Man, you never had a good week. What're you talking about? You're lucky to be riding the bus!"

Jimmy was just about to bust out his mean look when suddenly a knock on his other door startled him. He turned to see a boy waving at him. Jimmy ignored him like he had all the other curious spectators, but the boy persisted.

"Mister! Hey, mister!"

Finally, Jimmy gave him his sternest look and said, "Get away from this car, son. I'm not playing."

The boy looked exasperated and said, "Yes, sir, I know. But I just wondered who you were picking up."

Jimmy snorted and shook his head. Kid had a lot of nerve. "I'm sure it's none of your concern."

"Is this a Hospitals of America car?"

Jimmy looked at him inquisitively. "It may be."

"Well, I'm Charles Sullivan. I'm supposed to go to the Policy Advisory Committee meeting," the boy explained, his voice rising. "I thought maybe you might be here for me."

Jimmy frowned at him, anticipating a trick. "Say what? *You're* Charles Sullivan?"

"I'm Charles Sullivan," the boy repeated loudly, as if Jimmy were deaf.

The driver slowly stepped out of the car and noticed that the boy was dressed in a suit and tie and good shoes. He didn't look like a hooligan. "*You* are Charles Sullivan." It sounded like both a statement and a question.

Charles sighed. "Yes, I've been trying to tell you."

Jimmy looked at his instructions. It was then he noticed a note at the bottom of the printout: "Teenager." He shrugged. "I guess this is my passenger," he told himself.

"Well, if you're Charles Sullivan, then, yes, I'm here to pick you up. My apologies for the confusion." Clearing his throat, Jimmy didn't want to admit his embarrassment. There was a cough from off to the side. It was then Jimmy noticed an older man.

"Are you the boy's father?" Jimmy asked.

"No, no, I'm just a family friend. However, if you don't mind, I'd like to accompany him to and from the meeting."

Jimmy nodded. He guessed it wouldn't be a problem if the old man chaperoned. It made no difference to him whether he had one or five people in the car. He got paid the same.

Charles looked antsy. "Well, let's go. I don't want to be late for my first meeting."

Jimmy opened the door and motioned for Charles to get in the back. "Put your seat belt on, you hear?" the chauffeur said gruffly. He gestured for Oliver to climb in as well.

"Oh, I'll sit up with you, if you don't mind," Oliver said. "Let the boy enjoy the experience."

Jimmy shook his head as the old man opened the front door and got in. "Suit yourself," he said. He walked around the car, muttering to himself. What on earth was going on? He saw the old man lean out the window and wave up to someone in the apartment above. "What is this, a parade?" Jimmy thought. He climbed back into the driver's seat and started the engine. The old man extended his hand. "Reverend Oliver French," he said.

"Jimmy," said Jimmy gruffly. Now he had a chaplain in his car. He hoped he wasn't going to start hassling him about the last time he went to church. He sighed, put the car in drive, and pulled out.

As he drove, lots of questions were going through Jimmy's mind, but he didn't know how to find out the answers without appearing to be nosy. "A kid from the hood going to a committee meeting," he thought, smiling to himself. *"Ain't nobody going to believe this!"*

Charles's palms caressed the supple leather seats and his eyes took in the luxurious interior of the town car. "It's like a limo," he thought. He wished his friends could see him now. Craning his neck, he looked out the back window and saw people on the sidewalk gawking at the sleek, white car as it cruised unhurriedly through the neighborhood. He turned and waved as he recognized TJ sitting on the stoop in front of his building, but TJ looked right through him. "What's his problem?" Charles wondered out loud.

Jimmy glanced at the boy staring out the window. "Son? Those folks can't see you through those windows. They're tinted."

Charles felt a bit embarrassed.

"Look, just enjoy the ride. Is this your first time in a town car?"

"Yeah, it is," Charles admitted.

"Take a look in that compartment in front of you," Jimmy instructed.

Charles opened up the mini-refrigerator and gasped at the array of drinks and food. "Dang . . . I mean, look at all that stuff. People buy this?" Charles asked, reluctantly shutting the door. He had no money at all on him.

"It's on the house," Jimmy said, laughing as Charles flung open the little door. "Help yourself."

"I can have anything? You sure?" Charles looked greedily into the fridge.

"Anything except the alcohol," Oliver interjected. "Go on, take something."

Charles finally decided on a Dr. Pepper and peanuts in a blue foil bag. "Sweet!" he thought happily. "I could get used to this."

"Now, see that radio? We've got Sirius. Just about any channel you want, with any kind of music you want. Go ahead and pick something out," Jimmy added, hoping he wouldn't regret it. He expected the kid to find a station that played those rap songs and any minute the peaceful ride would be turned into a migraine nightmare.

Charles took his time sorting through the hundreds of stations streaming. He finally settled on one, smiling. Jimmy hunkered down in his seat, ready to step on the gas to make the ride go faster as he anticipated the harsh strains of gangster rap.

Suddenly the car was filled with the sweet sounds of The Temptations singing "My Girl," and Jimmy grinned widely. "You like The Temptations?" he asked Charles, who was singing along with the music.

Charles nodded. "Yeah, anything Motown. That's what we listen to at home."

Jimmy smiled his approval. "Turn it up a notch, son. I like me some Temptations." He added his alto tenor to Charles's soprano, and soon the reverend's bass, as they sang together pretty much in key. "I guess you'll say, what can make me feel this a-way. . . ."

―――――――

As they pulled around to the back of the HOA building, Charles looked at Jimmy, confused. "Aren't we supposed to be going to Hospitals of America?"

"This is the loading dock," Jimmy said. "I've been bringing Mr. Bradford to this entrance, what with all the protestors."

Charles nodded his head and looked around, unsure of where to go. Jimmy pointed him toward a security guard at a small rear-entrance door.

"I'll have the car here waiting for you when the meeting's over," Jimmy said. He held the door open so Charles could step out, wiping peanut crumbs from his suit. Jimmy had refrained from asking the boy why he was going to the Policy Advisory Committee meeting, because it wasn't his place, but he sure was curious. It didn't make any sense to him.

"Thanks, mister, that was fun," Charles said, holding out his hand.

Jimmy shook it gravely. "Call me Jimmy, and you're welcome."

Charles looked expectantly at Oliver. The reverend shook his head. "This is your meeting, son. I'll be right here."

Charles nodded and turned toward the building. The men watched as he strode confidently into HOA's headquarters without looking back.

Oliver looked at Jimmy and smiled. "I'll go get us some coffee," the reverend suggested. "How do you take it?"

"Black, two sugars," said Jimmy. As Oliver walked away, Jimmy smiled. Maybe today wasn't going to be such a bad day after all.

———

Charles took the folded piece of paper out of his pocket, even though he had its information memorized: seventh floor, suite 707, two p.m. Riding up the elevator, he suddenly wished he were back in the safety of the town car. "It's not too late to change my mind," he thought . . . but as soon as he thought it, the elevator opened to the seventh floor.

Hesitating inside the elevator, Charles waited until the doors started sliding closed again before he interrupted them with his hands and stepped out into the hall. Looking around, he noticed some people going into a room, so he slowly walked down the carpeted hallway toward the entrance.

"Can I help you?" a woman with stiff grey hair and piercing blue eyes asked him, as he paused in the doorway.

Standing up straight, Charles cleared his throat. "I'm Charles Sullivan. I'm here for the Policy Advisory Committee meeting."

The woman raised her eyebrows skeptically. She glanced at a roster and ran a red, manicured nail down the list until she located his name. Frowning, she noticed the birth date by his name. "You're *fifteen* years old?"

"Fifteen and a half if you want to get technical," Charles said, keeping a straight face. The lady opened her mouth, but had no suitable comeback. She had no choice but to give him his nametag and show him in.

As he entered the meeting room, Charles suddenly felt nervous and out of place. He stared at the long table with several people already seated around it, and wondered if he'd made a mistake after all. Rooted there, he was unable to move until someone gripped him on the shoulder, startling him.

"Charles! You made it. I wasn't sure you'd come," Ira Goldstein said.

"You're the one who helped me out." Charles struggled to remember his name.

Holding his hand out, Ira said, "Yes, I am. Ira Goldstein. Why don't you sit by me? I don't usually attend these meetings, but Mr. Bradford suggested I come. It ought to be quite interesting." Then, watching Charles's eyes wander around the room, he realized the boy might be bored out of his mind. "If you have any questions, don't hesitate to ask me."

Several people gave Charles surprised looks and whispered among themselves, but when he caught them staring, they smiled politely.

"Must be 'bring your kid to work' day, huh?" a beefy, red-faced man asked his companion, nodding over in Charles's direction.

"But whose kid?" the smaller man responded. "Ortiz's boys are already in college. Maybe it's some kind of gimmick." He shrugged, clearly not that interested.

The overweight man continued gazing over in Charles's direction, frowning. "Hope he knows how to behave himself. Teenagers get on my nerves."

Finally the meeting started and Charles sat straight up, paying much closer attention to the committee chairman than he ever had to a teacher in school.

"Let me get right to the point," the chairman said without any preamble. "HOA is having a public-relations crisis. Our PR is at an all-time low. The result is that our stock prices are steadily decreasing." Here the chairman paused, letting this information sink in. "I'm sure you've all seen the housekeeping staff and their supporters on the nightly news and in the newspapers. Ever since HOA announced that these workers would be outsourced they've been protesting, quite vocally, in the media. The more publicity they get, the more of them come out in force, it seems."

A woman with dark hair cut in a chin-length bob raised her hand. "What about the allegations of Medicare fraud?" she asked pointedly. "*That* certainly isn't helping our image."

"Hold on. I was just getting to that," the chairman answered a little irritably. "In addition to the protestors, we have recently come under fire for Medicare fraud, or, I should say, *alleged* Medicare fraud." Wiping his brow, the chairman looked at the unhappy and concerned faces staring at him.

"In our next few meetings," he continued, "it will be our primary job to counteract this barrage of negative publicity. We need to act quickly before more damage is done."

As was predictable, everyone had something to say and several people began speaking at once, resulting in chaos. Charles used this opportunity to tap Mr. Goldstein. "So we're going to be advising the company on how to look better in the press?"

Ira could see the boy sincerely wanted to understand, and this impressed him. "Yes," he replied, "we need to look good in the eyes of the public. If the public doesn't believe in us, the value of our company will continue to go down."

Charles nodded thoughtfully. "So if we just change people's minds," he concluded, "we can make more money again—is that it?"

"That's it, basically. HOA has always been a very successful corporation, Charles, and we'd like it to stay that way."

Suddenly they both turned as a large man got everyone's attention with his loud voice. "We need to get on the offensive and take control," he said aggressively. "Business is business; no one is owed a job. Layoffs happen when unions make it impossible for companies to do business. Should HOA go broke? Quit letting the housekeeping staff run the show."

The chairman interrupted him, not wanting the meeting to turn into a venting session. "What do you propose we do?" he asked.

"All right, then," the large man continued, now that he saw he had everyone's attention. "All the public has seen over the last few weeks is the nonsense from the housekeeping staff. The sooner that problem is solved the better. I think we should take out a full-page ad in the *Atlanta Journal-Constitution*, in the *New York Times*—heck, in *all* the major papers, if we have to— and let the public know about all the great things Hospitals of America is doing." He looked around for the committee's reaction. "We say things like, 'Our future has never been brighter.' It's called *damage control,* folks." He sat down with a satisfied expression on his face, again scanning the room for everyone's reaction.

"Yeah, we'll do an ad campaign!" someone shouted.

"Let's educate the public with facts," another man offered. "You know, so many lives saved, so many transplants performed, so many open-heart surgeries. You get the idea."

"But what about the fraud?" the dark-haired woman asked worriedly.

"*Alleged* fraud," the large, loud man retorted. "I'm telling you, we take out some ads in the Sunday paper and let the public know that HOA has never been in better shape. Say something that will restore the public's confidence."

"But we're in terrible shape!" she protested. "How's an ad going to change facts?"

The man glared at her, clearly offended. "So, what's *your* idea?"

Suddenly there was a shuffle from the back of the room. People began to turn their heads. Bill Bradford had entered the room.

The committee chairman rose up. "Mr. Bradford, this is unexpected."

Bill spoke as he walked to the front. "Sit down, I don't mean to interrupt." He saw Charles and gave him a warm smile. "I just wanted to come in and clear the air a little bit. I know there have been a lot of rumors around the office and in the news about what's going on around here. This committee is meeting to discuss how to put HOA back in America's good graces, but I thought, how can you do that without all the facts?"

He stopped at the front of the room and faced the committee. "HOA has committed Medicare fraud."

A nervous murmur went around the table.

"It was one manager leading a small group of people at a single branch," Bill continued. "This group is a tiny portion of HOA. He's been taken care of and we're working with the government to restore our good credit with them. But between the housekeeping layoffs and this, things have been blown out of proportion by the media. Our job is to find a way to get HOA back on America's good side."

Charles raised his hand. It took a moment for people to acknowledge him. He stood up and cleared his throat. The room went silent. "Um, so if you want America to believe in you again, what about just telling the truth?"

The chairman cocked his head as if he weren't sure he'd heard him. "What?" he asked.

"Well," said Charles, "Mr. Bradford just came in here and said that we could do a better job if we knew all the facts. And after what he said, I sure feel a lot better. I mean, every basket has a bad apple once in a while. But just because one person does something doesn't mean it should represent the whole group."

Ira leaned forward to tell Charles to quiet down. He admired his courage but couldn't believe he was telling the CEO and committee chairman what to do. But Bill waved him off: "You know, the young man has a point."

Everyone in the room looked at one another. Was he serious?

Bill paused a moment in thought before continuing.

"On Friday this week, I'll meet the press and tell them the truth: that Hospitals of America takes responsibility for the actions. That we don't run and hide behind our lawyers. When my father built this company it was to make a better way of life for people, through good medicine. Everyone makes mistakes, and we're fixing ours in the hopes that America can one day trust us again."

As Bill finished, he smiled at Charles. Charles smiled back. He'd made a difference, just like Mama and Oliver had said.

As the meeting broke up, the committee chairman nodded to himself. Bill Bradford sure was brilliant. As Bill walked by, the chairman shook his hand. "Great speech, Bill. America loves that goodie-goodie, 'Honest Abe' sort of thing." He leaned in conspiratorially. "I have to hand it to you, planting that kid here was even smarter. It really helped to sell it. You know all these people are going to start some positive buzz among the other shareholders."

But Bill Bradford didn't smile back. Instead he just looked the chairman in the eye and said seriously, "I meant every word."

The chairman stared after him as he strode out the door.

16

Charles gratefully entered the waiting town car and sank down in the seat, relieved to be out of the meeting and glad to be heading home.

"How was your meeting?" Jimmy asked as he started the car.

"Crazy," Charles answered. "A lot of people worrying about what other people think about them."

"Well, grab yourself a snack and relax. How about some music?"

"Sounds good to me," Charles replied, helping himself to a Coca-Cola.

Oliver walked toward the back door. "Mind if I join you back here, Charles?" Charles scooted over happily to let him in. "No offense there, Jimmy," said the reverend, laughing.

"None taken," said Jimmy, smiling. He knew Oliver was curious to hear how the boy did.

As they pulled out of the parking area, Oliver turned to Charles. "So, how was the meeting? I want to hear all about it."

"Man, it was confusing," Charles said, shaking his head. "People arguing. They care more about how the public sees them than doing the right thing . . . I don't know about all this, Reverend."

Oliver pondered. "Sounds like a complicated situation," he said. "Hey, how about we stop on the way home and pick up some food? The five of us can feast on some Chinese takeout tonight. How's that sound?"

"Sound great," Charles answered, realizing he was hungry after his long afternoon.

Oliver called up to the front, "Hey, Jimmy, you want some Chinese food?"

"Always. I can't get enough of those pot dumpling things."

"We're not taking up your time, are we?"

"No, sir, I'm on the clock another two hours whether or not you need me. So I might as well get myself some dinner."

"All right, sounds good."

"Hey, now, if you be wanting some good Chinese, I know a little dive off the highway that's right on the way back toward your place. The food is fantastic and there's a pretty little waitress that's not bad either."

Charles and Oliver shared a chuckle.

"That sounds perfect."

The three of them rode in silence for a while. Charles looked out the window, deep in thought, until Oliver said, "So, the committee meeting wasn't what you expected."

Charles sighed.

"You disappointed?" the reverend asked.

"I don't know. I mean, I'm glad. I think Mr. Bradford even listened to a suggestion I made."

"Mr. Bradford?" said Oliver in surprise. "Well, that's a good start."

"It's just that. . . ." Here his voice trailed off. The reverend waited while Charles struggled to make sense of the meeting. "People were stressing. I've never seen adults act like that! I mean, here I thought business-people were all professional; you know, wearing their suits and ties and talking to each other formally. But when they started arguing, well, they weren't any better than me and Gracie when we're fighting."

"Bet that was a surprise." Oliver chuckled.

"Yeah—and another thing," Charles said, warming up, his words eagerly spilling out. "The company isn't doing so good right now."

"Oh?"

"Yeah, the PR, the public relations, is at an all-time low. People have lost trust in the company."

"Probably the whole Medicare scandal," said Oliver absently.

"What does *Medicare fraud* mean, exactly?" Charles asked.

"Well," Oliver explained, "Medicare is what some people use to pay their hospital bills, like elderly people and those who don't have health insurance. Medicare fraud is when a hospital bills the government for something they didn't do. Let me give you an example. Maybe a person went to the hospital with pneumonia and stayed there three days. But the hospital bills Medicare for double pneumonia for ten days."

"So the hospital gets more money than it's supposed to?"

"Exactly."

"But . . . why would HOA do that when they've got so much money already?" Charles asked.

The reverend looked at the boy's worried face. "Charles, money makes people do strange things."

Charles thought some more about the meeting before he continued. "Mr. Bradford said that there was fraud but it was only in one branch, and that they fired the people who did it."

"That's good."

"So if they're fixing it, then why is everyone so mad at them?"

"I think in part because HOA has appeared to be covering something up, as if they're guilty. . . . They haven't told their side of the story. For instance, I didn't know that about the branch manager."

"Yeah," said Charles, "that's what I told Mr. Bradford. I said maybe if everyone knew the truth, they'd trust you again. But they said the housekeeping staff is protesting on the news, every day, and that makes the company look bad, too."

"Wait a minute," Oliver said. "Did anyone say *why* the workers are protesting?"

Charles stopped and thought. "No . . . they didn't talk about why. Just that the company was losing money.

But Aunt Etta said that a lot of it was that if she lost her job, she'd lose her health care and she's too old to find another job. I guess a lot of the housekeepers have worked at the company for years."

"Do you think it's wrong for them to protest?" Oliver asked as Jimmy pulled the town car into the restaurant parking lot and turned off the engine.

Charles thought about it. "Well, I guess if HOA is wrong to let them go, then no, they're not wrong to protest. Like, Aunt Etta has worked for them for twenty years. I guess that should count for something."

"So you think HOA is wrong?"

Charles was still uncertain. "One man said that not everyone deserved a job, and the company would go broke. And then no one would have a job, if the company doesn't have money."

The reverend nodded. "That's quite a hard decision. Do you take care of people who have worked for you most of their lives, if doing so makes the company lose money?"

Charles furrowed his brow. "But there must be a compromise."

Oliver looked impressed. "Compromise? Good word."

"Like when Gracie and I fight about stuff. Mama says we need to compromise. She says that we're both a little bit right and both a little bit wrong."

"Well, it sounds like you learned a lot today, my friend. That's business right there."

Charles sighed, thinking about it all. Then a voice popped up from the front. "You know what's an easy decision, gents?" Charles and Oliver looked up. They'd been in such deep conversation they'd forgotten Jimmy. "What we're going to order for dinner."

Several minutes later, the three walked back to the car, carefully setting the steaming bags of food in the front seat, and settled in for the drive home. Driver, chaplain, and committee member spent the rest of the trip in companionable silence, listening to the smooth sounds of Marvin Gaye.

As they arrived at the apartment, Jimmy looked back to see Charles stretched out on the seat, fast asleep. "That must've been some meeting," he murmured to himself.

"Wake up, son," Jimmy said to the sleepy boy. Looking at Oliver, he said, "Guess that meeting just plum tuckered him out." The reverend smiled as Charles slowly emerged from the car, yawning and stretching.

"That was one of the best rides I ever had," he said sincerely.

"Better than Bertha?" Oliver asked, teasing him. Charles grinned.

Jimmy helped them get their food out of the car. As he shut the door Charles stuck out his hand and said, "Thanks, Jimmy."

"Any time, young man." Jimmy gave him a firm shake and then he turned to Oliver. He shook Oliver's hand

and watched them walk toward the door. Then he called out, "Hey, Charles."

"Yeah?"

"You got a good head on your shoulders. I feel better about the future knowing you're in it."

Charles smiled. "Thanks," and he went inside.

Lorraine, Gracie, and Ramona were waiting for them when they got home. Lorraine gave her grandson a big hug when he and Oliver brought the bags of Chinese food into the apartment. "Hey, you're going to wrinkle my good suit," Charles said, squirming out of her grasp.

"And just *who* do you think bought you that oh-so-fine suit?" Lorraine said with mock indignation, hands on her hips.

"Aw, you know I'm just messing with you," Charles said, kissing his grandma quickly on the cheek. "Thanks again for getting it for me."

"Well, go change, son," Ramona said, wheeling into the room, "because we're about to start eating. Then you can tell us all about your meeting."

"That town-car ride, Mama! Man, that was—" Charles stopped mid-sentence, seeing the look on Ramona's face. "Okay, okay, I'm going to change."

The adults chuckled after Charles closed the door to his bedroom. "That boy sure is excited, Mona," Lorraine said. "This is a real adventure for him."

"And a real responsibility," Oliver added.

Ramona looked at him curiously. "Responsibility?"

Oliver nodded as he set the table and laid out the white boxes of steaming food. "I best let him tell it. The boy has a lot on his mind."

Ramona looked at him thoughtfully. "You think I made the right decision, Oliver?"

"Time will tell, but what he learned today you can't teach in school. I think it was real important."

"Gracie, turn that television off and come eat with us," Ramona called, noticing her daughter sitting cross-legged on the floor a foot away from the TV. Wordlessly the girl reached over, pushed the power button, and stood up with a heavy sigh.

Lorraine frowned at her. "What's wrong with you, girl? You haven't said two words since I got here."

Gracie shrugged. "Sorry, Grandma," she said listlessly.

"That's all right," Lorraine reassured her. "Let's eat and listen to Charles tell us about the meeting."

17

Bill Bradford pulled his Jaguar into the garage, turned off the engine, and sat in the dark silence listening to the clicks and sighs of the engine cooling down. He sighed, but he felt good. That Sullivan kid was something. Sometimes it took an outsider to point out the flaw in the whole system. Why were they hiding behind big words and misleading phrases? Why not come out and admit there was a problem, but they were fixing it? He was going to have to earn America's trust back. He was feeling good. This was the right way to go. Suddenly he realized he'd been sitting in the dark for a while. He grabbed his briefcase and went inside.

The house was dark, with just a small light on, over the stove in the kitchen.

"Paige?" Bill called out uncertainly into the silence. "Andrew?"

A note lay on the countertop in Paige's familiar handwriting: *Dinner's in the fridge. We'll be home by 8:30.*

Frustrated, Bill crumpled the note and tossed it into the garbage underneath the sink. He wanted to share with her all the things that had happened. To let her know that he was working to fix the Sullivan thing, and that he had a new direction with the Medicare problem. She couldn't even be bothered to tell him where they went!

He opened the fridge and grabbed the plate wrapped in tinfoil. As he closed the door he noticed the calendar stuck on its front. "Soccer finals" was written boldly, with a smaller "6 p.m." underneath. Guiltily, Bill remembered the schedule Paige had mentioned yesterday; at the time, he'd been distracted. A few weeks ago she had given him a list of Andrew's games. He had distractedly put it with a pile of papers, where it was promptly forgotten. In fact, he couldn't even remember the last time he had attended one of Andrew's games. There was always something else competing for his time and attention.

Bill couldn't remember ever feeling this alone before. Now that he actually wanted Paige and Andrew's company, it was nowhere to be found. Both of them had made excuses to avoid him for days. And once again Bill found himself alone in the big, silent house. He realized that for too long he had holed himself up in his study, ignoring their requests to attend soccer games, go on errands, or just spend time with them. Shaking his head, he thought about how many times he had scheduled golf games on the weekends, knowing that he would easily be gone five hours or more. Thinking he should have gone to see Andrew play today, he realized with a pang that he didn't have any idea where the games were even played. The park? The school?

Maybe Paige was right. Had he changed that much? What would his father think of him now? His father had died years ago, and Bill still missed him. When he was a boy he had idolized him. He loved hearing how his dad had grown up dirt poor but used his wits to build an important company. His dad had been one of a kind, no doubt about it.

Bill sighed. Although he had been famished when he entered the house, the desire to eat had left him. He put the food back in the fridge. Feeling exhausted, he headed for the family room, turned on the television without the sound, slumped on the couch, and fell asleep.

An hour or so later, Paige and Andrew clattered through the front door. "I still can't believe we won, Mom! Did you get a picture of that last goal I made?"

"What do you think?" Paige asked, laughing. Andrew often teased her about being "camera happy" because she liked to record every event, and their home had the photographs to prove it.

"Dad?" Andrew yelled into the quiet house. "Hey, Dad!" He headed for the family room, where he could see the glow of the television. "Dad?" he said uncertainly.

"Huh? What's wrong?" Bill said groggily, struggling to sit up on the couch. "Just dozed off for a minute," he explained, rubbing his face.

Andrew looked at his father's rumpled shirt and crooked tie. He couldn't remember him ever falling asleep in his office clothes on the couch.

"Are you all right, Dad?" Andrew asked softly.

Yawning and rubbing his eyes, Bill nodded blearily.

"We won the game," Andrew said, waiting for a reaction. "I made the winning goal!"

Looking at his son's hopeful face, Bill smiled and said, "That's great, son! What do you say we go out and celebrate?"

"Uh," Andrew said, hesitating. "We kind of already ate."

"Oh."

"But thanks anyway, Dad."

Bill tried to hide his disappointment. Paige walked in. As soon as she saw Bill, her face clouded over. She turned to Andrew. "Why don't you get cleaned up before you track dirt all over the house," she said to him gently. Andrew turned and left the room.

"Did you eat your dinner?" Paige asked her husband, who hadn't moved from the sofa.

"Wasn't hungry."

"Andrew's team won."

"He told me," Bill said, glancing at his wife standing uncomfortably in the doorway. "I offered to go out and celebrate, but he said you two had already eaten."

"We celebrated with the team."

Bill looked at his wife, searching for any signs of warmth.

"Paige, we have to talk," he said quietly. "We can't keep relating to each other like this."

Paige looked at him without any expression. "What do you want to talk about?"

He wanted to say he couldn't stand it, that he had always counted on her love and support and now that it was missing, life at home was intolerable. Everything, in fact, was intolerable. Why couldn't he just say that?

"Please, Paige . . . I'm your husband," he said instead.

When she didn't respond, Bill stood up and put his arms around her. She stood there stiffly, with her arms at her side. "I love you, Paige. Please talk to me," he pleaded. She refused to meet his gaze.

Andrew walked quietly down the carpeted stairs and stopped when he saw his parents embracing in the doorway. He wondered if things would get back to normal now. Not wanting to disturb them, but needing to see what would happen, he sat down out of sight behind the railing.

"What do you want me to say?" Paige finally asked.

"Oh, Paige. Act like you *care*," Bill said, still holding her, willing her to respond to him.

"Remember when I first met you?" Paige asked wistfully. "You were so idealistic . . . so proud of your father and the company he founded. But more importantly, you were proud of the kind of *man* your father was. You were proud of what he stood for . . . and you wanted to be just like him."

She paused. "I've lost respect for you," she whispered.

"I know," Bill answered sadly. "And I'm going to have to work to regain that. I've been trying to get in touch with Morrie. I've decided to settle with the Sullivans. You're right, it's the right thing to do."

"Really?" she said, finally meeting his gaze.

"It's important to you, and I respect what you think," he said. "That's important to *me*."

She gave him a warm embrace. From the hallway, Andrew nodded. Things were going to get better.

18

Thursday morning Bill arrived early at the office. He hadn't heard from Morrie while the lawyer was on his vacation, and he was eager to get this Sullivan thing off his shoulders. He waited not so patiently until nine o'clock. Morrie was never in before then.

At nine he knew Morrie would be in the office, and he placed his call. Before the lawyer could say more than a quick hello, Bill dived in. "Morrie, I've been doing some thinking. We should just settle with the Sullivan family. It was my fault as much as hers. More mine, really. I was grabbing my phone and not looking at the road. We should cover her medical expenses and disability. It's the right thing to do." Bill smiled to himself. Paige would be proud of him.

"Hey, hey, Bill—slow down. I was about to call you this morning myself. I just got off the phone with the Sullivans' attorney."

Bill sat back in his chair. "That's great, Morrie. So are we all on the same page?"

"No," said Morrie bluntly. "Listen, I tried to suggest a settlement, Bill. Their lawyer's playing hardball. He says they won't take less than a million. Now, you should know that the insurance can only cover so much before it comes out of your pocket."

"What?" said Bill, aghast. "But I thought that it would just be expenses. How much are we talking here?"

"Well, the insurance will cover up to one hundred thousand dollars if we're talking medical bills, loss of work, and legal fees. With a little pain and suffering thrown in."

"So, I'm looking at. . . ."

"Nine hundred thousand, yes."

Bill took in a sharp breath. "I thought a hundred thousand might be where it ended up," he said, "not where it started."

"There's more, Bill." Morrie paused. "I can't prove it, but. . . ."

"What is it?"

"Like I said, I can't prove it, but I'm pretty sure their lawyer is the one who tipped off the press to the Medicare issue."

Bill's good mood came crashing down.

"What?"

"And it gets worse. He's basically threatened to go to the press tomorrow with the car-accident story if we don't settle for a million."

"But I've got a press conference in the morning to take care of the Medicare scandal."

"I know."

"That's all they'll talk about. After this, they'll connect the car accident to me, and the Medicare fraud to me, and just assume the fraud is widespread and I approved it. This will destroy my reputation.

It'll ruin the company. It will kill HOA. Morrie, this is blackmail!"

"You could look at it that way. But there is freedom of the press. What can we do if he's just telling them the truth? I agree with you, though. With everything that's going on, a rich white CEO hits a poor black single mom and refuses to pay her? It doesn't look good, Bill."

"So, what are you saying, Morrie? Are you advising me to settle?"

"I wouldn't say that. I'm afraid there is no good answer here." There was a long pause as both men contemplated the options. "Listen, Bill. We have until the end of today to go back to this guy. Why don't you think about it?"

Bill was speechless and barely managed to get out the words, "Yeah, sure. Okay, Morrie." He didn't wait to hear Morrie's response and hung up the phone.

Bill still couldn't believe it. He couldn't believe that the Sullivans would do this to him. Had his wife been tricked? Was this whole thing a scam? Had the Sullivan boy tricked Paige into going to their apartment to feed her a sob story, angling for a million-dollar jackpot? Bill slammed his fist down on his desk. Charles and his whole family, with their crooked little plan—put the poor mama out on display with a broken leg to get Paige's sympathy. And Charles pretending to be a saint—"Oh, sir, I just wanted to return your wallet." Thoughts raced through Bill's mind: "Was it all just to make sure they weaseled their way into my life so they could rob me blind? Oh, they made quite a show of refusing my wife's money . . . when all along they were just waiting for a big payday."

He didn't know what to do anymore. Should he pay them? Sure, he was wealthy, but still a million dollars was big money. On the other hand, if he didn't, he could lose his reputation, his position, and his company. Suddenly Bill's big office felt claustrophobic. He had to get out.

He stood up, leaving his jacket and briefcase behind, and barely acknowledged Gladys and Sheila as he left. "I'll be on my cell. Cancel my meetings."

"But, Mr. Bradford—" called out Sheila. He was already out of earshot. The two women stared at one another. What was going on?

Andrew sat fixedly in front of his computer. He had newspapers spread all over the bed. Ever since he'd seen where Charles lived, he realized he didn't know much about anything. The world was such a big place with more to it than just sports and music and video games. It dawned on him that he didn't really know much about his father or his company. The news commentary was all about what a bad person Bill Bradford was.

Andrew read about outsourcing, and watched the protestors marching. The news said HOA was taking away their jobs. Was his father to blame for their suffering?

How could that *kid*, Charles, know that much about Hospitals of America?

Andrew had gone downstairs early that morning. He'd decided to ask his dad a few questions before work. Things had gotten better the night before, when his parents had made up. That morning his mom had still been sleeping, and he'd found his dad sitting at the kitchen table, eating breakfast and working on his laptop.

Andrew had looked seriously toward Bill. It had been a long time since the two of them had had a father-son talk. "Dad, can I talk to you?" he asked.

Bill had looked up curiously, wondering what could make Andrew seek him out like this, especially at such an early hour. He suddenly smiled with understanding. *He's got a crush!* Time to have that talk. . . . Preparing himself for a discussion on the birds and the bees, he focused on his son and gave him his full attention. "Go ahead, son. Ask me anything you want," he said generously.

"Dad, what does *outsourcing* mean?" Andrew said quickly, before he lost his nerve.

Bill gaped. *What?*

"Dad?" Andrew asked worriedly. "Did I say something wrong?"

"No, no. I just, uh, wasn't expecting that. Why in the world do you want to know about outsourcing?"

Andrew shrugged and said, "I dunno." Looking at his father's face, he said, "Well, actually, I was reading about it in the paper and I was, uh, you know, wondering . . . I mean, I don't get it."

Bill nodded, thinking something didn't add up here. The boy never read the paper—or anything else, for that matter. And in the *summer?* But he looked like he really wanted to know. It was nice to have his son's interest in what he did.

"And Dad . . . I'd like to know more about HOA," Andrew continued with seriousness. "You know, well, you're the CEO and all, and I thought . . . I should learn more about it."

Bill nodded thoughtfully. Andrew interested in HOA? Feeling flattered, he settled back in his chair comfortably and addressed his son. "Well, first of all, you know that HOA is one of *the* most successful corporations in America. Right?" Pride emanated from him as he boasted to his son. "Your grandfather, William Thomas Bradford, is responsible for making it the great company it is today."

"Sure, Dad," Andrew said. He'd heard this part before.

"One of the reasons we're so successful is that we're financially sound. Part of my job is to make sure we have the best team of financial advisors available. They make decisions about how HOA is run. You follow so far, son?"

"Yeah," Andrew replied. He didn't feel like his question was being answered, but he decided to be quiet.

"Now, about outsourcing: the simplest way of explaining that is to show you some facts and figures." Bill eagerly opened a file on his laptop. In a matter of seconds he pulled up a spreadsheet filled with numbers. "Okay, take a look. What you're seeing here is what it costs HOA to keep the housekeeping staff on board, and over here in this column you can see that by outsourcing those same workers we save *millions* of dollars."

Andrew frowned, trying to make sense of the rows and rows of numbers. This was much worse than any math assignment he'd ever encountered. "But, Dad . . . what does it really mean to outsource somebody? Their jobs still need to be done, right?"

"Instead of these housekeepers being employees of HOA," Bill explained, "they'll be employed by another company. Then HOA will hire them through that company."

"But how does hiring them from another company *save* HOA money?"

"Well, for one, we only have to pay their wages. See, if you look here," he said, indicating the screen, "this is what it's been costing us to provide benefits to these workers. Now, if you look down here, you can see how much we'll save. Pretty smart, huh?" Bill waited to see the look of admiration on his son's face.

Andrew dutifully studied the screen, knowing that it made his father happy. "Dad? Do you ever wonder about . . . you know, all those *people?*"

Bill shook his head. "What do you mean?"

Andrew thought back to meeting Charles. Didn't his great-aunt work for HOA? He thought about their families, and how they'd be affected. What did these numbers have to do with them? "How do *they* feel about being outsourced?"

Shrugging, Bill said, "Oh, people will always complain, son. It's the way of the world."

Andrew sighed. He felt like they were having a conversation about two different things. "If outsourcing is good for the company, why are the workers complaining?"

"Oh, Andrew," Bill said. "They're undoubtedly mad about losing their union and their benefits." Setting his mouth, he added, "They ought to feel lucky that this new company will hire them!"

"But Dad!" Andrew exclaimed. "The news said some of those people are too old to get hired again. They won't be able to find a job. Did Grandpa do that to his employees, too?"

Bill couldn't hide his irritation. "Why are you worrying about this nonsense? That's what they have social-service programs for. Those people know how to work the system. Trust me, if there's a handout to be had, they'll find it." He ignored the question about his father.

Andrew felt his frustration rising. "These are people who *want* to work, though. Haven't they been with HOA a long time? Like their whole lives, practically?"

"Son, what's your point?" Bill asked. He checked his watch, not wanting to miss the local early-morning news.

"It—it just doesn't seem right," Andrew said slowly.

"Right, wrong . . . there is no right or wrong, Andrew. This is a business we're talking about. A very *successful* business. If we worried about every little question we'd never get anywhere. You have to look at the big picture. Outsourcing makes financial sense."

Bill closed the spreadsheets on his laptop. "Son, can we finish this later?" Now that he'd reconciled with Paige, he didn't want to get into more arguments with Andrew. He figured his son would forget all this in no time.

Shortly after their conversation, Bill left for the office, but Andrew didn't feel satisfied. He decided to find more of the answers himself.

"Mom, where's the paper?" he asked Paige as she walked into the kitchen.

Paige looked surprised. "The *paper?* Since when do you read the paper? Not that I'm complaining!" She tossed it to him and he ran upstairs.

In his room, slowly scanning the national and local sections, Andrew found what he was looking for. He grabbed a pair of scissors from his desk and carefully cut out several articles. Then he went to the recycle bin and found a few days' worth of papers. While he was searching for articles he ran across a lot of other interesting information—it was like surfing the Web. Meanwhile, his pile of articles steadily grew. Had either of his parents discovered the collection they would have been quite surprised—not to mention dismayed, given what he was finding.

Andrew read and re-read the articles until he made up his mind.

He keyed in a few words on his computer, jotted something on a piece of scrap paper which he hurriedly stuffed in his pocket, and grabbed his backpack.

Andrew felt bad about deceiving his mother. He'd put on his pack and grabbed his bike, saying he was meeting the guys for a pickup soccer game.

A half hour of hard pedaling later, there he was, taking the city bus. It was the first time Andrew had ever ridden public transportation. It took all his courage to board the bus, after asking some teenage girls which one to take. He actually had the information on that piece of paper but didn't mind the few minutes of flirting. Boarding the bus, he felt scared and self-conscious—certain the other passengers could tell he didn't belong there. His brow knotted as he worried that he'd never find his way back. But after he figured out how much money to give the bus driver, he relaxed by a window and enjoyed the freedom and anonymity of the ride, relieved that no one paid him the slightest attention.

Andrew didn't usually encounter so many different kinds of people. As more and more passengers got on he realized he was going to have to share his seat pretty soon. Moving his backpack onto his lap, he watched as a chubby black kid, blue bandana tied around his head, made his way down the aisle and sat down next to him. The kid ignored him and turned up the volume on his earphones. Andrew stared out the window, unsure if he should say anything.

Suddenly the boy swore, ripping off his earphones. "Man, this is jacked up," he said disgustedly, glaring at his iPod.

Andrew glanced at him, unsure if he was being spoken to or if the kid was talking to himself. He decided that he must be talking to him. "Uh, what's wrong with it?"

The boy looked at Andrew and showed him his media player. The screen had gone dark and looked like it was stuck. "My nephew plays with it, thinks it's a toy. His mama doesn't watch him either, lets him get all up into my stuff," he lamented.

Andrew held out his hand in an offer of help. He took the iPod and tinkered with it; after a few moments it restarted. "How old's your nephew?" he asked politely.

The boy beamed, his anger forgotten. "He's only two years old. *Isaiah*," he said proudly. "My sister named him after me."

"Isaiah, cool name. I'm Andrew."

"What's up," the boy said, more relaxed.

Finally the screen loaded. "You know, you can lock up the screen so your nephew can't play with it."

"Oh yeah?"

"Yeah, here." Andrew handed the iPod back to Isaiah. "Just type in your code and boom. Little fingers can't do anything. Well, other than dump it in water, I guess."

Isaiah smiled at the skinny boy. "Thanks, man."

"What are you listening to?"

"Pitbull," Isaiah replied.

"That's cool," said Andrew, having little idea who that was.

Isaiah laughed. "What kind of music do you like?"

"Different things," Andrew said. "Lately I've been listening to some Motown."

"Get out. Now we're talking."

"Yeah," Andrew agreed. "A friend got me into it. Now I can't stop listening."

"Thought a dude like you would like Selena Gomez or the Jonas Brothers," Isaiah teased.

"Oh, like, totally," Andrew quipped, rolling his eyes.

"Well, now, if you like Motown," Isaiah said, searching his music list, "you gotta hear *this*."

Andrew took the earphone from him and listened. It had a scratchy sound like an old record. A great old trumpet played strong.

"That's amazing," he said.

Isaiah grinned. "That there is some Louie Armstrong. This music will make you feel good in a different way. Trust me."

Andrew closed his eyes and let the music take over. As the silky strains floated softly into his head he realized why Isaiah was grinning. It was somehow *perfect*.

Andrew looked up and realized his stop was ahead. "Hey, man, that's where I'm going," he said, taking out the earphone. He pulled the stop cord and stood up, carefully stepping around Isaiah. "Thanks for letting me listen to your music."

"Thanks for fixing my iPod."

"No problem," Andrew said, and he exited the bus.

Gracie was standing precariously on the side of the bathtub. She leaned against the wall so she could turn around. She looked over her shoulder at her reflection and admired the way her new skirt looked from behind. She had spent several hours last night getting her hair painfully braided, but the result looked good. She had even managed to sneak a dab of Ramona's makeup— just a little mascara and some lipstick. Her mother would make her wipe it off her face if she saw it. She'd have to make a quick exit from the apartment.

Charles banged on the bathroom door. "Gracie, come on! Before summer is over, please. Let's go."

"Coming," she said. Perfect; she could rush out of the apartment now. She opened the door quickly and followed Charles, being careful to walk beside him as they passed their mother.

"See you in a while, Mama," she called out.

Ramona was reading a magazine and didn't look up for more than a second. "Bye." As they were closing the door she said, "Charles, take care of your sister and be back in time for dinner."

"Yes, Mama."

As they exited into the hallway Charles looked at Gracie and laughed. "What's wrong?" she asked, suddenly afraid she looked stupid.

"Mama is going to kill you if she finds out you were prancing around the neighborhood in makeup."

"Well, it's a good thing no one is going to tell her," she said, and she turned to march down the stairs.

Andrew looked around at the apartment buildings. Finally he saw the one he remembered to be Charles's. He started up the stairs only to bump into the brother and sister halfway.

"Hey, Charles," he said.

Charles was surprised. "Hey, Andrew. What are you doing in this part of town?"

That was a good question. Andrew wasn't so sure himself. "I don't know," he admitted. "I had to get away from my house and think."

"Well, we were just headed to the park to play some basketball. You want to join?"

"Sure," he said. "I'm more of a soccer player, though."

"A ball is a ball." Charles laughed. "Just don't kick it too many times and you should be okay."

"Sounds good." Then he noticed Gracie's clothes and hair and makeup. "You sure look dressed up," he said.

Gracie eyed him warily. What did that mean?

"I mean, you look nice."

She gave him a grin—and gave Charles an "I told you so" look. Together they all headed out.

As soon as they got to the park, Gracie ran off to catch up with her friends. They sat giggling on the picnic benches under some trees as they watched the boys. Gracie tried to look casual although her goal was to catch Kayden's eye. She knew he'd been watching her when she first arrived.

Charles and Andrew wandered over to the basketball courts, where three intense games were happening all at once. Charles stopped to talk to a couple of guys lounging on the bleachers, but Andrew was so awed by what was happening on the courts he nearly walked right out into the middle of the closest game. He'd played basketball before, of course, but he'd never seen anything like this. Guys were throwing behind-the-back passes, flipping alley-oops to teammates, and dunking on nearly every trip up and down the court. And the game seemed more vicious than any he'd ever seen. In the NBA games he'd watched from his dad's corporate suite, it seemed like they called fouls on every other play. But here there were no fouls at all. One kid, streaking in for a fast-break layup, was shoved so hard he ended up two rows into the bleachers.

"All right, we're up next," Charles said as he joined Andrew on the baseline. "My boys need two more guys."

"I don't know, man. I'm not that good." Andrew looked so nervous that Charles almost laughed. He didn't know why Andrew was acting scared all of a sudden.

"Come on, it's just street ball. You'll be fine. Let's go shoot a few on the side court to warm up."

Charles led the way to a small half court with an old rusty rim and backboard. He stepped up to the free-throw line, bent his knees, and sent a perfect shot ripping through the net. Andrew grabbed the ball and fired it back out to Charles, who drained another free throw with the same smooth motion.

"So you like to play soccer, huh?" Charles asked as Andrew returned the ball again. He took another shot, which bounced up off the rim and over to Andrew.

"Yeah, I've been playing since I was five. We won finals last night. I scored the winning goal!" Andrew took a shot from the baseline, but the ball barely made it to the rim and bounced off toward Charles.

"Great job, dude," said Charles as he deftly caught the ball and buried a jump shot from the three-point line. "You sound good."

"Not as good as you are at basketball," Andrew said.

"Yeah, sure, I guess," Charles returned, as he set up for another throw.

Gracie was laughing a little too loudly at her friend's joke. She wasn't even sure it was that funny, but she wanted Kayden to see her having fun. Being the center of attention. She caught his eye and he smiled at her. Suddenly he broke away from his friends and came over. Gracie panicked; she had only thought as far as looking nice and making him notice her. She hadn't thought of what happened if he actually did.

"Hey, Gracie," he said, smiling confidently.

"Hey, Kayden." Her friends giggled behind her. She shot them a quick side-eye.

"You look pretty today."

She blushed but said nothing.

"Listen, I was thinking, we're all going to a barbecue at Trey's house on Saturday. Around 4. If you and your friends want to come."

Gracie had a hard time speaking. *Pull it together, girl, and be confident.* "We'll think about it," she said, trying to act like she wasn't excited.

"All right, then," he said, and went back to his friends.

As he walked away her girlfriends let out shrieking giggles. Gracie barely noticed. She felt all warm and fuzzy inside.

"Charles! Yo, Charles! Let's go, man! We're up." A tall, skinny kid was yelling and waving to them from a spot under the basket on the far court. Andrew fought the butterflies in his stomach as he and Charles headed over to join the rest of their team. The skinny kid eyed them suspiciously as they approached.

"Who's the white dude?" he asked.

"Relax," Charles said. "He's cool."

The tall boy stepped up a few inches from Andrew's face. "You shoot hoops?" he asked.

"A little," Andrew replied. "But actually soccer is my game."

"Well, we don't play soccer here. We play a real game and there's no refs and there's no free throws or any of that other crap."

Andrew, still feeling a little intimidated, said nothing. He looked over at Charles for help.

"I've seen him play before," Charles said to the ring-leader, fibbing. "Give him a chance."

Before anybody could say anything, a loud voice called out from the court. "Okay, you stiffs, it's your turn to be humiliated."

The skinny kid sighed. "Okay, I guess you'll have to do."

Charles saw Andrew's face and could tell his friend was nervous. He stepped out to midcourt where the other team was waiting "Give us a minute or two to warm up, will ya? We just got here."

"Warm up while you play. First to eleven, win by two. Take the ball."

As Charles brought the ball up court, Andrew looked over the guys on the other team. Most of them were taller than him, but the guy guarding Charles was about Andrew's height and skinny, too. Andrew didn't think his team had any kind of set offense so he decided to try to set a screen for Charles. As Charles took the ball across the center line, Andrew stepped up and set his screen. Charles's defender blew right through him, elbowing him in the face as he went by. Andrew brought his hand to his mouth, and was surprised to see a trickle of blood appear on the back of his hand. Charles pulled up for jumper at the top of the key, but the shot bricked off the front of the rim and into the hands of an opponent.

The rest of Andrew's team was still under the basket as two of the opposition raced down the court in the opposite direction. Only Andrew stood in the way of a quick basket for the other team. He broke back toward his basket, trying to keep himself between the ball carrier and the other player coming down the court on the other side.

Andrew stayed tight on the ball handler's right side, hoping that, like a lot of soccer players he knew, the guy could only play on his dominant side. At the top of the key, the guy whipped a fast pass over Andrew's head to the other player coming toward the basket. Andrew turned and tried to block the guy's access to the basket. The man with the ball took two long steps and left the ground to slam the ball home. In the process, he ran right over Andrew, knocking him to the ground.

As Andrew picked himself up, the scorer turned around and stared down at him. "There ain't no charging in this game, boy," he sneered. "Unless you wanna call a foul?"

Andrew just shook his head. He might not be the best ball player out there, but he knew enough to keep his mouth shut. Better to let the loudmouth who'd run him over do all the trash talking.

And talk he did. The loudmouth was clearly the best player on either team, and he never shut up. With the ball, without the ball, made shot or missed shot, winning or losing, the running commentary never stopped. As the game proceeded, it actually became amusing—it even helped Andrew get over his initial nervousness. As the game went on he got more and more confident, and by the time the teams took a quick water break, his team was leading thirteen to twelve.

As the game got underway again, the other team took the ball and stormed down the court looking to tie it up. "Push 'em to the outside," Andrew yelled, surprising himself slightly by taking charge. He could tell the other team was tired. Passes became more strained, and hands were swatted away by each player as the opposition tried to create space against a tight defense. Finally, out of sheer frustration, the loudmouth took a long shot from the corner. It circled around the rim, but wouldn't fall through. Five separate players batted at the ball before it fell into Charles's hands.

He quickly cleared the ball brought into the frontcourt. Down by a point, the other team was as tenacious on defense as Charles's team had been the possession before. But Andrew knew he could rely on his soccer conditioning; he was in better shape than anyone else on the court. He tried to outrun his defender, darting in and out of the paint, to the basket, along the baseline. Charles was passing the ball around the perimeter, looking for somebody with an open shot.

The opponent covering Andrew was breathing heavily now. Andrew made a move to go back outside and then cut back to the basket. Charles saw him and threw a dart. Andrew took the ball in one stride and then laid it home—fourteen to twelve, game over.

A short time later Charles and Andrew sat cooling off by the side of the court. Andrew laughed, and squinted up at the sun, which was beating down on them. "I'm thirsty. Can I buy you a lemonade?"

As they relaxed, drinking from cool bottles, Andrew suddenly asked, "Do you hate my dad?"

"What?" said Charles, choking back some lemonade.

"I mean . . . he hit your mom. I just wondered, you know, if you hate him. It seems like everyone thinks he's a bad guy."

Charles looked thoughtfully at Andrew, carefully choosing his next words. Did he hate Mr. Bradford? On one hand, yes, he had hit his mom, which made him angry; but on the other hand, the man had given him an opportunity to do something he'd never done.

Finally he answered. "No."

"Hmm," Andrew sighed, taking it in. They watched a player sink a shot after a layup. "It's just I've been reading all this stuff in the paper about how HOA is laying off all these people, and, well, they keep talking about my dad. They say some pretty mean things. And he was explaining it to me today but it was just all these numbers and I thought . . . I don't know."

"Well, money makes people do some strange things," Charles said. "You have numbers, and then you have people. I guess after a while you can get so high up in your tower you forget the people."

Andrew looked serious.

"I told you," said Charles, "my mom's aunt works for HOA. She's been working there for over twenty years and now she's being fired in the outsourcing."

"My dad said all those people would just get another job."

"Well, that's true, I guess, for some of them," said Charles. "But my aunt, she's older and she has some health issues. She's worried no one will hire her. But she's not old enough yet to get help with her medical expenses. So. . . ." He trailed off.

Andrew echoed what he'd told his father that morning. "It just doesn't seem right," he said.

Charles nodded in agreement. "Lots of people. Lots and lots of people are losing their jobs, their benefits, their medicine . . . everything."

Andrew looked around at the park. These were the people who worked for HOA.

He and Charles drank their lemonade and settled into silence.

After his phone conversation with Morrie, Bill left his corporate headquarters and took a long drive through the city. He didn't know where he was going—only that he needed to get out of the office. He took off his tie and unbuttoned his collar and drove. Slowly the iron-drab downtown opened up to the suburbs and then eventually to the outskirts of town where nature crept in.

His phone buzzed. He glanced down at the caller i.d. It was the office. He hit the button to decline the call, sending it to voicemail. Then he just turned his phone off. He was hiding, running from it all, and he knew it.

Right now he just didn't want to be found. He needed to clear his head. Get some air.

Suddenly Bill realized where he was going. He took an exit off the main road and headed north.

Paige was getting worried. She'd talked to some of Andrew's soccer buddies at the grocery store as they were piling out of a mom's car. They asked where Andrew was—as if they hadn't seen him all day. Paige wondered if there were any other boys he would have been with. She made casual calls to a couple of the other moms under the pretext of planning a barbecue. She didn't want them to know she didn't know where her son was. But none of them had seen Andrew. She'd called Bill at the office and was told he'd left unexpectedly earlier. "What is going on?" she wondered.

Bill turned in to a driveway that led through two tall, imposing iron gates. As his car passed through, the words on the gates became clear: MONT CLAIRE CEMETERY.

He drove slowly. He hadn't been here in some time, but he knew the way to the family mausoleum. He saw the white stone structure up ahead and parked under an ancient weeping willow. As he got out and stepped onto the lawn next to the car, a low-hanging willow branch softly caressed his cheek.

Bill wasn't sure why he'd come here but he didn't know where else to go. The dry earth crunched beneath his dress shoes as he walked. Weaving between the headstones, he made his way to the family plot, and there he read the inscriptions he knew so well: "William Thomas Bradford" and "Cecilia Carroll Bradford."

His parents had always been so vibrant and full of life. His father, working hard to build his company—and his mother, creating a safe and nurturing home. Bill never had any siblings . . . a strange thing in the 1960s, when every family seemed to have at least four or five kids. After he was born, his mother had been unable to have any more children, and so they'd spoiled him. Giving him every opportunity, every desire. Bill remembered his childhood as a time of feeling safe.

His parents had died barely a year apart. He shook off the memory of it but it enveloped him. How he longed for his father's advice now—he'd know what to do. And for his mother's embrace—she'd always had a way of making him forget a scrape or a harsh word.

But they were gone.

He felt the cold hard stone of the mausoleum and looked up at the marble angel over the building's doorway, its arms lifted to the sky. He raised his eyes to the heavens, blinking away the sun, and fell to his knees, crying.

―――――――

A few hours later, Bill was headed toward home. He wanted to talk to Paige. He still didn't have all the answers, but he felt clear-headed enough to make a decision. He knew the direction his father would have pointed him in.

As Bill pulled into the driveway he saw Paige rush out, her face streaming with tears.

The sun was going down as Andrew pedaled back toward his house. He was relieved to have found his bike still intact after he got off the bus—and a little impressed that he'd managed to even find his way back to it. Overall, he was floored by everything he'd learned today. He'd found out a lot about his father's company. He'd formed a better understanding of the world he lived in. He'd gained some insight from Charles.

Lost in his thoughts, he didn't notice the two worried grownups standing in front of the house, or the police car parked there.

Bill and Paige stood together in their driveway. Bill had come home with his mind full of childhood memories and racing with ideas, but those thoughts evaporated when Paige ran out and told him she couldn't find Andrew.

"He left this morning," she sobbed. "He said he was meeting some friends to play soccer. Is it too soon to file a missing-persons report?"

"I don't know," Bill said, holding her, "but let's call the police and at least see if they can send someone out here."

The officer had just finished taking all the information down when they saw a figure riding a bicycle up the street.

Paige put her hand to her mouth as the two men looked over.

Bill raised his hand, gesturing toward his son. "There he is," he said.

The police officer put his pen back in his clipboard. "I'll wait here if you think you'll need me?" he said, as he prepared to get back in the cruiser.

Paige looked at him. "We're so sorry to have troubled you, officer."

The officer tipped his hat. "No problem, ma'am. I'm just glad to see him back home."

As Andrew got closer he noticed the police cruiser and his parents in the driveway. This was not good. He was tempted to turn around and pedal back the other way. He was obviously in trouble. He slowed down and made his way toward his doom.

The officer pulled away when it was clear the Bradfords had the situation under control.

"Where have you been, young man?" Paige scolded harshly.

Andrew wasn't sure what to say.

"Answer your mother," Bill said. "You've had us worried sick."

"I'm sorry, Dad."

"Don't just apologize to me."

"Sorry, Mom."

"Oh, Andrew," Paige said, almost weeping, "Where were you? I had all these thoughts running through my head."

"I'm sorry, Mom. I should have told you."

Bill and Paige looked at him expectantly.

"I went to see Charles."

"What?" they both exclaimed in unison.

Bill was angry. "You've been running around the south side all day without telling anyone where you were? I can't believe this. What if something had happened to you?"

"Andrew, go upstairs and take a shower," Paige ordered their son. "You're covered with dirt."

She turned to Bill and sighed with a mixture of relief and frustration. Then: "Oh! Our dinner reservation tonight—I just remembered. Should I cancel?"

"It was supposed to be our celebration for his soccer-finals victory," Bill said, frowning. "The whole family, together." He thought for a moment. "Paige, at the very least Andrew deserves a stern conversation about personal responsibility," he said. "But let's keep that separate from the soccer celebration."

Paige nodded in agreement. "They're two different things."

"Besides," Bill thought to himself, "it's not only Andrew I'm upset with."

Bill shut the door to his study. He'd been feeling good after going to the cemetery and spending some quiet time there in reflection. "Dad never took the easy path if it meant compromising his values." He knew that his father would have wanted him to admit his responsibility in the car accident and help the Sullivans. But that thought got harder to hold onto when he learned what Andrew had been up to. Not only had he gone alone to the south side of town, far from home, but he'd lied to Paige to go there.

Now Bill's thoughts were far less charitable toward the Sullivans. "These people are turning my family against me. First it was Paige, and now Andrew. And they're letting their lawyer blackmail me into a huge payoff? Who do they think they are?"

No. It was time to take a stand. "I won't sit back while they attack my company and my family," Bill thought. With determination, he picked up the phone and called Morrie.

"Hey, Bill," Morrie answered. "I've been trying you all afternoon at the office."

"Yeah, I'm sorry, Morrie, I had to find some space to go think."

"You okay?"

"No, but I've made a decision. Tell them no."

"What?"

"The Sullivans. Tell them no. The offer is off the table. Not only will they not get their million dollars, but they also won't get anything at all. I wanted to do the right thing, Morrie, and it backfired. You give these people an inch, they'll take a mile."

"Are you sure, Bill? They may go to the press."

"Let them. I'll expose them for what they are: a bunch of money-hungry opportunists."

"Okay, Bill." Morrie nodded to himself. This was the old Bill Bradford.

19

Ramona was woken from a nap by a harsh ringing. She quickly sat up and realized it was just the telephone. She'd been having a very strange dream that was on the tip of her consciousness. She felt uneasy.

The phone rang again.

"Hello," said Charles in the other room. "Yes, I'll get her." She heard his footsteps coming down the hall and the soft swish of the phone cords being dragged. She tried unsuccessfully to shake the sense of dread she was feeling.

Charles entered the room with the phone receiver pressed to his chest. "Mama, you up?

Ramona nodded her head groggily. "Yeah."

"It's your lawyer. You want him?"

Ramona propped herself up on her pillows and gestured for the phone. "Hello?"

On the other end of the line, Mason Smith paced anxiously, waiting for Ramona to pick up. He hadn't anticipated Bradford's move. It had been a possibility, of course—but with all the scandal surrounding HOA he'd felt sure the man would cave to avoid more bad press. Bradford must be completely insane. And now Smith was going to have to make good on his threat to go to the media. He had no qualms about the way his actions might disrupt the Bradford family. The board would fire Bradford, for sure. But now, Smith had to deliver the bad news to his client. An out-of-court settlement had been their only hope; in court, Bradford's attorneys would skillfully argue that Ramona had been jaywalking. "No judge or jury would make Bradford pay if she's at fault." He felt a moment of remorse, but it was brief; mostly he was disappointed he'd lost. He'd really wanted that new car. "Oh, well," he thought, "there'll be other cases. And now at least the other attorneys will think twice before crossing me. Let it be known that Mason Smith keeps his word."

Ramona could barely hear what Mason was saying to her. The moment he'd started to explain, a ringing had started in her ears. She could hear her blood rushing— her heart pumping loud, faster and faster.

"I'm sorry, Mrs. Sullivan, they've withdrawn their previous offer," he said.

She managed to weakly ask, "So what does that mean?"

"It means we're done. Unless you want to file a civil suit."

He talked on and on about high-powered attorneys and easily swayed juries. And something about the press?

But Ramona stopped listening. This was it. She was back to square one, her hopes dashed. She'd spent the last couple of days feeling better—confident that her bills would be paid. Now how was she going to get out from under this?

The money from her church friends was helping, but it barely amounted to what she'd have made if she'd been working these last weeks. "No matter how many jobs I work," she thought, "I'll never be able to pay my bills."

She heard Mason wrap up the conversation and give an awkward goodbye. With trembling hands, Ramona hung up the phone.

Gracie, Charles, and Lorraine had been sitting on the couch watching a movie when the phone rang. They'd stared at one another in anticipation when Charles came back from his mother's bedroom and told them it was Mason Smith on the phone. They had turned down the TV to hear the conversation, but it seemed like the lawyer was doing most of the talking, and soon the conversation was more like a monologue: Ramona was saying nothing at all. Charles and his grandmother had exchanged concerned looks.

Finally they heard a click as Ramona set the phone down. A long moment passed while they waited for news. Then Lorraine heard soft, muffled sobs coming from Ramona's bedroom. She and Charles got up at the same time. Lorraine gestured for her grandson to wait.

"Let me handle this, sugar," she said softly. "Sometimes we all just need our mama."

As Lorraine walked down the hall, Charles turned to Gracie. He whispered, "Go over to Juanita's and call Reverend French."

Gracie looked put out. "What's going on?" she asked.

"Move it." Charles gave her a shove off the couch.

"Why can't I use our phone?"

"Because I said so. Now go."

Gracie stuck out her tongue but got up to do as she was told. People were acting strange and it seemed like it might be a good idea in this instance to get out of the apartment. "What do you want me to tell him?"

"Just tell him I asked him to come," said Charles, with an exasperated look. "Please."

She shook her head as she walked out and mumbled under her breath, "Whatever you say, boss-man."

Lorraine sat rocking Ramona in her arms as she cried. She hadn't seen her daughter cry like this since she was a little girl. It made her heart ache. Ramona told her what happened; Lorraine got bits and pieces through the tears and sobs, and slowly it was all coming together. Finally the sobs turned into quieter sniffles.

Lorraine gently pulled her daughter's head up to look at her. "We're going to get through this, you understand? Now, you'll move in with me. It will be a little cramped but we can do it. I've got some money saved and together we'll get through this. Your leg will heal soon and you'll be back on your feet. You'll see."

Ramona didn't answer but simply laid her head against her mother's shoulder. Finally she said, "I don't want to be a burden on you."

"You could never be a burden."

They sat in silence for some time until they heard a man clear his throat in the doorway. Lorraine looked up and saw Oliver. She didn't realize she'd wanted him there the whole time. She mouthed a silent "thank you."

Charles had whispered to the reverend what he needed to know when he got there. Oliver took one look at the scene and exclaimed, "I think I need to take you all to dinner."

Lorraine and Ramona both looked up in surprise.

"I insist. It's my treat. I won't have you all sitting around feeling sorry for yourselves."

"Feeling sorry for ourselves!" returned Lorraine. "If you knew what the—"

"Now, Lorraine, I didn't mean to offend you. I just find that sometimes our troubles feel a bit lighter with a full stomach and time with those who care about us."

"Hmmph," said Lorraine, half placated. She was annoyed but not enough to wave off a kiss on the cheek.

Ramona surprised herself by smiling. "I guess it's settled, then. Thank you, everyone. Let's spend some dinner time together."

20

A short time later, the five of them were piled into Bertha. Ramona's leg was on top of Gracie and Charles in the back. Her face and eyes were puffy from crying but she seemed okay. Charles was glad Oliver was there to help. He felt lucky to have him around. He could tell his grandmother was thinking the same thing. She was looking at him as he drove.

They pulled into the parking lot for Minnie's Diner ("Home of Minnie's World-Famous BBQ and Fried Chicken"). Charles's stomach rumbled. He was hungry.

As the family walked in, Charles spotted Jimmy sitting at the counter. He waved. Jimmy sauntered over to the family. He looked more relaxed out of his driver's uniform.

"Hey, y'all. What are you doing here?"

"I'm taking these lovely ladies and this fine gentleman to dinner," said Oliver. He made introductions all around and explained how they knew Jimmy.

"You eating here, too?" asked Charles.

"This is my sister's joint. I eat here almost every day."

"Your sister is *the* Minnie?" asked Oliver.

"Yes, sir," he said, patting his belly. "Why do you think I'm so fat." Jimmy gestured to the waitress. "Hey,

Carla, these here are my friends, so make sure to treat them really well." He winked at Oliver and said, "Dinner's on me."

"No, we couldn't," said Oliver.

"I insist," Jimmy replied warmly, as the waitress ushered them away.

She seated them near the front window. Lorraine and Oliver sat facing the street. Ramona was at the head of the table; it accommodated her wheelchair with ample space. Gracie and Charles sat on the other side. After they'd placed their orders, the reverend raised his glass. "I'd like to propose a toast." He waited as the others picked up their glasses.

"To Ramona Sullivan. You might just be one of the toughest, bravest souls I've ever met. And you've raised two wonderful children with good hearts and minds. We are lucky to have you with us today."

The group clinked their glasses as Ramona smiled happily.

"Oh, and let's not forget Lorraine Jackson," continued Oliver. "One of the most beautiful and caring ladies I know." Lorraine elbowed him playfully and then gave him a kiss on the cheek.

Ramona looked at her family and silently thanked God, closing her eyes briefly.

Jimmy watched them from across the restaurant and smiled. He'd asked around the neighborhood after he dropped the Sullivan boy off the other night. He'd learned all that they'd been through with the accident.

Buying that family dinner was the least he could do. Besides, Minnie gave him half off.

As soon as their meals were served, Oliver had them all join hands while he led them in prayer. The other patrons looked on with interest as they spoke their thanks and almost applauded when the group gave a heartfelt *Amen*.

Across the street from Minnie's was another restaurant—one significantly more upscale. Bill Bradford maneuvered his Jaguar into its driveway and handed the valet the car keys. Paige stepped out as the valet opened her door, while Andrew jumped out eagerly, looking forward to eating. He was starved, having skipped lunch.

Paige wasn't sure they should be going to dinner after Andrew's behavior earlier that day. They were supposed to be celebrating, but she didn't think he needed to be rewarded for scaring her to death. Traveling all by himself down to the south side, without telling anyone where he was? But Bill was in a mood and insisted that they keep their original plan. He wasn't going to have his life dictated anymore. He seemed determined to celebrate, and so here they were.

Andrew, meanwhile, refused to let his parents' moods bring him down. It looked like he'd gotten out of trouble for the time being. On top of that, this was one of his favorite restaurants and it had been a long time since the Bradfords had dined here.

Inside, they were greeted warmly and the maître d' gave them prime seating, by the window overlooking the garden. Bill ordered a bottle of wine for himself and Paige, while Andrew hungrily read the menu. Paige tried to relax and enjoy the garden view.

As Lorraine was about to put the last piece of tender fried chicken into her mouth, she stopped with her fork midway and stared out the diner window. Three people had just piled out of a Jaguar at the restaurant across the street. She recognized the man's face as he turned to give his keys to the valet—it was none other than Bill Bradford. Lorraine seethed and watched as they took their seats inside by the window and opened up their menus.

"Look at them," she thought icily. "In their big grand car at their fancy restaurant. Not a care in the world! And here only an hour ago I was consoling my poor daughter."

Only Oliver noticed the change in Lorraine's mood. He followed her gaze and saw what she was looking at. Everyone else was too busy savoring their delicious meals to pay attention.

Suddenly Lorraine stood up, and everyone took notice.

"Lorraine, sit down," Oliver said quietly.

"I'll be right back," she said. "I just need to go to the ladies' room."

Lorraine didn't want to upset her daughter, and Oliver wasn't sure what to do. He placed his hand over his face to guard his expression and muttered a quick prayer.

Across the street, Paige Bradford tried to make small talk at the table, but it was forced. Andrew seemed to be playing it safe, knowing he was lucky not to be in trouble, and kept his head down. Bill seemed to be mostly concerned that they were enjoying themselves.

"Doesn't the menu look good?" he asked. "Paige, it looks like they've added some new desserts."

Suddenly, they heard a commotion behind them.

"I'm sorry, ma'am, but if you don't have a reservation—"

"I'm not here to dine, I just need to have a quick word," said Lorraine as she stormed by the fragile maître d'. He was genuinely afraid of her and made a minimal attempt at resistance—just enough to look like he'd tried, but not enough to get run over by the woman. She made him think of an angry rhinoceros.

Standing at the Bradford table, Lorraine looked up and down the corporate CEO in his expensive suit. Bill wondered why the woman had stopped at their table, and, more importantly, why she looked like she was about to blow a gasket.

"Can I help you?" he asked.

"Sir, I tried to stop her," said the maître d' meekly, making sure to keep himself out of reach of the woman just in case she got violent.

"That's okay," Bill replied. "I'm sure we're fine."

"Mr. Bill Bradford? My name is Lorraine Jackson."

Bill searched his memory. Was that name supposed to mean something? She was obviously upset about something. Maybe she was one of the housekeeping staff? He squinted his eyes. He was getting a headache. He really didn't need this tonight. He braced himself for the accusations he felt were sure to come.

"I am Ramona Sullivan's mother."

Lorraine waited for the information to register with Bill. She stood there and faced the man who was the cause of all their recent problems. For all her faith in the Lord, she suddenly felt very angry at their situation.

"You should be ashamed of yourself," she said.

Bill's face paled. Paige looked at her husband. Why was this woman so angry? Hadn't Bill said he was settling with the Sullivans?

Other patrons in the restaurant turned casually to sneak a peek at the confrontation. It was obvious that something was happening, and Lorraine was making no attempt to keep her voice down.

Paige stood halfway up and gestured to an empty chair at their table. "Mrs. Jackson, I'm Paige Bradford. Would you care to sit down?"

Lorraine looked at the woman. "Thank you, ma'am, but no. I'll say my piece to your husband and then I'll be on my way." She waited for Paige to sit back down.

"Mr. Bradford, you've been hurting my family quite a lot these last few weeks. My sister has been an employee of HOA for almost thirty years. She started there when your father was in charge. It sure was a different company then."

"Is that right?" Bill said, wishing they had gone to a Wendy's drive-through.

"She's one of the housekeepers you're laying off next week. And you know my daughter, Ramona; you hit her with your car only a few weeks back. You never wrote or called or asked how she was. And then you fill my grandson's head with big ideas about his future, all while your lawyers cook up ways to cover your behind. My daughter is destitute and can't work. She'll be out on the street if I don't take her in. Meanwhile you just sit here driving your fancy car, eating your fancy meal, without a care in the world."

Paige could take no more and jumped to Bill's defense. "Mrs. Jackson, surely there's been a mistake. Just last night my husband told me that he was going to settle with your daughter and pay her expenses. Right, Bill?" Paige turned hopefully toward her husband.

Bill tugged at his collar, feeling strangled. Paige took a breath when he didn't confirm her words.

"Look, I don't have to listen to this," he said, desperately signaling for the waiter.

"Bill?" Paige said carefully. "You did settle, didn't you?"

"Stay out of this, Paige," Bill whispered at her. "It doesn't concern you."

"How dare you dismiss me like that?" Paige tossed her napkin in the direction of her husband, not caring that she was now contributing to the scene.

The restaurant's owner had now appeared, and he and the maître d' hovered by uncertainly. What in the world was going on?

Lorraine looked from Bill to Paige, to the owner, to the maître d', to poor Andrew, and then back to Paige, who sat waiting to hear whatever else she had to say. Then she made the mistake of looking around the restaurant and realized that all eyes were on her. What had she started? *Be careful of what you wish for,* she admonished herself. She'd wanted someone to listen, and now she had *everyone's* attention. "Oh, Lord, help me get out of this one," she prayed.

"Go on," Paige urged. She sensed that it was only a matter of seconds before Bill or the owner swept them all out of the restaurant. "Talk to me. Please."

Lorraine gathered up her courage. "Well, not two hours ago, my daughter's lawyer called to say that you aren't going to pay anything. Not a single dime. You know, my daughter didn't expect a penny from you. She's a good girl. But this lawyer filled her head with the idea that he'd be able to get enough to help her pay her bills. She didn't want more than that. But now, well, like I said, she'd be on the street if I couldn't take her in."

Instead of feeling satisfied, Lorraine felt sick. This Bradford woman had no idea what her husband was up to, that much was clear. She felt like she had just told Paige that her husband was cheating on her. Lorraine couldn't look at her anymore; she felt ashamed at the amount of pain she had just caused. Being mad at Mr. Bradford didn't give her the right to hurt Mrs. Bradford and that is what she had just done. *Oh, Lord . . . forgive me.*

Oliver watched Lorraine as she walked back to Minnie's. She looked shaken. The others hadn't noticed her go out the side door and he wasn't about to point out her coming back. She simply walked quietly back into the restaurant and pleaded silently with Oliver to not say a word. She sat down and grabbed his hand beneath the table. He could feel that it was shaking.

Somehow the Bradfords managed to leave the restaurant (Bill left a huge tip, fearing that he wouldn't be welcomed back for a long time) and drove home without uttering a single word. Paige sat huddled in the front seat, leaning as far away from Bill as she possibly could without falling out the door. Andrew sat in the back seat behind his mother, staring out the window, avoiding his reflection in the window. Bill drove with hands clenched on the steering wheel. He was furious—but the question was, at whom?

Finally the unhappy trio arrived home and Paige and Andrew scrambled to get out of the car. No one could stomach the thought of having to say another word. Who knew what would be triggered? Paige brushed her teeth quickly, undressed in the dark, put on her pajamas, and climbed into bed, all in a matter of minutes. Exhausted and miserable, she fell asleep immediately, the covers pulled protectively around her. Andrew lay awake for some time with his earphones in, the strong beat of the music comforting him.

Bill remained sitting in the car long after his wife and son had gone indoors. It was well past midnight when he finally pulled himself out of the Jaguar and made his way upstairs to bed.

21

Bill Bradford awoke to the shrill sound of his cell phone. His heart pounded, and he realized he had a splitting headache. Not bothering to answer the phone, he massaged his forehead to ease the pain and tried to remember what he'd had to drink last night. Suddenly the humiliating events at the restaurant came flooding back to him. It didn't seem fair to feel this sick when all he'd had to drink and eat was water and a dinner roll.

Reluctantly, he opened his eyes and peeked through his fingers. Why was the room so sunny? Groaning, he turned to his bedside table and squinted at the clock, which glowed "9:15."

Nine-fifteen?! But the press conference was at noon! Headache or not, he had to get up and get to the office. His cell phone had quieted, but now started to ring persistently again. That was probably someone from work calling him.

"Where's Paige? And why didn't she wake me up?" Bill silenced his phone and sat up, ready to tell her how he felt about these childish games. She knew he had to be at work. "This passive-aggressive behavior has to stop," he thought angrily. Then he realized how upset she'd been at him. Groaning, he swung his legs out of bed and sat there for a few seconds, waiting for the throbbing in his head to stop. He stumbled into the bathroom and clumsily rummaged in the medicine cabinet and found the aspirin. If he could just swallow three of these he'd feel better. The cap wouldn't twist. *What the—? Oh for crying out loud, it's one of those child-proof caps.* Bill slammed the small plastic bottle against the bathroom tile in frustration. It rolled behind the toilet, undamaged. Apparently it was tile proof, as well.

He stood there, one hand on his forehead, the other gripping the edge of the sink to steady himself. Finally, he knelt down and reached his arm around the bowl to capture the bottle. He succeeded in knocking it over to the tub, where it wobbled, urging him to try again. Crawling now, around the side of the toilet, he reached out and roughly grabbed the bottle before it could escape. Sitting on the floor, his back propped against the tub, he tried to align the arrows and push up. Nothing. He looked very closely at the cap and the bottle, making sure that the arrows were lined up *perfectly*. Almost afraid to try again, he held his breath as he pushed up. *Hard.* Finally the lid popped off, but not before it scraped the top of his thumb. Peering inside, he saw only one aspirin. Not wanting to take any chances of losing it, he emptied the bottle directly into his mouth and bitterly chewed the pill.

It was only after he'd taken a very hot shower, and brushed his teeth, shaved, and combed his hair that Bill realized how quiet the house was. Now that his head was slightly better, he wondered where everyone was. Maybe Paige or Andrew had left him a note. He wrapped a towel around his waist and walked out of the steamy bathroom into his sunny bedroom—and froze. There on the bed was his suitcase with a newspaper folded neatly on top of it. He had been too groggy to notice it before. Without taking a step further he yelled, *"Paige! Andrew!"*

Please answer, he begged silently. Answer me. . . .

Bill tossed the newspaper aside and grabbed the suitcase by the handle to move it off the bed. He was startled by its weight—it wasn't empty. Opening it, he saw that several shirts and pairs of slacks were neatly folded inside, along with socks and underwear. With trembling fingers he searched carefully through the clothing for a note. *Nothing.* He didn't take out the clothes. It was obvious Paige wanted him out of the house, plain and simple, and dumping out the suitcase wouldn't change a thing.

He began dressing automatically, trying not to think.

Andrew hopped off the bus, swung his backpack over one shoulder, and headed quickly down the street with a sense of urgency. Early that morning, while his father still slept, Paige had barely acknowledged Andrew as he told her he was going outside. After the previous day he expected more questions, but his mother was clearly upset and preoccupied. He'd left without her giving him a second glance.

Rounding the corner, he was taken aback by the crowd of people, the music, and the air of festivity. He had expected a group of sad-looking, down-and-out people, but the protesters in front of HOA were singing with passion. Uncertain, Andrew slowly walked over, blending in with the crowd. It was difficult to make out who were the protesters and who were the onlookers. Music from a saxophone was accompanied by the beat of an African drum and everyone was either singing or clapping their hands to the rhythm. "Why," Andrew wondered, "are they so happy?"

A man with a hotdog cart had even moved from across the street to join the group. The aroma enticed many people, who stood patiently in line waiting to order a late breakfast. Andrew studied some of the faces around him. Even though they didn't know him, he felt like he knew them. Each article he had cut out of the newspaper featured the story of one of these people. A reporter had interviewed several workers in depth to find out how outsourcing would affect their lives.

Today's article had inspired Andrew to come here, because today was the last day they could protest. Next week all of them would be outsourced. Now that he was here he had no idea what to do. They certainly didn't need manpower; there were hundreds of people. Finally the song ended and the workers linked arms and bowed their heads. Not familiar with the rituals of prayer, Andrew looked around questioningly. Suddenly a rich baritone voice rang out. Andrew bowed his head and listened as a tall man thanked the Lord for all their blessings. Only once did he make reference to HOA and that was to ask God to guide Bill Bradford to make the right decision.

People slowly let go of one another and began picking up signs that had been propped against benches and trees. The crowd thinned out as the onlookers continued about their business. Finally Andrew got up enough courage to approach an older black woman standing by herself.

Hesitantly he asked, "Why isn't everybody upset?"

Surprised by the question, she laughed. "Upset? How's that going to help? It's in the Lord's hands. All we can ever do is try, but all things are up to the Lord," she said, smiling at the serious young man in front of her.

Andrew wanted to say it wasn't up to the Lord, that it was up to his dad, and these people didn't have a prayer because as far as he knew his dad didn't talk to—much less *listen* to—any higher power. Instead he nodded as if he agreed.

"You look mighty worried, son," she said kindly. "Are your folks going to lose their jobs?"

"Uh, well," Andrew faltered. "I just don't think it's right that everyone's being outsourced. I've been reading about it and I just had to come down here."

She studied him thoughtfully. "I see. You want to show your support?"

"Yes," Andrew said, grateful that she understood.

Putting her arm around him, she led him toward the group. "Here, sugar," she said, handing him a sign that said *NO to Outsourcing!* "Hold this and just stand with these people right here. Let me know if you get tired. I'll understand."

Andrew held his sign self-consciously until he realized that no one was paying him any special attention. The twinge of guilt that he wasn't an authentic part of the group was slowly replaced by a feeling of pride. People smiled and nodded at him and eventually he felt the rightness about what he was doing. He felt like he belonged.

Bill picked up the newspaper from the floor and glanced at the headlines as he bounded down the stairs. While the front page still held a story about HOA, there was nothing about the car accident.

He jumped into his Jaguar and turned on the radio. He wanted to hear any other news he should know. The newscasters were down on the streets interviewing protestors.

"And what's your name?" he heard a woman reporter ask. "Why are you here today?"

A boy's voice answered, "My name's Andrew." Bill blanched. That was his son! He was picketing in front of HOA? "And I don't think the outsourcing is right."

"Do your parents work for HOA?" the reporter asked.

"Um, sort of," said the boy. Bill silently pleaded for Andrew not to say it.

"Is your mom or dad going to be laid off?" she asked.

"Well. . . ." The boy paused as the reporter seemed to put two and two together.

"What did you say your name was again?"

Andrew took a breath, unsure, and then said, "Andrew. Andrew Bradford."

This was insane. Bill turned the radio off. He could barely restrain himself from stamping his foot on the gas pedal, weaving in and out of traffic, and blaring his horn at the hapless drivers who got in his way. It took a supreme effort on his part to keep the speedometer hovering just under the speed limit. He had no idea what he was going to do about Andrew protesting, or about Paige kicking him out of the house, but he knew *exactly* what he was going to do when he arrived at HOA. Just thinking about something he actually had control over slowed his breathing down and he loosened his grip on the steering wheel. Thank goodness all that nonsense with the protesters would be over with soon. After today he'd never have to deal with them again. "It would serve them all right if the new company didn't hire them," Bill thought vengefully.

He pulled into his parking stall, cut off the engine, and looked in the rear-view mirror, smoothing back his hair. He straightened his tie, seized his briefcase, and jumped out, slamming the door shut. He was ready to get this over with. Impatiently waiting for the elevator, he barely glanced at the people around him. A few gave him curious looks, but no one dared approach him. Bill gave off energy like a tiger ready to pounce.

From the ground floor up to the twenty-sixth, the only person with enough chutzpah to even speak to him was Sheila. That bubble gum really was a de-stresser. "Good morning, Mr. Bradford," she chirped when he walked by her desk. "You're awfully late this morning."

Narrowing his eyes at her, he was on the verge of delivering a scathing remark when she blew an enormous purple bubble that burst with a loud pop all over her face. All he could see were her blue eyes, which flew wide open. She managed to peel the gum off (no easy task) and stick it all back in her mouth. "Oops!" Sheila giggled. "I hate it when that happens." She continued chewing, looking at him with anticipation. "Did you want to say something, Mr. Bradford?"

"Sheila," he said in a growl, "if you intend to keep on working here I strongly suggest you get rid of that bubble gum. You're not a sixteen-year-old schoolgirl. You're a thirty-year-old woman, for God's sake. Act like it. If you can't be professional then pack a box and leave."

Without waiting for her to respond he strode into his office, where the morning paper was neatly placed on top of his desk. He threw it into the trash.

Gladys came in and quietly set a stack of pink memos on his desk, and quietly walked out, shutting the door behind her.

Bill leafed through a few of the messages, realizing it would take him all morning to respond. He winced at some of them. There had been ten from various press organizations in the last twenty minutes. Probably asking about his son. He opened his briefcase, took out a sheaf of papers, and reviewed his already memorized speech. In just a few minutes he would go downstairs to the conference room, face the media, and let America know once and for all that *he* was still the CEO of this company.

When Charles had asked Oliver the night before for a ride in the morning, the reverend hadn't asked any questions. He arrived early to find the boy waiting on the front steps of the apartment building, in his suit. Oliver knew without being told where to go. Now they were approaching HOA headquarters. He found a parking spot on a nearby street, carefully avoiding the commotion of the front entrance.

Charles got out of the car and cleared his throat and said, "I'd like to go up alone, if that's okay with you."

Turning off the engine, Oliver nodded his okay. He sat looking after Charles long after the door of the building had swung shut behind him.

Inside the building, Charles walked quickly and got on the elevator with several other people. He pressed button 26 and the elevator ascended; he watched anxiously as the floor numbers lit up. If he had any doubts about what he was about to do, he knew he only had a matter of minutes to change his mind. He recognized a few of the members of the Policy Advisory Committee, some of whom smiled at him. He stood in the back and kept his gaze straight ahead. Everyone gradually exited until he was the only one left. He waited in silence as the elevator continued climbing. Then the doors opened and Charles stepped out onto the landing.

Willing himself to move, he woodenly took a few steps in the direction of Bill Bradford's office. This was harder than he'd imagined. He had made up his mind last night, during dinner. After coming home from the park he'd rummaged through his drawers, found what he needed, tucked it away in his jacket, and laid out his suit. But now that he was here he didn't know if he could follow through.

"Charles!" Sheila said, bumping into him as she came out of the women's restroom.

Charles noticed Sheila's eyes were red and puffy, as if she'd been crying. "Are you okay?" he asked.

She sniffled and then hiccupped. "Yeah, thanks. What are you doing here, sweetie?" She used an already damp tissue to dab her eyes.

"I came to see Mr. Bradford."

"Hmm," she said. "I assume you don't have an appointment?'

Charles just shook his head.

"Today is not the day for me to rock the boat with Mr. Bradford," she said hesitantly. She couldn't believe he'd been so mean to her: *Pack a box and leave?* Still, seeing the anxious look on Charles's face, she said suddenly, "Well, let's see if he's got a minute, anyway." Linking her arm with his, she strode down the hall to Bill's office and knocked sharply on his open door. "Mr. Bradford? There's someone here to see you."

"Sheila," he snapped. "Don't you know I'm busy?"

He could see out of the corner of his eye that Sheila was not moving. Annoyed, he looked up, and just as he about to make another angry remark, he saw Charles standing quietly in the doorway. Sheila gave him a small nudge. He took a step forward but made no move to enter further. She quietly shut the door, leaving the two of them alone.

Inside his office, Bill tried to mask his confusion at Charles's presence. What on earth could this kid want? Another scene. Was it possible to make a bigger one than his grandmother had made last night? He made no attempt to get up or shake the boy's hand.

"Charles Sullivan," he said coldly. "What brings you up here?"

Charles noticed that Bill glanced at his watch. "You don't have to worry," he said. "I don't plan on staying long at all. I'm sorry for disturbing you, Mr. Bradford. I know you have a lot on your mind."

"Here, take a seat." He offered a plush chair and looked at Charles. On the outside, he seemed like a good kid. It made sense that he had trusted him—"been fooled by him," is what Bill thought. He had that trustworthy demeanor. "How was I supposed to know he was just like any other con artist after a quick buck?"

But looking at Charles now, Bill wondered for a moment if he'd gotten it all wrong. Maybe the kid had genuinely just wanted to return his wallet. He shook his head; no. But then, what was with their lawyer? He couldn't make up his mind what to think about it.

Gulping, Charles said, "I came to tell you thanks for giving me the share and for giving me an opportunity—"

Bill interrupted him. "Oh, no need to thank me, Charles. No need at all." *Okay, here comes the big sob story*, Bill predicted, and waited for the boy to lay it on thick.

"Well, I came here to resign."

"You what?" Bill asked stupidly.

"I'm resigning from the committee. And I'm giving you back my share." Having said that, Charles stood up, reached inside his jacket, and withdrew the original stock certificate that Bill had given him. It was a little worse for wear, having been folded up numerous times. Handing it over, Charles wondered why Bill had such a funny look on his face.

Bill took the folded piece of paper and stared at it. "*Now* is he going to ask me for money?" he wondered. "Should I pay him for the stock?" He reached into his pocket to pull out some money.

"I'll pay you for the share."

Charles waved him off. "That's all right, sir. You gave this to me and I'm just giving it back."

Bill put his wallet back in his coat pocket. When he didn't say anything further, Charles rose and said, "Well, that's all I came for."

"Wait," Bill said, wondering if he'd really understood what the boy was trying to say. "I don't understand, Charles. I thought you liked being on the policy committee?"

"Oh, I do! I mean I did, Mr. Bradford. I've learned so much about business and about the hard decisions you have to make. And you have some hard ones."

"Is this about your mother?" Bill asked. That must be it.

"No, sir. My mother never expected anything from you. Maybe you were driving fast or distracted but she walked into the street without looking. I guess in some way, you were both at fault. Then she got smooth-talked by that lawyer. She was worried about paying her bills and so she let him take care of things. She got her hopes up and now. . . ." He trailed off. "But I don't blame you, Mr. Bradford. I guess if you don't think my mom deserves money, well, it is what it is. We've never had a lot. We'll figure it out."

"So, where do we stand, then?" asked Bill. Was what the boy was saying true? Had the shady lawyer been pulling the strings all along? A weight fell on him. What had he done?

Charles stood there uncomfortably, wishing that he could just go without more questions. "Like I said, Mr. Bradford, you have to make a lot of hard decisions. Like with the layoffs. You have to weigh the good of the company against the good for its employees. That can't be easy. But that doesn't mean I have to agree with your decisions. I thought I could make a difference, but it seems like nothing will really change. You're going downstairs soon to your press conference, and you'll be honest about the Medicare fraud, but you're still going to lay off all those housekeepers. I guess I just don't want to be part of this company. I don't like what HOA stands for."

Bill was floored. He looked at his bookshelf. On it was a picture of him and his father. Next to that was an older photo of his father breaking ground on his first HOA building. He was surrounded by a group of smiling, happy employees.

"And tell me," Bill said quietly, "what does HOA stand for?"

"I don't like what you're planning to do to folks," Charles began. "I know now that you have shareholders and public opinion, but where would a company be without its employees? You're outsourcing workers who've been real loyal to you. I know that people are going to be hurting bad once they can't work for HOA. You really aren't doing the right thing by them or their families." Charles spoke without any trace of nervousness. In fact, now that he was here talking face to face with Mr. Bradford, he felt strong.

"My mama always taught me that for every argument there are two sides. I just don't feel like you're listening to any side but the one with dollar signs."

Bill couldn't say anything. He just stared at the boy, amazed by what he'd said and having a hard time denying the truth in his words.

Charles looked at him levelly for a moment. He'd said his piece. "Goodbye, Mr. Bradford." With that he got up and walked out of the office feeling much lighter than when he walked in.

Stepping into the bright sunlight of the late morning, Charles stopped to look at the crowd gathered outside. He shielded his eyes from the sun, and let his gaze wander over to the group holding up signs, walking slowly in a large circle. "That's funny," he thought, "that kid looks just like Andrew. Hey, wait a minute—that *is* Andrew!" He walked over to his friend and tapped him on the shoulder. "What are you doing here?"

Andrew greeted Charles but then paused, wondering how to explain his presence at the protest. "You know, the other day? When you were telling me about these people? Well. . . ."

"Yeah?"

Andrew looked away uncomfortably. "I didn't want to believe it at first, but you're right about the outsourcing. So I just wanted to come down to see for myself. To help out."

Charles nodded, secretly impressed.

"Here, take my sign," Andrew said abruptly. "I'll go grab that one over there." He went to get an abandoned sign lying face down on the sidewalk in front of the building.

Charles held his sign and waited for Andrew to return. Then both boys joined the group, holding their signs proudly. Suddenly a startling flash of light went off right in front of them.

"Sorry about that, guys," said a young man with a large camera around his neck, as he fiddled with its controls and snapped a couple more photos. "Should have turned my flash off."

They continued walking on with the group.

Aunt Etta came around the picket line and saw Charles. She walked out and went to give him a big hug.

"Hey, Aunt Etta," said Charles.

"Good to see you here supporting your old aunt," she said.

Oliver had seen Charles come out of the building and he followed him into the crowd. "Charles!" he called out loudly, trying to get his attention, but Charles was deep in conversation with another boy and didn't hear him. Striding over, Oliver stood in front of the boys, causing Charles to stop in mid-step.

"Hey!" Charles protested. He froze when he realized who it was. "Oh, Reverend French. . . ." he said.

Oliver didn't say anything, waiting for Charles to explain himself. "Sorry, I saw Andrew over here and forgot to come find you," he began, embarrassed.

"I'm Andrew," the blond boy said to Oliver, before the man had a chance to question him.

"So, Andrew," the reverend said, "what's your reason for being here today?" He looked at the boy curiously.

Exchanging a quick look with Charles, Andrew said, "It was just the right thing to do."

"Well, it seems like you're both very concerned about your fellow man."

"And fellow *woman*," Charles added quickly, thinking of poor Aunt Etta.

"That's a very admirable trait, especially in young people," the reverend conceded. He shook Andrew's hand. "Pleased to meet you, Andrew. I'm Oliver French, a friend of Charles." Looking over at Charles he added, with a smile, "Apparently I'm his chauffeur today."

"Oh," Andrew said. "Are you leaving?" He seemed disappointed.

"Do you need a ride, too, young man?"

Before Charles could say anything, Andrew set down his sign and said eagerly, "That would be great. Thanks."

"Actually," said Charles, looking over at Oliver, "would it be okay if we stayed a little while longer? I'd really like to go inside and hear the press conference." Then, to Andrew, he asked, "Can you stay?"

"Yeah, sure," said Andrew, wondering whether or not he should.

The reverend picked up a sign. "Might as well do some good work while we wait," he said.

They all picked up signs and marched into the crowd.

Back in his office, Bill stared out the window and down at the people below. Had he ever really tried to talk to them? He'd been up here so long he had no idea. He'd misjudged the Sullivan boy incredibly—more than once. He wasn't a thief. He was a good, honest kid. Better than most. Was he right about what Hospitals of America had become?

Bill looked down again and had an idea. It was different—but it just might be what this company needed. What *he* needed.

"Gladys, get George from Public Relations on the phone."

A moment later Gladys spoke over the intercom. "He's on line two," she said.

"George," said Bill animatedly, "I need you to move the press conference. No, not from today to another day. From the boardroom to outdoors. Get on it!"

22

From where they were standing, Charles noticed a lot of equipment being moved out in front of the building. There were big, tall scaffolds draped with banners showing the HOA logo. And it looked like they were bringing out a platform and a lectern? Something big was going on. A microphone was brought out, and men carried long extension cords.

"I thought the press conference would be held inside," Charles said to Andrew.

The housekeepers had begun to notice the commotion as well. They stopped marching and began to congregate around the podium. Charles saw more media vans pulling up, their sides marked with various station identifications.

Andrew was surprised to see his mother off to one side, walking toward the crowd. He ran over to her, and she gave him a big hug.

"I heard you on the radio," Paige said. Holding his face in her hands, she pulled him again into a hug. "I came right away."

"I'm sorry, Mom, I didn't mean to scare you again."

"No, that's not what I mean," she said. "I came to walk with you."

Andrew smiled and walked her over to Charles and Oliver.

"Hello, Charles," she said warmly. And then, more seriously, "I'm really sorry about what's happened to you and your family."

She didn't know what else to say. Charles took her hand in silence, bidding her to say nothing more.

A short time later, Bill entered the elevator to descend to the lobby. His PR man, George, was sweating bullets. He'd tried hard to dissuade Bill from doing this. He could control an audience of professional reporters inside the confines of a boardroom, but a public crowd outside the building? "Mr. Bradford, they're unpredictable," he warned. "They could ask or do anything."

"I know," Bill had replied. "But it's time to talk directly with the workers. It's time for transparency. If we want America to trust HOA again then we have to talk to them, face to face. No more hiding behind glass doors and security. We're going outside."

And so George had rushed to get the word out and move the crew and setup outdoors.

As they got into the elevator he said to Bill, "I still don't like it."

"Don't worry," Bill replied. "This is my decision. I'll stand by it."

The elevator reached the lobby. Bill fixed his tie and smoothed his hair one last time before the door opened. He looked down at the index cards in his hand and handed them to George.

George looked apoplectic. "But, sir, your speech."

"I don't need it," Bill replied.

George wiped the sweat from his forehead and tried to breathe. He was going to lose his PR job. He knew it. "Then who will hire me?" He made a mental note to update his resume as soon as he got home.

As Bill exited the front door of the building, the quiet from inside was replaced by the noise of a protest. As the people standing near the podium saw him, boos began to ring out. Flashbulbs went off all around and camera shutters clicked as the press photographers shot as many photos as they could. Each one jostled for position in front of him. Bill saw Charles standing in the crowd and then saw that his wife and son were both there. He made eye contact with Paige. Her face told him nothing.

Finally, George stepped up to the microphone on the podium and introduced Bill. A few claps, but mostly shouts and boos, went up from the crowd. Bill hesitated for just a moment in front of the steps leading up to the podium. This was it. He could very well lose his position after this. But he was tired of running. He lifted his chin and walked with squared shoulders to face the crowd.

Standing stiffly, Bill surveyed the audience before him. The day had turned overcast and still. While the boos had continued for a moment longer, as soon as he walked up a hush fell over the group, and signs were either set down or propped half-heartedly against shoulders.

"Good morning!" His voice boomed over the public-announcement system. There was a sharp squeal of feedback. He watched a technician fix the system and then scurry to the back.

Then the only sound was that of cameras clicking away. News reporters were placed strategically around the crowd so the cameramen could get good shots. Even the traffic noises seemed subdued this morning. A baby wailed once, but was quickly shushed by his mother.

Bill spoke. "As you all know, in the fifty years since my father started this company, Hospitals of America has had a sterling reputation in the hospital industry. As one of America's most successful corporations, HOA has helped bring better health care to our country and to other countries around the world." He paused to take a drink of water. There was some shifting of feet, a few coughs, but no applause or nods. They waited patiently for him to finish what he came here to do.

He swallowed, wiping his hands on his jacket. He looked out at his wife and son. The expressions on their faces were solemn. Paige had her arm draped protectively across Andrew as he leaned against her. They made a self-contained unit that left no room for anyone else. When Paige saw Bill looking at her she unconsciously tightened her hold on their son.

Bill's eyes blurred for a second and he silently admonished himself to *get a grip*. The crowd started getting a little restless, but still no one spoke. Bill coughed, and loosened his tie, as it seemed to have tightened on his throat. He gripped the sides of the lectern to steady himself. For some reason his heart was pounding and sweat was trickling down his forehead. *The humidity*, he thought, wiping his face irritably.

Adjusting the microphone, he let his gaze drop. Normally he was an accomplished and eloquent public speaker, and he couldn't remember ever in his career having been nervous in front of a crowd. In fact, even as a child he had thrived on the attention of an audience. He loved going to work with his dad and meeting all sorts of people. He remembered his father introducing him proudly to everyone—from the top managers to the food-service workers to the housekeeping staff. An image of his father warmly greeting everyone he met came to him and he had to shake his head to clear the memory. His father had felt comfortable with everyone. He had respected *everyone*, Bill remembered. He felt a knot in his stomach grow bigger.

Finally a woman toward the front broke the silence. "Is it true that HOA commits Medicare fraud on a regular basis?" she asked loudly.

Another reporter called out. "What do you think about your son being out here today, protesting against you?"

Then others joined the questioning.

"Did you really hit Ramona Sullivan with your car and then refuse to pay her medical expenses?"

"She's a single mother, isn't she, Mr. Bradford?"

"Is this what Hospitals of America stands for?"

The situation was going south, just as George had warned. Bill had been ready to explain everything, but his wife's presence had thrown him off. He couldn't think clearly. He stopped for a second, letting his gaze wander briefly over the crowd, when he caught the eyes of Charles Sullivan staring back at him. His expression was inscrutable, but he stood there confidently, at ease, waiting for Bill to continue. Was there hope in the boy's face?

Bill couldn't find his voice. He couldn't tear his gaze away from Charles, and one by one the hundreds of people standing there turned to the source of Bill's attention and discomfort. *It was just a kid.* People exchanged curious looks with one another, shrugging their shoulders, wondering what in the world was going on. The barrage of questions reached a boiling point.

"Uh, excuse me," Bill choked out. Wiping his damp forehead with a handkerchief, he took a deep breath and steadied his gaze into the crowd as if he were trying to make eye contact with every person there.

"Have you ever had someone try to teach you something," he asked, looking expectantly out at the crowd, "but you weren't ready to listen?"

No response.

"Have you ever had something right in front of your nose, but you couldn't or wouldn't see it?"

Again he waited, but no response.

Bowing his head, he tried to collect his thoughts, but now they were coming so fast he had to be careful not to stumble all over himself.

"There are people in my life who tried to teach me, but I was too blind to see and too deaf to listen." Another pause, and this time there was definitely some murmuring.

"A few weeks ago a person came into my life who tried to teach me *integrity, character,* and *courage*—values I had learned long, long ago as a boy. This person tried to teach me by example, just as my father had done." Bill's voice rang out clearly.

Now the energy of the crowd was charged. What was Mr. Bradford trying to say? What was he getting at? Paige and Andrew pushed their way closer to the podium.

"They say the true test of character is in what you do when no one is watching. And that following your conscience takes courage. Not because someone is watching, and not because you hope to benefit from it or be rewarded in some way." Bill looked at Charles directly. "But only because following your conscience is *the right thing to do.* That it would be unthinkable to live and act otherwise. I have only met a few people who have had the courage to live their life with that kind of dignity.

"Hospitals of America has let you down. I have let you down. This company was built from the ground up not by one man, but by many people. My father believed in giving people good health care so that they could live long lives, enjoying the bounty of their families. But some of us here forgot that message. Yes, the Medicare allegations are true."

A gasp went up from the crowd.

Bill continued. "Medicare fraud did occur at one of our branches. We have since terminated the responsible parties and we're paying fines for the mistake while we work with the government to make sure this never happens again. No, fraud was not a company policy, but when part of a machine is broken the whole thing falls apart. I stand here today to let you know that we will not stop until we have earned back your trust."

Charles smiled up at Bill. A reporter's hand shot up but Bill respectfully held out his hand to tell him to wait. "You asked about my son being here today with the protestors." He looked into the crowd and met Andrew's eyes.

"How do I feel about that? I'm proud. My son is a good, intelligent young man and I'm here to say that I agree with him." Flashbulbs popped as he said the words. Paige, choking back tears, nodded in approval to her husband.

"My father built this company with his employees," he continued. "Some of the people here today have given most of their working lives to Hospitals of America. We should not overlook their loyalty in favor of saving a few dollars. I am here to tell you today that tomorrow I will sit down with the heads of the housekeepers union to bang out a deal that keeps them here at HOA."

A loud cheer rang out from the crowd. The protestors were jumping up and down and hugging one another. Inside the crowd, Oliver looked at Charles with amazement. What exactly had this boy said to Mr. Bradford today?

"Moving forward, Hospitals of America will adopt a policy of transparency—for everything, from costs associated with our hospitals to policies affecting our employees."

He paused and then continued. "Finally, since you asked about my personal life. Yes, I did hit a woman a few weeks ago, but I want to reassure everyone that I will do everything I can to take care of her and her needs."

Motioning with his hand, Mr. Bradford beckoned Charles up to the podium. Charles looked at him, surprised, and mouthed, "Me?" Bill nodded and Oliver gave him a gentle push. "Go on," he encouraged. "Go on up." Charles straightened his suit coat and made his way in the direction of the podium. The crowd parted to let him through and the camera people scrambled to get him in view. Finally he reached the steps and climbed up to stand with Bill at his side.

Putting his arm around the boy, Bill faced the crowd and said, "This young man, Charles Sullivan, has taught me an important lesson over the past few weeks. He had the courage to speak up for what he felt was right even when no one would listen to him." Bill paused and took a deep breath. "And I am ashamed to say I *ignored* him. I *dismissed* him without ever really taking the time to listen. I made assumptions about him and his character, and I want to say I'm sorry."

Looking slowly across the sea of upturned faces, Bill said, "And you—all of you—tried to get me to listen to your fears, your concerns about your futures and your families. You came here day after day, but I wouldn't listen. My own son—" Bill shook his head and glanced over at Andrew. "My own son tried to tell me outsourcing was wrong. And my wife, Paige, was . . . appalled that I could do such a thing. She made me wonder what my father would have done in this situation."

The audience made no sound.

"Well, they were right. HOA is a great corporation *because* of its employees. *That* is the lesson my father taught me. All of you have been extremely loyal and I will not punish that loyalty by letting you go. As of today, I hereby state that there will be *no outsourcing*. Your jobs are safe here."

Again the crowd rose up in cheers.

Impulsively Charles threw his arms around Bill. No one could hear what he said because the applause that followed was thunderous. People began hugging one another, wiping their tears, shouting, "Amen!" and "Thank you!" Paige and Andrew made their way through the crowd, angling their way up to the podium. Breathlessly, Paige stood in front of her husband. "Bill. . . ."

Wordlessly, he included her and Andrew in his embrace. Finally, he emotionally waved at the crowd.

"About your share, Charles," he said, taking the certificate out of his jacket pocket and handing it back to him.

Charles laughed. "You know I'm down for HOA, right?"

━━━━━━━━

Bill, Paige, and Andrew stood on the platform in front of the headquarters a little awkwardly, not quite knowing where to go from there.

"Dad?"

"Son, I can't begin to tell you how—" Bill began.

"It's okay, Dad," Andrew said, knowing where his father was headed. "I love you and I forgive you."

━━━━━━━━

Back in the apartment, Ramona, Gracie, and Lorraine all sat around the television. Ramona and Lorraine had tears in their eyes. Oliver had called them and told them to turn on their TV right away. They'd turned it on and been shocked to see Mr. Bradford and Charles on the news. They hadn't moved during the entire press conference. Ramona couldn't have been more proud of her son. Gracie cheered aloud, "Woohoo! Good job, Charles."

Lorraine put her arm around Ramona and proudly said, "That boy's going to change the world."

Ramona choked back a happy sob. She couldn't disagree.

EPILOGUE

Five months later.

Bill Bradford leaned back comfortably in his chair, waiting while the young newspaper reporter opened up her briefcase and extracted a yellow legal pad and a small tape recorder. Snapping the case shut, she placed it on the floor, turned on the recorder, and wrote a quick note on her paper. Looking at Bill expectantly, she was ready to begin the coveted interview.

"It's a pleasure to meet you, Mr. Bradford," she said, trying not to gush. After all, he was the CEO of one of the most successful businesses in the country. "How much time do we have?"

Bill glanced at the digital clock on his desk and said, "We have less than fifteen minutes."

The reporter nodded, knowing someone like Mr. Bradford must have one important meeting after another. "All right, then," she began bravely. "You've had quite a year, between allegations of Medicare fraud, accusations of unfair workplace practices, and pressures in your personal life. How did you make it through it all to get back on top?"

Bill chuckled at her eagerness. "You don't waste any time, do you?"

"Well, we only have a few minutes," she explained.

Bill nodded.

"The people who committed the fraud," he began slowly, "did so in part because of the climate of greed we had here at HOA. Even though I personally had no idea that Medicare was being defrauded, I do hold myself accountable for creating that climate and thus encouraging it to thrive."

The young woman scribbled furiously, in spite of her tape recorder.

Bill continued. "Since that time, we've paid all our fines and our record has been spotless. It's important to me that HOA be known worldwide for its high ethical standards, and that this *is* the company my father started."

The young reporter nodded. "It's been said that you've become somewhat of a trendsetter since you reversed your outsourcing decision last summer. What's your opinion about that?"

"A trendsetter?" Bill asked modestly. "Yes, it's a fact that a number of corporations have since revisited their outsourcing policies. Here at HOA we put people first. After all, we are here to *help* people."

"Do you find it ironic that by putting people before profits your stock values have risen dramatically?"

"No," Bill said, shaking his head, "not at all. Our company is successful because of its employees, so it stands to reason that the happier our employees are the more successful our company will be."

"Just one last question, Mr. Bradford. What can you tell me about the newest member of your board of directors?"

Smiling at her, Bill snapped shut his briefcase and said, "He's a bright young mind and a promising new leader."

"Isn't he also fifteen?" asked the reporter skeptically.

"Nearly sixteen, if you want to get technical," Bill retorted.

"Mr. Bradford, isn't that a bit young?" She looked at him, confused.

"A good CEO concerns himself more with what the message is than where it comes from." He looked at his watch, sending her the hint that time was up.

"Do you have holiday plans, Mr. Bradford?" she asked, as Bill stood up and she began gathering her things.

"Yes," he said, "I'm heading out as soon as we finish here. I owe my wife and son a vacation so we're taking a cruise in the Caribbean."

The reporter rose. She extended her hand. "Thank you, Mr. Bradford, for your time."

"My pleasure," he said as he shook her hand in return.

———————————

A few minutes later Bill prepared to leave the office himself. He'd already given most of his employees their holiday gifts, but he had two more. With his coat draped over his arm he walked out and closed his office door.

He took an envelope from his pocket and handed it to Gladys. It contained her usual bonus for the year. Then he stopped in front of Sheila. He handed her an envelope and set a plain rectangular box on her desk.

Without another word he walked out the office toward the elevators.

Gladys looked at Sheila, suddenly expecting the worst. She'd heard all about Mr. Bradford's angry comment about professionalism and packing a box and leaving.

Sheila cautiously opened the box—and found a huge stash of watermelon bubble gum.

Standing at the elevators, Bill heard Sheila's telltale shriek and smiled.

Gracie went up the walkway through the snow, holding on to Kayden's hand. They had officially been boyfriend and girlfriend for more than a month now. They'd spent the whole afternoon ice-skating at Centennial Olympic Park downtown. Her cheeks were rosy. She laughed and teased him, "I can't believe you almost knocked over Mrs. Pietrowski."

"Yeah," said Kayden, "I guess I shouldn't have taken that turn so fast."

"She would have failed you this year for sure."

They stopped in front of her doorstep. Neither wanted to say goodbye. Finally Gracie glanced up at the apartment window to see her grandmother looking down.

She nodded her head upward and said, "I gotta go."

From inside his coat, Kayden pulled out a small box. "Merry Christmas," he said. "Open it up."

Gracie had a sharp intake of breath and she ripped the package open. Inside a very delicate necklace with her name in gold. Kayden took it out of the box and placed it around her neck. "To the most beautiful girl I know," he said, and gave her a peck on her cheek.

"Kayden, thank you!" She smiled and then looked up to see her grandma tapping at the window.

"I love it," she said, impulsively hugging Kayden before she ran up the stairs, grinning from ear to ear.

Inside the apartment, Lorraine gave Gracie a stern look. Then she saw the happy grin on Gracie's face and decided to let it go.

Most of the apartment was in boxes, but they'd managed to clear space to put up a Christmas tree and a table. The Sullivans were scheduled to move the following week, to a much larger apartment.

Ramona walked into the room carrying a pie straight from the oven. She put it on a rack to cool. She looked at her daughter.

"Gracie, you aren't even ready for church," she said reproachfully. Then she spied the glittering necklace adorning her neck.

"Did Kayden give that to you?" she asked, smiling at Gracie.

"Yes, isn't it beautiful?" she exclaimed.

Ah, young love, thought Ramona. "Yes, baby, it's lovely. Now get ready. I don't want to be late."

Oliver and Charles were sitting on the couch watching some football. They'd both been dressed and ready for a while.

Charles shook his head. "Girls take forever to get ready," he said.

The reverend chuckled. "Get used to it, son."

A few minutes later, and after several reminders from her mother that they were going to be late, Gracie emerged ready for church. Everyone grabbed their belongings and piled down the stairs and then into Bertha.

The church was packed. As usual, everyone wore their warm coats inside. "It doesn't matter how much heat they pump in there," Ramona thought with a smile, "this place is always drafty in the winter." It seemed only days ago she'd been complaining the church was too hot in the summer. As she sat quietly in the pew she reflected on the past year. She thanked the Lord for how lucky she was. She looked at her beautiful children, her mother, and Oliver. Her mother had been so happy these past few months—happier than she'd seen her in a long time. She looked down at her leg. No longer was she stuck in a heavy cast. With lots of walking and a little therapy, her leg was fully healed, and tonight she wore a new pair of bright-red pumps. Her money troubles were over, too. After the press conference, Bill called Morrie and made him put their offer to settle back on the table, plus some. Ramona remembered the call from Mason Smith. He'd seemed flustered and was muttering about getting threats that he'd be disbarred. She had just listened politely. The money from the settlement had paid all of Ramona's bills, including the ones from her previous hospital visit. She'd put most of the rest away in savings and into accounts for Gracie and Charles. She looked at the children and thought of their future. She didn't know what it held in store but she looked forward to being with them every minute she could.

The congregation rose up and the church and choir began to sing. Ramona raised her voice loud and strong: "Hallelujah, Hallelujah, Glory to God in the highest."

Later that evening, the family sat around the table for their last dinner in the old apartment. The food had been fantastic. They all leaned back, too stuffed to think about dessert yet. Suddenly, Oliver picked up a spoon and clinked his glass.

"I'd like to make an announcement, if I may?"

Everyone looked up, wondering if he was about to say what they'd all hoped for a while.

"Well, you all know that some months ago I met a beautiful woman, Miss Lorraine Jackson. I've been a widower for some time, and she brought life back into my life. These months have been some of the happiest this old man could ever hope for. And because I can't imagine a world without her, I've asked this beautiful, loving, spirited, opinionated lady to marry me." He paused for effect and laughter. "And she said yes."

A cheer rang out from everyone. Glasses were raised in a toast. Tears ran down Ramona's cheeks. She looked at Charles, who shook the reverend's hand in congratulations, and at Gracie, giving Lorraine a hug. All was right with the world.

Neil Shulman, M.D., is the author of more
than thirty books for readers of all ages. His
adult fiction includes *What? Dead . . . Again?,*
which was made into the 1991 Michael J.
Fox movie, "Doc Hollywood." Some of his
medical books (such as *The Black Man's
Guide to Good Health* and *The Real Truth
About Aging*) have improved the quality of

life of thousands of readers. Others (such as *101 Ways to Know
if You're a Nurse*) heal with laughter. Neil's books for children
include *Don't Be Afraid of the Dentist; Kid Power: The Great
Face-Off!;* and *What's in a Doctor's Bag?* He is a past president
of the Patch Adams nonprofit organization (the Gesundheit!
Institute), and is also a highly sought-after speaker for Fortune
500 companies and other large audiences. He devotes much of
his time to charitable causes and finding ways to improve the
lives of others; among his most recent effors is involvement in
the Global Health & Humanitarian Summit.

"I've had the opportunity to have friends who are very poor
and friends who are billionaires," Neil says. "I've learned a lot
from both groups, especially the ones who are caring, ethical
human beings. The characters in *The Corporate Kid* are ficti-
tious; however, the lessons I've learned from my remarkable
friends have helped me in the writing of this book. Any resem-
blance between characters in the book and real folks is purely
coincidental."

Susan Wrathall has been a teacher in the
field of special education for more than
twenty-five years. She lives in Salt Lake City,
Utah, with her two daughters, Sophia and
Simone, and their two Yorkshire terriers.
"Between work and home," says Susan,
"there is never a dull moment." *The Corporate Kid* is her first novel.